Mother Country

Mother Country

✳ ✳ ✳   A NOVEL   ✳

Irina Reyn

Thomas Dunne Books
New York

THOMAS DUNNE BOOKS.
An imprint of St. Martin's Press.

MOTHER COUNTRY. Copyright © 2019 by Irina Reyn. All rights reserved. Printed in the United States of America. For information, address St. Martin's Press, 175 Fifth Avenue, New York, N.Y. 10010.

Excerpts from *Mother Country* have appeared in *Ploughshares* and *Bennington Review*.

www.thomasdunnebooks.com
www.stmartins.com

Designed by Donna Sinisgalli Noetzel

Library of Congress Cataloging-in-Publication Data

Names: Reyn, Irina, author.
Title: Mother country: a novel / Irina Reyn.
Description: First Edition. | New York: St. Martin's Press, 2019.
Identifiers: LCCN 2018039822| ISBN 9781250076045 (hardcover) | ISBN 9781466887374 (ebook)
Classification: LCC PS3618.E95 M68 2019 | DDC 813/.6—dc23
LC record available at https://lccn.loc.gov/2018039822

Our books may be purchased in bulk for promotional, educational, or business use. Please contact your local bookseller or the Macmillan Corporate and Premium Sales Department at 1-800-221-7945, extension 5442, or by e-mail at MacmillanSpecialMarkets@macmillan.com.

First Edition: February 2019

10 9 8 7 6 5 4 3 2 1

For my mother and my daughter

But wars of independence have a second step and that is a war for borders.

—SENIOR SECURITY OFFICIAL IN KIEV AS TOLD TO TIM JUDAH, FROM *IN WARTIME: STORIES FROM UKRAINE*

Mother Country

Prologue
WAR

We wake up at four in the morning to explosions. Once the bombing begins, we may as well get up and start the day. The windows, fortified by tape, are rattling with enough force to shatter into a million pieces. Everyone in the apartment building is awake, you could hear us breathing through the walls. We want to go back to sleep, hard-earned sleep we've forced upon ourselves with tranquilizers and alcohol, but what can we do? We still have to get ready for work. We rise, we pick out our clothes, we brush our teeth, we put on makeup. We move to the one room with no glass walls. The entire family gathers in the bathroom, babushka, cat, and all.

If we start seeing that flare crossing the sky, if the shelling sounds like it's moving closer, that's the signal bombing is coming, and we are more frightened when bombing happens during the day than under the shroud of darkness. Such flagrant daytime bombing makes us think all of humanity has been extinguished. Even the cat is traumatized, and nothing we can do, not even the promise of wet food we no longer have, will tease him from out of the space behind the toilet.

Inside the bathroom, we dress in our best bras and panties. They are not the cotton, granny kind but our finest, without the holes, with a little scalloped silk to the elastic. The girls from work joke that if we don't survive the walk to school or back and our bodies are splayed out on the sidewalk for all to see, it's far preferable to be discovered in respectable underthings. Of course if the building goes down, if a single shell hits the nearby chemical factory and sets off a calamity worse than Chernobyl, neither the bathroom nor nice underwear will save us. But controlling our appearance is all we have.

We never make the twenty-minute walk to work alone; at each block we gather more and more colleagues until an entire row of women are walking with linked arms, flashlights illuminating the road. We exchange the kind of nervous banter that would appear to the eavesdropper as the normal gossip of young women. We recount the highlights of our weekend in entertaining detail, we even laugh at one another's jokes. But even as we are concentrating on taking one step and then another, we are aware of being watched. Snipers are hiding on the roofs of buildings, at block posts, behind blockades. Tanks with the Ukrainian flag are rolling beside us.

Soldiers can stop us anytime to search through our bags, so we bring only the essentials, no rucksacks or duffel bags. A small feminine purse. We don't want to be like Yana, who was trying to head west for a short trip. At the blockade, she was forced to turn her bag inside out. Of course nothing incriminating was found in there, but the soldiers told her, "Who leaves their own region when everyone's dying? What kind of a patriot are you?" She was so nervous, she pressed her foot on the gas instead of the brake. Well, what do you think happened? She was shot to death. This happens all the time. Sometimes the soldiers get so loaded up with booze, they just shoot at one another, and who wants to be caught in the middle of that nonsense? No one wants their death to be the result of a drunken brawl.

Today, the principal ushers us all inside the school with a chuckle. "Hello, good morning, ladies, come in, come in. Don't worry, all will be well. They won't kill us today."

"Well, that's a relief, Pavel Mikhailovich," we say, tagging our own laugh onto the end of his. We tuck away our lunches and peel off our cardigans. We try to concentrate on that day's lesson plan.

There is no choice but to settle in to work. We are earning eighty a month and rent is fifty a month, and everything we squirrel away goes toward emergency doctors' visits. We know if something happens to us or our parents or grandparents, the emergency personnel will first ask, "And how old is your babushka?" and "Do you have the cash to cover this?" Even if poor babushka is having a heart attack right in front of them! To draw blood, we know to go to the hospital with our own cotton, our own syringe, our own alcohol. All that requires cash. No, not a day of work must be missed.

Our students are so young and frightened. Some have been well informed by their parents about what's going on but others are sweetly, innocently protected. We go over the protocol, the emergency drill, the evacuation plan in case our school is shelled. Japan or some other country has managed to slip in some relief supplies, blue rucksacks with notebooks and pencils, some medicine. The kids caress the pencils like the most precious of toys.

At least some part of the day is devoted to talking about the war. We hand out photographs of mines, so they know what they look like on the ground. We've heard stories of kids who've stepped on a mine while running around outside. We will not let it happen to any of ours if we can help it. A classic game like Old Woman Kutsia—where a blindfolded child must find his friends by following the sound of their clapping—is strictly forbidden. We feel so sorry for these kids. What kind of life is this? As children, we used to spend hours playing in the woods but our students must come directly home after school. So must we.

On the way home, we see the soldiers from the west, the ones sent here to "protect" us from separatists, we see the ones from Russia, slipped in to rescue us from western Ukrainian occupation, and we see the separatists, who insist we need to wrestle control of our region, that we have never belonged to Ukraine. To be honest, we're tired of all of them. We want nothing except an end to this war.

These poor men, how can we not pity them? They have been sent to a region they do not know. The ones from the west are in flip-flops, poorly outfitted. Their guns are foreign objects for them, bigger than their scrawny forms. They are so incredibly young for their jobs, six-teen or seventeen, or so incredibly old, in their fifties and sixties. They are hungry and cold. We give them food from our garden plot, eggs and potatoes. They make makeshift homes for themselves in the woods, rickety planks held together by twine that collapse at the first threat of wind. They keep saying, "the junta is coming," "the bandera." The words tumble out of their mouths, do they even believe them? Most are just knocking on our door, asking for showers, for a spare bandage for their bleeding feet.

When we return to our cold apartment, there is no warmth even among family. We are all divided east or west. Cousins and uncles stop returning phone calls. They remove your friendship and block you on Odnoklassniki. Other than Mongolian common cold recipes and cats running on treadmills, the only posts we like on the site are:

> *If you have Russo-Ukrainian families, husband, wife, mother, father, grandfather, grandmother, like this post. If you have relatives in Ukraine or in Russia, like this post! Let's show the whole world that we are not just two coun-tries that share a common border. We have mutual families and relatives!*

121K comments   4K shares   536K likes
And:

Let's make a common wish for New Year's: so our parents live a long life, our children don't fall ill, our loved ones don't leave us, friends don't betray us, salary should grow, prices should not. And the most important thing: no war.

Posts like these make us feel less alone and less crazy.

We know this: we are poor. No one wants us in Europe. Everyone tells us it will get better, but our life is worse, way worse. We are trapped here. We are living as though in medieval times with no light or water, or medical care. We walk around with candles. Everyone is abandoning the city. You think you hear the sound of footsteps, but it is the dragging paws of an abandoned dog. Anyone who can, leaves.

And we know all too well, a Ukrainian winter is coming. The days will be shorter at least, which means more bombing in the dark where it belongs. But there will be no heat, and we will be starving and jittery and half crazed with fear all day. War is so loud; you have no idea how loud war is. You're just not prepared for the noise. And the agonizing passage of time. We spend those hours trembling with the cat in the bathroom, washing our underthings in the sink, drying them on the side of the tub. Drinking neat spirits. Preparing for the next day's walk among the rubble.

TRANSCRIPT OF AN INTERVIEW CONDUCTED WITH A
TWENTY-SEVEN-YEAR-OLD SCHOOLTEACHER LIVING IN
THE DONBASS REGION OF UKRAINE

—*THE ATLANTIC*

1

First-World Problems

❋ **Brooklyn, April 2014**

In this Brooklyn neighborhood, Nadia was sure she was the only nanny from Ukraine. She preferred to think of herself as an observer, a temporary traveler, someone waiting for a new life to begin, rather than who she really was: a worker executing an invisible task within the neighborhood's complex ecosystem.

She generally liked the cheerful chaos of the park playground. Children were tooling about on sea legs, clutching green pouches of pureed nonsense. Older kids swished about on those dangerous scooters, babies giggled their way down slides. The sudden eruption of tears, the squeaky hum of the swings, the sound of women droning into their cell phones. By this point, Nadia was capable of pulling out a few phrases in English—Come here, No, Don't touch—but the rest congealed into a soupy blur behind her eyelids.

One eye trained on Sasha, Nadia was listening to a song her daughter emailed her by some *blondinka* pop singer with preternaturally tanned skin. On first glance, this Vera Brezhneva was yet another Ukrainian starlet who had magically transformed herself into one of "*Russia*'s sexiest women." On the other hand, the song had a melancholy strain Nadia couldn't resist and the music video, three generations of blond girls, mothers, and grandmothers in white shifts embracing one another on breezy seashores, made her cry. The song was a mother addressing a beloved daughter, advising her to uphold inner strength during the most difficult times and promising that, no matter what, she would always be by her side—two ways she was currently failing her own daughter. "Don't fall apart, my dearest girl," Brezhneva breathed into Nadia's earbuds.

She was tugged into the song's plaintive chorus, the tide of hopelessness for her own family's situation, when she noticed Sasha scissor across the wooden slats of the jungle gym to yank a stuffed rabbit out of the hands of some crouching toddler.

"Sasha," she called out, shutting the music off.

Sasha had an identical rabbit at home. The same pewter-white, exorbitantly overpriced bunny with cloth of pink flowers sewn into the insides of his flapping ears. The other child had a look of shock on her face. Her encounter with Sasha was clearly a first in a series of life's arbitrary cruelties.

"Mine, mine!" Sasha cried, clawing at the little girl's enclosed fist.

Vera Brezhneva was rendered mute. "Enjoy, Mama," wrote Larisska when she sent her the link to the song. Nadia hoped this was the beginning of a thaw in their relationship, a sign that Larissa was softening to her. But this message was the last Nadia received from her, the final one from home before the fighting moved there. According to the news and friends who'd escaped to Kiev or Odessa, Rubizhne was devastated—no electricity, no water—just the sound of shrapnel and random shooting. Every time she heard fire truck sirens on Court Street or the metallic thrash of a shutting grate, she felt her heart burst free from her chest. That her daughter might be dead—shot by a sniper on her

walk to work, say—is a thought she refused to form, but its outline, the inconceivable blackness of it, gripped her several times a
day, sometimes several times an hour.

She caught up to Sasha—"*Shto ty delaesh?*" What are you
doing?—and pried the rabbit out of Sasha's hands. The little girl
and her nanny looked satisfied with the rabbit's homecoming—
"Say thank you, Gwendolyn"—but Sasha burst open a livid wail
that turned all eyes toward them. The girl scrunched up her face,
zigzagged her mouth, and exploded.

This kind of thing happened often now. Nadia struggled to employ American methods that Sasha's mother clearly preferred
while ignoring her own certainties on how to curb this behavior.

"Maybe, Nadia, if you just try to explain to her why you need
her to act a certain way, if you . . . how to say . . . 'empower' . . . her
with choices. I think positive parenting works better than our old
Soviet methods, don't you?" Regina had shyly pointed to a row of
parenting books on her shelf. There were way too many of them,
on every basic facet of raising a child—pooping, sleeping, walking, discipline. Of course, Nadia knew "positive parenting" was
laughably worthless, basically handing children keys to the house
and begging them to discipline *you*.

She decided to try the American method first. She plucked
Sasha gently by the elbow, crouched at face level like Regina demonstrated for her, and tried to make eye contact with the girl. Most
of those books recommended offering children two acceptable
choices.

"Would you like to go home right now or in five minutes?" she
tried. Everyone in the neighborhood was using this technique, and
even if she didn't understand the words, she felt the tormented seesaw of those choices in the voices of adults all around her: Would
you like an apple or a carrot? Juice or milk? Your pink jacket or

green sweatshirt? Your kale pouch or your cheese bunnies? Often what she really wanted to cry was, *Look at the choices facing the greater world! Would you prefer life or death?*

Sasha was avoiding her, the hollering growing operatic and accusatory now, the nannies and mothers pretending they weren't stealing glances in their direction. If this were Larisska, she would have swatted her a few times on her behind, told her in no uncertain terms that this was unacceptable behavior. She would have marched her home and shoved her directly in the corner. Not that a public tantrum of this sort would have even occurred to Larisska, whose sense of rules and boundaries were inscribed into her from birth.

A terrible thought now assailed her: had Larisska sent her the song out of an outpouring of love or bitter irony? As in, "Look how you abandoned me here. Some mother you turned out to be." Or, "I've realized they gave you no choice but to leave me behind" and "I know you are doing what's best for me"? It wasn't clear, but Nadia chose to interpret the sharing of this song in the most positive light. *Enjoy, Mama.* It was the first unsolicited email she had received from Larisska in six years and she could not afford to doubt its sincerity. Not when they were so close to finally getting her here. Or at least she prayed they were close. For the past six years, since arriving in America, Nadia labored for a single goal: to bring her daughter here. Her sick daughter, her diabetic daughter, a daughter that, despite being in her twenties, still desperately needed her mother. For God's sake! She had been on a waiting list for seventeen years!

The letter to the state senator was in her purse right now, scrawled in careful Russian for Regina to translate. "Dear Mrs. Senator. I am writing you urgently with the hope that you will help speed up the immigration process of my daughter who lives in war-torn Ukraine. Her application to join me in America has been stalled for five and a half years now and the current situation has become very dangerous for her. I worry that with the escalation of the war, my diabetic daughter will no longer have access to insulin. . . . Is there any way to please speed up her application, to grant her asylum . . ."

Sasha had pulled free and was running away from her, ducking under the swinging tire.

"*Sashenka, Sashenka, idem ot syuda.*"

"No, no no!"

There was a reason no sane Ukrainian mother presented children with silly choices. Sasha had was digging in her heels, turning her body floppy and heavy, immovable. It was as if the very sound of Russian was irritating to her.

"You must stop speaking Russian," Sasha had commanded her the other day. Her chin was thrust out, a three-year-old landowner overseeing a stable of serfs. "I want you to speak only English."

"Your mama wants I speak Russian," Nadia tried to explain then, as if the girl could understand why her Russian-born mother wanted her to speak Russian while speaking it so badly herself. But who listened? As she headed toward her fourth year, Sasha's personality changed. As a two-year-old, she was charmed by the Russian language, by the simple messages behind classic Soviet cartoons, the books they read together about birds who withheld porridge from lazy animals, and songs about raffish bandits saving princesses from dull, bourgeois lives. Sasha was only too happy to immerse herself in Nadia's lap and count in Russian, her dimples deepening with each pronunciation—*odin, dva, tri*. But once she started part-time preschool, she wanted nothing more to do with the language. Insisting in her own way that everyone that mattered now spoke English.

Sasha moved away from the tire, wiped her nose with her sleeve. It seemed like she'd concluded with her protests, had made peace with the bunny's surrender. She returned to the jungle gym, her long eyelashes matted with tears. But then the little girl toddled by again, pushing the bunny in her pink baby stroller.

"Give. Back. Bunny!" Sasha launched into a renewed scream at the top of the slide, blocking any other child's access to its mouth. Nadia started to climb, tiptoeing her way past babies who, frankly, did not belong in this section of the playground.

"Sasha, Sashenka," she pleaded.

She was about to resort to good, old-fashioned Russian tactics when a mother holding a tall, straw-colored drink rose from her bench and slowly approached the slide. She was the type of woman Nadia saw more and more in Sasha's neighborhood, a gaunt chicness in monochromatic shirts. Her hair was slicked behind her diamond-studded ears. She wore leg-hugging pants that ended before the ankle and a pair of gold ballet flats with no arch support. The kind of clothes her Larisska used to fantasize about as a teenager, clipping pictures of them from Moscow magazines. These women didn't walk; they glided like porpoises.

With one fluid crook of the finger, the woman gestured for Sasha to go ahead and slide down, and to Nadia's amazement, the girl instantly obeyed. Then the lady whispered something in Sasha's ear, a speech so calm, and so directed, Nadia could barely see the mouth moving. How she envied this power language could wield. With each whisper, Nadia was being diminished, pushed out of sight. It was clear from the way Sasha looked back at her with newly wise eyes. Nadia was being swept aside by some higher sphere of native authority.

As if by magic, Sasha transformed back into a calm, self-possessed little girl. The other kids began circling down the slide, the parents and nannies became immersed in their former conversations. The girl with the bunny offered no more provocation. Sasha dutifully placed her hand in Nadia's palm.

"Tank you," Nadia said, but the woman barely acknowledged her. Her lips were pursed. To her, Nadia embodied nothing more than hundreds of ineffectual nannies at New York City playgrounds. What would be the point of telling her that Nadia had once served as head bookkeeper at an important gas pipe manufacturer? That she had her own family on the opposite side of the world? That her life was far rounder than the reflection in the woman's eyes?

"I want water," Sasha commanded. Nadia dove into a bag filled with Sasha necessities—a hat, sunscreen, bug spray, snacks, change of clothing, princess wand, safari stickers, "organic" fruit chews. She handed over the water bottle. The morning was turning toward noon, the babies bundled back in their strollers, toddlers chasing after dogs. Nadia noticed that the water spray was turned on—way too early in the season if you asked her—and she watched in horror as kids in clinging bathing suits and wet faces ran around in twenty-degree Celsius weather. Sasha drank her water with an imperious lilt to her throat, and when she handed it back and their eyes met, it was clear she too knew that Nadia could easily be erased. That even though the girl once wept inconsolably when Nadia left for the day, and had clung to Nadia's thighs in countless baby music classes and ran to her in the morning with joy-suffused cheeks, a wispy thread connected them that Sasha alone had the power to snap.

"Let's go," she said, sighing, and Sasha complied.

A quick backward glance told her the woman and her son had disappeared beyond the trees, the expensive shops, the clutch of chatting nannies from exotic, warm climates Nadia would never know.

Sasha's mother came home at six fifteen. Every day, Regina interpreted "six o'clock" in a novel way. She returned wearing the same gym clothes from the morning and dropped a heavy canvas bag to the floor. On days like these, it was easy to forget Regina was anything but American; what Russian woman would dare dress like this in public? What Russian woman would fail to notice that her often absent husband was probably sleeping around on her and maybe she should try a little harder with her appearance if she wanted to hold on to him? That Regina was born in Moscow and emigrated with her parents when she was seven seemed only to lend her an air of general melancholy, an uninformed grasp on Russian politics, and a smattering of grammar-school Russian words she often wrested out of their proper contexts. Immigration in childhood had been Regina's biggest trauma and Nadia sensed that this narrative shielded the woman from life's more pressing tragedies. But she was like family now, and family was to be scrutinized under a microscope with affectionate exasperation.

"Mommy, Mommy, you came back," Sasha cried, leaping into her mother's arms. Her happiness was so acute and genuinely surprised, you'd think the girl was abandoned during wartime, her mother returned from the front to fetch her at an orphanage.

"Of course Mama came back, Mama always comes back," Nadia said gaily, rising from their puppet show of animals. She gave Regina an affectionate kiss of greeting. Sasha ignored her, her usefulness concluded. She immediately started engaging her mother in English, presumably about the details of her day. She hoped the girl was leaving out the tantrum, the bunny, the haughty mother that had so swiftly altered the tenor of their relationship.

"Oh, wonderful." Regina nodded, clearly half listening, slipping out of her sneakers. "Sounds great, honey." She was always, in Nadia's view, distracted. She was a woman who never seemed to live in the present; she was like Chekhov's "Lady with a Lapdog" without the tormented lover or decrepit husband. Her American husband, Jake, had a youthful, athletic physique, and was suspiciously good-looking and rarely at home.

When Nadia once asked Regina what she did for a living, Regina replied that she was a "writer." Nadia assumed this meant journalist or secretary or even a professor of literature. But Regina insisted that she wrote *romany,* that she was in fact a novelist for a living despite having never published any actual novels. This "occupation" baffled Nadia. As far as she was concerned, a true novelist was Tolstoy or Pasternak or Bulgakov or even, if you had to grope around for one in the present, Valery Shevchuk. Tormented geniuses huddled over their desks, pens scratching across yellowing reams of paper, or great orators performing to rapt crowds, hosts of salons where big ideas circulated along with Georgian wine. Dignified graying women with sober cropped haircuts or, at least, alcoholics. Not this anxious woman in workout clothes and hot pink sneakers, whose haircut was way too long for someone her age. Not this woman, who at forty-two was about fifteen years too old to have small children, who whiled away the day at some rented cubicle just down the street staring into a computer screen, presumably waiting for divine inspiration to strike.

Regina sat down heavily on one of the kitchen stools, Sasha on her lap. Her stalk-green eyes settled a bit fearfully on Nadia's. She switched over to her usual schoolgirl-level Russian. "So what happened today?"

Nadia launched into the details of the girl's rigorous education, feeding, sleeping, and pooping schedule, highlighting Sasha's triumphs of good behavior while glossing over the incident at the playground. She had eaten pureed vegetable soup, almost half a head of broccoli, and one of Nadia's famous farmer cheesecakes studded with fresh blueberries. They had accomplished some simple addition with the help of cherry tomatoes, read two Russian books, memorized half a poem, and practiced writing "Sasha" in Russian and English.

"Nice job!" Regina said to Sasha, a bit of hollow American praise she overused. "Great, *spasibo,* Nadia. Sounds like a . . ." She searched for an appropriate Russian word. "Good day."

Nadia had been looking forward to an entry, a natural pause in the conversation where she could take out the letter to the senator, but Regina was already being pulled toward a game on the rug and she was left standing by the door. The letter she had drafted lay at the top of her purse's opening, folded carefully between the pages of a book to avoid creasing.

She considered whether to interrupt the game, to insist on Regina's help. But Sasha had already enveloped her mother's attention, and the tantrum was still fresh in Nadia's mind. She slowly rose to leave, giving Regina every opportunity to encourage the little girl to bid her a proper good-bye at the door.

"See you later," she called out, lingering. "Don't forget tomorrow I work at Grisha's."

But mother and daughter were firmly ensconced in the living room/bedroom, the mother taking on the ludicrous persona of Peppa Pig (or Svinka Peppa, as she would only allow Sasha to watch the Russian-dubbed version of the British cartoon). Regina was emitting unfeminine snorting noises.

"See you next week, girls," Nadia tried again.

"Oh, bye, Nadia," Regina called out from the play rug, giving no indication of rising herself. Well, what did Nadia expect? Like mother, like daughter. Such a different understanding of manners here. If Regina were not so vulnerable, so easily bruised and defensive, she would have reminded her of the importance of modeling good manners.

She had never allowed Larisska to skip the ritual of the greeting or farewell. "Say good-bye to Tyotya Olya" or "Say hello to Dyadya Yasha." By the time Larisska was five, she no longer needed to be dragged to the door; she knew the proper way to bid someone farewell.

But that was then, of course. When the world was right side up.

Nadia locked the door behind her and trudged down all those stairs to let herself out of the brownstone and into a Brooklyn so different from her own slice of the borough it might as well be a different nation. In this Brooklyn, the stores were not warehouses for cheap plastic junk, but elegantly and neatly presented to pedestrians. They were museums, spare and gutted of any actual wares. She loved walking into them with Sasha, inspecting wispy and decadent items. Useless frippery like soaps wrapped in twine, delicate swan-shaped moisturizer bottles, silky spaghetti straps dangling from velvet hangers. Some stores bartered only in nuts, while others churned out "artisanal" mayonnaise. She marveled at the civilized exchanges between owners and customers. No one was groping at vegetables, suspiciously sniffing them for freshness. No one was hobbling about with grim expressions, hauling cheap flowers in yellow disposable bags. No babushki sitting outside their high-rises in plastic chairs, volubly commenting on passersby— "Maybe you should put a sweater on that child before she freezes to death" or "A real man never lets a lady carry heavy bags." On her stretch of Kings Highway, it was dubious produce and "Italian" fashion, trinkets with which to entertain children, pharmacies with their Polish creams and *matryoshki* and other sentimental ornaments from the former Soviet Union, nothing more than tourist bait.

Here, no one was haggling over pennies or chastising her for asking stupid questions. No one raised their voices the way they did at her local pharmacy this morning. (The pharmacist had yelled "Get out of here, *narcoman*!" to a customer trying to push a prescription of Vicodin across the counter. Couldn't she have simply said "I'm afraid we cannot fill this particular prescription"?) It was a country of too much and not nearly enough.

And there were so many restaurants in this fake Brooklyn, people always tending to the business of eating in public. Back home, no one went out to dinner. Any Russian or Ukrainian woman worth her salt could cook a better meal than the expensive ones in restaurants. But here she saw the same people out night after night for no good reason, licking their fingers after fried potatoes, fishing into bowls of black shells with tiny forks, actually waiting on sidewalks in order to get in and be divested of their money! Passing these idlers on her way to the subway, she couldn't help remembering that awful January in 1988, Larissa just born and refusing her breast milk, waiting two hours in line at the cooperative in case there was a single can of baby formula. No one here could grasp that kind of desperation.

The train was predictably crowded but she could mark the exact places where it would start easing up. Carroll Street, Fourth Avenue, and the biggest exodus of all: Seventh Avenue. Women in workout clothes and comfortable shoes. Dark-skinned men with tattoos who seemed to be the only segment of the population who rose for pregnant women. Orthodox Jews. Five years before, she had never seen people like this—all these shades and religions.

Back home, she had only read about Orthodox Jews and Muslims and black people and gay people, saw them on television in ominous broadcasts on life in America.

Her first few months here, she was afraid of them all, clutching her purse tightly to her chest. Her heart raced with every stop until the scary people got off the train and she could breathe again. When someone broke out drums or begged for cash, she would find her blood pressure rising, newly alert, pepper spray clutched tightly in her fist. But after a year or two, she started relaxing, seeing a new beauty, a new collegiality with all that color. Now she rode with them backward and forward, from deep Brooklyn to la-la Brooklyn and she thought of them as private comrades in life and war.

The following Monday, Sasha was being obstinate by refusing to roll her Russian *rs*. "Tree" she kept attributing to the number three, the *t* way too soft, the *r* carpeting out of her mouth. And then, "I did it, okay? Can I have my lollipop now?"

Nadia tapped on the blackboard with a wedge of chalk. "Try another time, yes? *Odin, dva, tri. Trrrrrri.*"

The girl said something in English that may have been the word "tired" or even "buzz off," an unfortunate addition to both of their English vocabularies thanks to an unfortunate new gift of a book. Sasha's attention kept returning to the fire escape, where a squirrel was nibbling an acorn to shreds.

"Tired," she said again.

"No tired. Try one more time."

"Stop? Sew dog."

Nadia sighed. Back home, kids younger than Sasha were counting and repeating and memorizing. (*Praying for their lives and countries in underground bunkers!* But she refused to think about that.) By Sasha's age, Larissa could recite Pushkin's "On Seashore Far a Green Oak Towers" or a smattering of Shevchenko. Here, on the other hand, children were passively entertained at all times; no wonder they were ill-equipped for boredom. Even the adults were untrained for the basic hardships of life.

How often had she watched Regina lugging poor baby Sasha, her stroller, and a bag of groceries? The effort took on a comical cast, with Regina struggling with Sasha on one hip, the stroller pressed against the other, and the groceries dragging pitifully behind her. When Nadia hoisted three bags, she was able to lift the stroller under one arm, the groceries firmly in hand, and Sasha around the waist. By contrast, Regina was often overwhelmed by the smallest of domestic tasks: how to wash urine from a sheet in the sink, sew the split crotch of a pair of pajamas, scrub mold from a tub corner. It was as though her own mother had failed to teach her tools of basic survival.

She pitied Regina for raising children in a culture that promoted her helplessness, a culture that made her doubt her own instincts, forcing her to research how to be a parent rather than boldly and unquestioningly raise her own daughter. Even Sasha's name made no sense to her! On one hand it was a nod to Regina's Russian heritage, but no girl in Russia would be named Sasha. It was a nickname, an affectionate truncation of Alexandra, just like Nadia was short for Nadezhda. Imagine her name being Nadia on a birth certificate! To name a child Sasha was to strip the word of any coherent connection with the past.

When she first interviewed for the job, Nadia handed to Regina a list that summarized the correct approach to child-rearing.

1. The child will always be strapped into the stroller on city streets.
2. The child will not be given any cold beverages or ice cream.
3. The child must spend at least a half hour out-doors breathing fresh air.
4. An exception to the above rule—if the child is sick. Then all her activities must be canceled so she can recover.
5. Naps will be orchestrated at precise times each day so the child has a strict understanding of her daily schedule.
6. Nadia will puree as many foods as possible to avoid choking, and each meal will include a veg-etable, a grain, dairy, and a fruit.
7. There will be two educational activities each day, including time for the child to play independently.
8. Toilet training will begin at nine months.

The list continued in this vein, and as she read on, Regina appeared both thrilled and intimidated by Nadia's rules. It was clear that this was precisely what she was looking for, a person to bring order to a wishy-washy household, to erect strict boundaries to a formless world of self-doubt brought on by a sea of parenting manuals.

"When can you start?" Regina had said, putting down the list. And now, three years later, they were enmeshed together in a tight cocoon of love and fear and language confusion.

Sasha was shoving at her a red dog split at the belly because her coddled mother had no idea how to thread a needle.

"Okay, okay, I do." She took the disemboweled dog and reached for the sewing kit.

Her phone rang; she put down the wounded dog and Sasha took advantage of the interruption by moving away from the chalkboard with the Russian letters and toward the dollhouse in her tiny alcove.

"Allo."

"Nadia, hello." It was Regina's apologetic voice. Regina was always apologetic, deferring to Nadia's competence or to Sasha's impetuous outbursts. She acted as though she had a hard time being seen. "I'm so sorry. I forgot to mention this morning that Sasha has a playdate with this girl from her preschool, Mila. Would you mind meeting up with Mila's nanny today? She speaks Russian too, so I thought it would be a great . . . plan."

"Of course, no problem." She wrote down the address in clear block letters. "We go to them, yes?"

"Oh yes, of course. There's no room for both girls at our place."

"No problem. I will put on her jacket now." She hung up, and called, "Sasha, Sashen'ka! Come here."

Not that she had far to walk to find Sasha, which was the reason friends were never invited here. Another thing Nadia would never understand about Regina's life was the size of this apartment. Who ever heard of an American family choosing to be squashed like this? A little girl in a room with no door while the parents slept in a pull-out couch in the living room? Her own parents had lived better than this under communism! Her mother and Larisska lived in a much bigger apartment in Rubizhne. (*If it was still intact. If they were still alive.* Not now, she refused to dwell on that.)

"It's worth it for us to . . . how do you say, sacrifice? To live in this neighborhood," Regina explained to her on more than one occasion.

"Why this neighborhood? Because of mayonnaise store? You cannot live without fresh . . . what is it? Rhubarb mayonnaise?" she asked in disbelief.

But Regina just smiled and shook her head. "Nadia, you don't understand."

Regina and Jake's apartment consisted of two rooms and a kitchen on the fifth floor of a brownstone in desperate need of renovation. The bathroom was tiled in mustard yellows and browns with a leaking claw-foot tub and a shower curtain not long enough to contain pools of spraying water. The kitchen cabinets were almost all off their hinges, the rusted hardware loose, the oven lit only when you jiggered the knob and helped it along with a match. The ceiling in the "living room" was stamped with an amoeba-shaped water stain.

Was any neighborhood worth this discomfort? It was clear to Nadia that Regina and Jake had no time alone together, their marriage frayed by the sardined living conditions. And poor Sasha was always losing friends when Regina never reciprocated the invitations of other families. The pattern was always the same—Sasha would be invited one or two times to some classmate's house, then Regina would volunteer they meet in a public place like the park. When the weather deteriorated she was forced to invent excuses for why Sasha was unavailable for any more playdates. Eventually, the friend drifted away, Sasha heartbroken, repeating, "When I go to Isabella's?"

All this to stay in a neighborhood that sold yarn and expensive handbags and eyeglasses, ice-cream shops with six-dollar scoops that had lines around a velvet rope. More than once, she wanted to shake Regina and tell her that her entire life would improve if her family moved to a neighborhood they could actually afford.

She peeked around the corner into Sasha's "bedroom." The girl was crouched on the floor, squeezed in between bed and white dresser. "Okay, Sashen'ka. We go Mila's house."

"Too busy." The dolls were seated in high chairs, eating in a restaurant, of all things. (Nadia's dolls had once explored nature or cooked elaborate meals. They sewed and danced and studied their multiplication and marched in parades. It came as no surprise to Nadia that American dolls whiled away their own pampered days in restaurants.)

"Yes, I see you very busy. But Mama said . . ."

"Ramen, please," one inappropriately busty doll commanded from a solicitous waiter.

The phone rang again. "Nadia, sorry, it just occurred to me." Regina's meek voice was being drowned by the screech of ambulance sirens. ". . . you mind putting a new outfit on Sasha?"

"New outfit? But she is dressed already."

Nadia quickly scanned Sasha. The little girl looked fine to her in her jeans and pink tunic, a pink sequined headband sweeping back her long chestnut hair.

"Actually, I'm thinking that Tea dress with flowers and Hanna Andersson leggings, and the Primigi Mary Janes?"

"She is warmly dressed for the weather. Do not worry, she will not catch chill."

There was a pause. "Oh, I know. I have no doubt you dressed her . . . good. But I'd like her to look especially nice for this play-date. Mila's mother is on the . . . how do you say . . . committee . . . of this school, and . . ."

"Oh, I understand. No problem, Reginochka."

"Sorry to bother you. Thank you, Nadia." Regina sounded relieved, as if she had expected Nadia's stern objections and was happy, if only in that moment, not to be judged.

+ + +

This Mila's brownstone was one of the gleaming, renovated ones on Strong Place, an idyllic, tucked-away block that Nadia enjoyed strolling. Unlike Sasha's loud corner just off earsplitting Smith Street, this was a hideaway of leafy perfection, of brownstone after elegant brownstone illuminated by perfect sunshine by day and gauzy lanterns in the evenings. At night, when the interiors exploded with light, Nadia enjoyed staring into the cavernous, curated lives within, owners gliding between windows with books or trays, glasses of wine. Contorted, modern chandeliers reflecting light on enormous works of modern art. It was even better than television, gaping at these foreign worlds.

They lingered at the steps, the windows large and open, the brick exterior clean, the door painted an inviting, unchipped cherry red. It was clear by the single buzzer that Mila's family owned the entire house. At her side, Sasha lingered. She was gripping Nadia's hand, her thumb making an indentation in her palm. Nadia let her press the buzzer with a single uncertain finger.

The door swung open and a voluptuous, dark-haired woman in coral lipstick waved them inside. "Come in, come in," she said in Russian, and just the sound of those familiar words filled Nadia with hope. It occurred to her how rarely in her long days with Sasha she heard the mellifluous flow of the Russian language.

"I hope we're not late."

"No, no, we were just finishing a late lunch."

The woman's bosoms receded to another room, and the two of them were abandoned in the foyer with this Mila. By glancing the little girl over, Nadia understood why she was asked to change Sasha's outfit. Mila was wearing an expensive-looking printed herringbone dress, sunflower sandals, and a satin headband with a

floppy bow. She also looked to be older than Sasha, at least five
years old.

"Follow me, Sasha. Let's go." She was leading Sasha onto a different floor, one that was presumably all hers. Her dictates held
an even more officious ring than Sasha's.

"Tea?" the nanny called from the other room.

"Thank you, that would be most welcome."

"Come join me."

Usually, she dreaded the necessary socializing during these so-
called playdates. ("Can you explain 'playdates'?" she asked Regina
in the beginning. "I know, the very word is ridiculous, isn't it?"
Regina had laughed, empathizing with her confusion.) Not that
she was able to properly socialize with the other nannies or mothers.
The nannies were usually from lands incomprehensible to Nadia—
Dominican Republic or Trinidad or Saint Lucia. After the initial
tortured chitchat with the few English words Nadia had at her
disposal, they silently agreed to type on their own phones for the
remainder of the "playdate."

But now, she followed this Russian woman into a gleaming
kitchen straight out of a magazine. A kitchen embellished with
steel and marble, with a refrigerator the size of a car and an
industrial-sized oven with charming burgundy knobs.

"It is so beautiful here, *pravda*?" the nanny said. She was pulling
down marked glass jars decorated with a soothing array of Indian
prints. "There are many tea options. Lemongrass, verbena, something called Golden Monkey, chocolate mint truffle, rooibos, South
African red bush, green, green lavender, green mango, green peppermint."

"How about just plain tea? Normal tea."

The nanny smiled. "I know exactly what you mean." Her smile

was as generous as the rest of her, framing mostly straight white teeth. She selected the jar with loose black leaves, and sifted some of its contents into a strainer. Nadia tried to gaze away from those breasts but they were tightly encased, conical orbs peeking out of striped cotton like the smooth curve of a baby's bottom.

Running footsteps overhead sounded like a pair of galloping horses. The nanny turned her head to the ceiling. "Mila, you know pine floors are sensitive. Walk, please."

The footsteps halted.

"Okay, nanny, I won't do it anymore," came the perfectly fluent Russian response.

"Amazing," Nadia marveled. "I can't get Sasha to speak to me in Russian for the life of me."

The nanny gave her a sidelong glance, a quick flicker that Nadia couldn't entirely interpret. "So what's your story? There's an accent. From where?"

For some reason, Nadia was starting to feel uncomfortable. She wished the tea would steep faster. "Ukraina. Lugansk area."

The nanny whistled. "That's tough now, eh?"

"It's horrible." It was all she could do not to confide in this stranger. Her daughter, her mother, her friends. The one word she received was from a cousin who'd made it to Kiev. He told her over Skype, "It's impossible to explain to you, Nadenka. The bridges are gone, the hospital. Bodies just left to rot in the streets." Last time she saw Larissa over Skype it was at night, and outside the window, she could see the arc of flares shooting across the sky. Her mother said they took turns sleeping in the tub.

The galloping resumed upstairs, but this time the nanny didn't correct it. "I can't imagine. A nightmare over there. You must have relatives." The nanny served the tea and they sat silently among the gleaming stainless steel surfaces. Nadia became aware of a street leached of sound, so unlike what she had become used to in Brooklyn.

"I do. We're all terrified. Of course all we want is to be left alone." The last thing she meant to do was wade into politics. That most immigrants from the Soviet Union were Jewish in this country was a fact that took some getting used to—in Ukraine she had met one Jew, maybe two. But here weren't they all simply immigrants? "What about you? Where are you from?"

She heard giggling upstairs, the slamming of doors. The turquoise tiles above the stove gave the wall a look of a picturesque cobblestone street.

The nanny was no longer smiling. "Moscow. But my parents were from a small town in central Ukraine called Dzhurin."

"Oh really? I know where that is." With immigrants it was better to talk about anything but Ukraine, a touchy subject for Russian-speakers, western Ukrainians, and Jews. "This is such delicious tea. What flavor is this?"

"Of course eventually they had to leave with the other Jews."

Nadia set down her tea. "Well, I dream about one day getting to Moscow. It's a beautiful city, isn't it? When I save up some money, I might meet my daughter in Moscow. It seems like the only way I'll ever get to see her again. I couldn't take her, you see."

"You left your daughter behind?"

In the woman's voice, she perceived a snap of hatred. It was too bad. She had been looking forward to the possibility of a nanny friend. Child-caring hours were so long and monotonous and she envied the nannies she saw passing their work time in pairs, their braids swinging in unison as they pushed strollers down Smith Street.

"I think you misunderstand me. I didn't leave her. I came so she could join me here."

"You left your own daughter?" the woman repeated. "You left your own child in the middle of war?"

"There was no war then. She aged out of the application and I had to fill out a new application for her when I landed here. This was the only way she could leave. I send her money every month." Nadia was shocked. Did civilized people speak so rudely to strangers?

But this nanny kept talking. "You know, my parents were forced out of Dzhurin. Once my father grew beets instead of corn, and he was arrested. Can you imagine being arrested for growing beets? Of course, there was a famine, the region needed beets, but who cared about that?"

"I'm sorry."

"At the collective farm, they would report my father for any infraction. Turned him in and everything, slapped his many war medals down on the table and said he had a 'Jewish mug,' a *zhidovnia morda*. And that was after he survived the ghetto and the Soviet army. He died today, my brother's dealing with all the arrangements. Mila's parents couldn't find a substitute babysitter, so here I am."

"That's terrible. Do you want me to stay and watch Mila for a few hours?"

The woman slid a row of cookies from a tray as if they were engaging in pleasantries. "They would freak out. No, I will wait for them to get home. I don't know why all this came out. Look, try this one. It's dipped in chocolate with a raspberry filling. You'll lick your lips. These cookies cost more than my purse."

"No, thank you."

The nanny bit into a cookie. "They said he was not a bad guy for a 'zhid.' Believe me, I have no cozy feelings toward either Russians or Ukrainians, and you should feel exactly the same way."

Nadia rose suddenly, a loud scrape of the stool against shellacked bamboo floor. She felt her breathing speed, one breath bumping up against the next. The familiar feeling of being impotent. Or worse, being vaguely, impersonally hated. So often, the most incisive, externally imperceptible abuses in this country came to her from the mouths of other immigrants.

"Maybe it's best that I check in on Sasha." Before the nanny could protest, Nadia was halfway up the stairs. "Sashen'ka," she called out. "It's time for us to go."

Finding the kids was not easy. There was a long hallway flanked by three closed doors and she tried them all. One was a master bedroom with French doors that opened out to a balcony. The other two were children's bedrooms connected by a walk-in closet exploding with voluminous clothes. One wall was devoted to children's shoes, strappy and buckled, toes neatly pointing outward. An entire section of the closet consisted of costumes: witches and princesses, tutus and ladybugs. She stood there for a minute, a burning sensation in her throat, a pulsating twitch in her right eye.

She heard voices overhead so she climbed another set of stairs into an enormous loft drenched with toys. Her first reaction was to marvel at the hardwood floors, at the broad windows framing the first pussy willow buds of the season. The room was splashed with luxuriant light, the dappled color of which, it seemed to her, only rich people could afford. When she turned her attention to the kids, the sight that greeted her did not entirely make sense. The girl Mila was holding real scissors, long and silver, with inlaid pearl handles. And Sasha was sitting underneath them, among a constellation of hair lying in feathery layers on a shaggy white carpet.

"Dear God, what did you do?" She ran to Sasha and inspected

her head. Half of it remained intact, beautiful waves curling down her shoulder. The other side was hacked into wisps and spikes snarling around her ear.

"We're playing salon," Mila explained. "I am the hairdresser from Salon de Quartier, Sasha's my client."

Sasha was blinking up at her, suppressed fear beneath a need for . . . what? Collusion? Sympathy? Guilt?

The nanny was behind them now in a cloud of sugar and lavender perfume, wringing her hands. "Oh no, Mila. What did you do? We're going to have to tell your parents. Sashenka, please forgive Mila. Mila, say you're sorry."

"You should have been watching us better, nanny." Mila sweetly put down the scissors.

Nadia picked Sasha up in her arms. It had been many months since Sasha allowed herself to be carried in this way, crumpled and small, pressed against Nadia's chest. She was visibly scared, the way she was when the consequences of her own naughtiness solidified and were presented to her. It reminded Nadia somehow of walking on the edges of the Kremina Forest with her own Larisska where the air smelled of pine. They called the vast wooded area "Green Pearl" because of its fecund lushness, and at one point, not long after the diagnosis, she imagined a deep inhale of pine would cure her daughter of diabetes. How simple their relationship was then.

She descended with Sasha down the stairs, picked up her purse and stroller. "Thank you for having us."

She could hear the nanny behind her apologizing for the disaster of a morning. She was emotional, she hoped Nadia could forgive them all.

"Of course," Nadia said. "I wish I could help, but we really should go. I'm sorry for your loss."

She cradled Sasha and the stroller and Sasha's bag filled with nonchemical sunscreens, organic dried fruits, filtered water, and sun hat, and her own bag, heavy with her lunch and letter to the New York senator and change of shoes and a paperback. She hoisted all of them at once and suddenly felt immensely strong again. As if she could carry much more, half the world, in her steely, female grip.

On their way home, they walked past the new ice cream shop. A line was already formed at its front doors, children emerging with their cups of fancy treats, parents with their own cones. This time, she took note of Sasha's crumpled face. Instead of veering Sasha right past them as she normally did, they joined the back of the queue. Once inside, she watched the people in front of them as if through a clouded window, adults tasting from tiny plastic spoons and contemplating which flavor to choose as if the fate of entire nations rested on it. When they inched closer, she lifted Sasha up to peer inside the display cases. No tubs of plain vanilla, mind you, but chunks of caramel or chunky peanuts covered in chocolate or entire candy bars shoveled into barrels of what appeared to be frozen hazelnut. Sasha pointed at a spotted vat, which turned out to taste of peppermint and a haze of chocolate flecks. Sasha seemed to be cheering up. As she reached over to take a cone from a young man, she didn't appear to notice that the waiting hordes were staring at her asymmetrical hairstyle.

"Very punk rock," the cashier said, whatever that meant.

"Let's go." She paid the ridiculous six dollars and winced as Sasha submerged her entire mouth in the freezing dessert. Larisska's ice cream, like her own when she was a child, had been heated in a pot until lumps succumbed to soupy broth. How she would chase those orbs of ice around with her tongue! But Russians would never give children ice cream or drinks laced with ice cubes, and in her bones Nadia believed this to be right. It couldn't be good for throats or stomachs to be exposed to cold like that. But here was an entire culture that felt differently, and she was part of it now.

Ice cream consumed, they let themselves into an apartment that looked even shabbier than the one they left, the floors more sloped and stained than before, the caulking more visible in the corners. She became aware of how wide the wet splotch on the ceiling had spread, how it made the expensive furniture look cheaper. On top of the air conditioner, pigeons were putting the finishing touches on their nest, earsplitting cooing competing with the honking of snarled traffic. Regina would be horrified, would blow the entire thing out of proportion. Preschool pictures were looming and she would treat the matter as if it were a national tragedy. It would be up to Nadia to situate the haircut as a child's prank, to calm the hysteria.

Sasha, her mouth still sticky with peppermint, slipped off her shoes without being asked. She even placed them in the cubby designated for this very purpose. She looked puny with half a head of hair, her shoulders and rib cage slight, belly protruding.

"What do you want do? Shall we play restaurant with your dolls? Did they ever get that *soupchik* they ordered from that no-good waiter?" Nadia asked quietly.

Sasha walked directly to the chalkboard and contemplated the numbers scrawled there in Nadia's careful, florid penmanship.

"*Odin, dva, tri, chetyri,*" she began to recite. They were a team again, the solidarity of the wounded with a secret. Nadia nodded vigorously at "tree" and at "cheteerie." She praised Sasha's pronunciation. She volunteered hot dogs for dinner, but framed them with pureed carrots, and when Sasha ate every bite, she held the girl close, listening to the stubborn consistency of her beating heart.

When Regina came home at almost seven o'clock, Nadia put on a brave, cheerful face. Even before Regina set her canvas bag down and slipped off her sneakers, Nadia was working on easing the severity of her reaction.

"Don't worry, Reginochka. Her hair was so beautiful, but it will return to its length in no time. It'll probably be even thicker and healthier."

Regina looked confused, then her eyes fell on her daughter. She screamed, "What happened?"

Nadia explained what she had mentally prepared, making sure to level her tone. The girls were left alone. It was the way of children. It would grow back. This should only be the worst thing that happens to you, she thought privately.

"I don't understand this at all." Regina was winding her fingers around the cropped stalks and phantom hair that used to curl behind the ear and onto the girl's shoulder. "You were there, weren't you? You were watching her? How could this even have happened?"

"I'm sorry. Forgive me."

"But her hair was perfect. We just got it cut at the salon on Atlantic. It took so long to find a style she liked."

Sasha, overwhelmed by her mother's emotion, broke into a fresh round of tears. The two rocked in the tight wedge between living room and "bedroom." Nadia watched them, a struggle waging inside her. Once, her Larisska returned from a day with her friends with her hair completely caked in mud; they'd all taken turns "shampooing" one another out of roadside puddles. But so what?

She'd slapped Larisska halfheartedly across her backside, and sent her with a towel to the bathroom.

This was not the best time to emerge with the letter to the senator, but was there ever a good time?

"What's this?" Regina looked up at the envelope, uncomprehending.

"Would you please translate into English and type up for me? I wrote it just as I want it to say. My daughter is trapped in Lugansk region. Right where fighting is."

Regina unpeeled herself. "I didn't know you had a daughter."

She guessed it was true. She had never mentioned Larisska to Regina. At first, it was out of caution with a new employer who might use a sentimental connection like this one against her. Then it seemed easier to immerse herself in Regina's life, to mother her and Sasha instead.

"Look, as you can see this isn't a great time." Regina sighed, visibly irritated. "And I'm not very good at reading Russian. What is it you want me to do?"

This was a Regina she did not understand. The only way to make sense of it was to love her even more, for all her frail, childlike extremity of feeling. After all, she was living her life with no idea that there was a war going on where innocent people were dying, where the threat of death occupied their every thought, where they had no idea if they could find enough food to feed their children. How could this lucky American woman possibly comprehend that a bad haircut was not the end of the world?

Nadia spoke succinctly, like a history teacher. "I don't know if you have been reading the papers. But it is a complete emergency. A civil war and all the fighting is in my region. There is a referendum on the future of our region and my mother cannot vote in our town. She will have to be driven outside of Donetsk to find open polling booths. Even then she is not safe and her vote is probably useless. Every day, there is heavy artillery, bombing. Tanks around the perimeter of the forest, blockades, snipers shooting. I need to do something. I need to save them, and my best and only chance is to start with Larisska. She is like you, you know? Young but not young. She can't take care of herself."

The speech did seem to land with Regina. Her face took on a fresh compassion, perhaps even lending her more perspective on the haircut debacle. She kept stealing looks back at a Sasha still entwined around her leg, thinking. "I had no idea. Well, Nadia, I guess I don't really understand the situation in Ukraine . . ."

"You are writer. If you could write me that one letter in English in a nice florid way, in the way of a native English speaker. Maybe then the senator will pay attention to me."

There was no room for all of them and this fresh sadness inside this minuscule kitchen. "Okay. Why don't you leave it with me and I'll take a look later."

Nadia slid the letter onto the table and gathered her things. She was surprised to hear Regina's laughter.

"You want to hear something funny? The more I look at it, I actually like it," Regina said. She was holding up Sasha's other side, evening the two parts into a projected whole. "It's kind of . . . how do you say . . . In English, we say 'funky.' It will be easier to brush for sure. Wait until I tell Jake. We may be able to rescue it after all."

"Very punk rock," Nadia said, which made Regina laugh even more. They embraced good-bye after the envelope of cash was exchanged.

At the door, Nadia turned. She put her heavy purse down and gestured for Regina to come closer. "Before I go, I need to tell you something. Something very important. What just happened with Sasha, you should not make such a big deal of it. There are worse things that could happen."

Regina had this faraway smile on her face, as if she really had recovered. But Nadia saw her soul clearly. It was no different from that of their beloved little girl in the playground, outwardly composed but silently devastated over the loss of a ridiculous, expensive white rabbit. And how could Regina possibly know her daily, pressing, constant palpitating fear? This was one thing she owned, an emotion native to her, the one that gave her strength and resources that Regina was lucky enough to lack.

She bent down and repeated the main Vera Brezhneva lyric into Regina's ear—"Don't fall apart, my dearest girl"—in the calm, confident manner of that American mother at the playground who knew exactly what to say in a crisis, who somehow possessed the ability to make whole what was recently broken.

2

The Western Ones

When she arrived at her second job at Grisha's, Nadia heard the fierce sound of clanging cookware. This meant Aneta was angry again and the transition would be a headache.

To hear her tell it, Aneta hated being a home attendant, detested old people and their smells, found Grisha a dissolute lecher, and couldn't stand dirty Brooklyn sidewalks. Their employer, VIP Senior Care, punished her with the occasional overnight shift, which she attributed to pro-Russian biases in former Soviet Union immigrant circles, as if there were a Putin-led conspiracy to push ethnic Ukrainians out of the most desirable elderly caretaking jobs in America. She was angry for a million other reasons Nadia could not even begin to fathom.

"Your Majesty, waltz in at ten like nothing," she huffed as soon as Nadia turned the key. Lately, Aneta insisted on speaking English exclusively even though none of them had a decent grip on it.

"I no late." Nadia pointed to the clock on her phone. It said 8:58.

She heard Grisha call out in Russian from the catacombs of his bedroom, "Thank God, you've come to save me from this monster. It seems your beleaguered but proud country of Ukraine has elected a new president and now this one's become insufferable."

Aneta was a ruddy woman from some village outside of Berdy-chev. Stocky and square, she dressed in floral muumuus, scraggly hair tightly pulled back into a bun the size of a child's fist. Her face could be vastly improved, Nadia often thought, by just a few more teeth or at least the occasional smile.

She wagged her finger at Nadia. "Speak English. English. With me, always English. Or, if you like, Ukrainian. You should be speaking mother tongue. Are you not Ukrainian too, you separat-ist Putin-lover?"

This was not the time to explain to Aneta that though Nadia's mother tongue was Russian, she prayed every day that both west-ern Ukrainians, separatists, and Russians would leave her home-town in eastern Ukraine alone. In her worst nightmares, she never imagined it would come to war. How she wished the two sides of her fractured country could talk to each other, come together peacefully to find a way forward for a united Ukraine that served west and east. That dream was as far away from reality as it would ever be. But this was definitely not the time to remind Aneta where her actual allegiances stood (with America, naturally, the country that has saved both of their lives, not that Aneta expressed any ap-preciation!). It was best to distract her or wait for her to leave. Or at the very least, change the subject.

"How was Grisha night?"

"How could it be? I was trapped with this *idiotka*." Grisha wheeled himself into the living room. He whistled, looking her up and down. "My, my. You are height of female beauty, Nadia An-dreevna. Your hair is magnificent today. You look like a firebird. Or at least Tatyana from *Evgenyi Onegin*. Young and spritely."

"Thank you, Grisha."

He ignored Aneta, who was gathering her things on the coun-tertop and shoving them into her beige handbag. At one time or another, Nadia glimpsed empty yogurt containers, sweets they were forbidden to bring inside the homes of diabetics, earplugs, stockings, used tissues, nasal spray, even a change of underwear. When Aneta was this worked up, her hands shuddered. In her attempt to shovel possessions back into her purse, a cell phone slipped out of her fingers and crashed onto the linoleum floor.

"See what you people did?"

"Let me help you," Nadia said.

Before the Maidan protests began, before Yanukovych was ousted, before the "Lugansk People's Republic" declared their independence from the rest of Ukraine, Aneta didn't protest that Nadia and Grisha spoke Russian. Aneta's own Russian was quite fluent, if thickly accented. Back then, they all communicated fluidly, imparted important information about their shifts, went over the medication schedule, and even enjoyed the overlap in their hours by watching addictive reality television shows on the Russian cable station together. But as the war continued to rage and news of the election results was imminent, Aneta began pulling away, as if their very existence was an affront, demanding they all speak Ukrainian. What was poor Grisha supposed to speak when he was from Saint Petersburg and emigrated with a good-for-nothing son at the age of sixty-four? Was he to learn a new language? And what about Nadia, growing up in an ethnic Russian enclave in the Lugansk oblast'?

On the floor, the cell phone's cracked face showed a picture of an attractive girl Larisska's age, framed by blond curls. Nadia reached for it.

"She's beautiful. Is this your daughter?"

"You not touch. Nothing." Aneta wrapped her bruised phone in a scarf. She made a final sweep of the apartment and at last shoved open the front door.

"Bye, Aneta. Have nice day," Nadia said, in English, through her teeth.

"'The breaking of a wave cannot explain the whole sea,'" Grisha intoned to Aneta's back. He was always displaying his erudition by quoting Great Russian Writers.

Aneta froze, a hand still on the knob. The back of her neck practically sizzled with rage.

Just be quiet, Nadia silently ordered Grisha. *Let her go.* "What that mean, eh, old man? What you say?"

Two older women were slowly making their way across the hallway to the elevator. The one with the cane complained about a granddaughter that never called to ask after her health, the other with the rolling walker had an entirely different monologue going about the deteriorating quality of the produce at NetCost. They were, naturally, conversing in Russian.

Aneta lingered in the door frame. But then, as they listened to the pure Moscow cadences disappearing down the hall, she seemed to reconsider. Before Nadia knew what happened, Aneta traversed the room and slapped her across the face. The shock of it was the initial sting, Aneta's ringed, creased, foreign hand at her skin. But then the pain initiated in her chest, up the neck, and exploded at the place of attack. Her eyes filled with tears immediately, her very sockets burning from the heat of it.

"*Slava Ukraini,* traitor," Aneta said, noting her surprise and anger with satisfaction, and stormed out. They could hear the stomp of sensible heels against linoleum floor.

"*Nu, nu,*" Grisha clucked. "'However stupid a fool's words may be, they are sometimes enough to confound an intelligent man.'"

"What?" she said. It was a question aimed toward the universe at large. The outlines of the room were losing its focus. "I could kill her."

"That's Gogol, in case you'd like to be more cultured. I prefer my women cultured. Especially before we undertake the most beautiful act a man and a woman can enjoy together." Grisha wheeled himself to the cabinet where his medication was stacked. Myriad orange bottles for any imaginable ache. Back home, old men were being blown up in daylight; here old men took pills to marvel at their erections. "Shall I take the little blue one now? Or shall we be patient until after lunch?"

She tried to gather herself, bring her own anger under control. The apartment was cleaned in a hostile manner, items of contradictory functionality all whisked together in messy little piles. Candy and pills, glass cleaner and room spray, old photographs and bills. She wished she could yank that Aneta back here and punch the rest of her teeth out. *I'll show you my mother tongue!* But she had dropped the letter to the senator in the mailbox only yesterday, and without this job, the official, documented nature of this job, Larisska would never be allowed to come.

She found the nursing uniform in her tote and slipped her arms through it. "I don't understand that miserable woman. In the best country imaginable and she's not happy."

"Would you be happy if you had that face to carry around?"

Nadia suppressed a smile. "Let's go breathe some fresh air, shall we?"

The mirror displayed a thick head of copper-blond hair in desperate need of coloring, glistening eyelashes, an inflamed cheek, already swollen. Looking down, she saw that Grisha had reached up into the freezer and folded some ice cubes into a waffled kitchen towel.

"Speaking of face, go ahead and press it," he said, wheeling over. "Bring the swelling down. Our magical lovemaking will just have to wait."

+   +   +

That night, like every night, she anxiously opened Skype. Oh, how beautiful it was, that undulating *S* floating in a cloud of blue. It was the vein that pulsed its way to her beloveds. The technology had been a godsend, soothing the sting of those first years in the country. Her mother's face filling her screen, the slope of her forehead, her gray-stranded bob, drooping eyelids, even the gold crowns at the back of her mouth. Her mother would call Larisska over, and sometimes her daughter would comply, arms crossed at her chest. That silent act of defiance used to infuriate her.

But, ah! The contours of their faces, the darling sounds of their voices. On Larisska's twenty-third birthday, she was able to witness her girl blow out candles, a self-conscious huff, the lights extinguished. Through the screen she could examine Larisska's profile, probe the depths of her gray eyes for unhappiness or loneliness, satisfy herself with her daughter's weight, her pallor. She could pepper them with questions: if Larisska was diligently monitoring her insulin, if her mother's blood pressure was being carefully overseen by her doctor. Larisska never answered these queries directly, of course. She made it very clear that she was only fulfilling her filial duty by allowing her own mother to view her on Skype. Once that was accomplished, she edged away into the peripheries of the apartment, untracked by cameras.

But now Nadia would be more than satisfied with Larisska's cranky voice in the background. It had been two weeks since the power and internet went out in Rubizhne, and Channel One flashed pictures of bombed-out hospitals and bridges and deserted apartment buildings. Bodies covered in blankets in broad daylight, people returning to houses torched to the ground. Twitchy gunmen patrolling the streets. Abandoned factories engorged with chemicals just waiting for the spark of gunfire to explode into the skies. And America granting no asylum.

And there were her daughter and mother as grayed-out boxes on her computer screen, unreachable. Still, she powered up Skype a few times a day, searching in vain for that green check mark. A check mark meant her mother or daughter was safe. A green check mark meant life.

The following morning, she pushed Grisha in his wheelchair under Brighton Beach Avenue's rattling subway tracks. They had just bought a satchel of potatoes and the afternoon was crisp, free of humidity. If she had her Larisska waiting for her at the apartment, Nadia would be perfectly content. A tumble of potatoes swinging on the handle and the kind of sunny late-May day that magnified the few trees bursting out of concrete, deepening and sorting their unique shades of green—heaven! At the corner grocery stands towers of pineapples, underripe mangoes, and black cherries were practically spilling onto the sidewalk. Women in ruched dresses wound arms around the elbows of open-shirted, buttoned-down men. Teenagers guffawed and plotted the weekend in groups, their gold necklaces swaying. Outside Russian restaurants, smokers in black sunglasses accepted car keys, finished their cigarettes, and disappeared screeching around the block.

Grisha was greeted from all directions, women bending down to him, grasping his hand. "If it isn't the poet Grisha," they said, gently mocking. He took advantage of these exchanges to evaluate spilling cleavage. Firm-lipped babushki cracked smiles at him, and he called them seductive ladies, a true coven of Sophia Lorens. The Sophia Lorens ignored Nadia entirely; to them, like to most people she encountered these past six years, a paid helper was the most insignificant personage, a ghost.

"Good morning, Gospodin Poet," called out yet another woman of a certain age, not even glancing Nadia's way.

They stopped for a red light. "Are you really a famous poet?" she asked Grisha. "How come I've never read a single poem if you're such a celebrity here?"

He swiveled around in his wheelchair, eyes moist at their pink corners. "I will be whatever you want me to be, Nadezhda Andreevna. For you, I will be Alexander Blok himself." Grisha was growing an uneven scraggly beard, more filled in at the cheeks than chin and neck. Nadia had offered to shave it, but he said it lent him imperial distinction. He liked holding a cane as they rolled along, sometimes wielding it as a conductor's baton.

She smiled. "I'll take Okudzhava. I'm not picky."

"I love women who aren't too picky. How do you feel about men of the Jewish persuasion?"

"You're ridiculous, Gregory Markovich. Recite me a poem of yours."

"And eradicate my entire mystique? What if you're not educated enough to appreciate it?"

A pair of ridiculously dressed middle-aged *babas* stalked right by him in bare legs and gold sandals shimmering in the sun, and he swiveled to better appreciate the receding promenade. She felt strangely rejected, as if Grisha were conspiring against her with the rest of the borough.

"Recite one for me. Please?" She pouted, a rusty, coquettish act. But it worked. Grisha's attention returned to her.

+ + +

Every surface in Grisha's apartment was littered with medicine. Pills clustered in days-of-the-week containers, white ovals outlined on the dining room table. At home, she used Russian Google to figure out what purpose all the pills performed. There was depression medication and nitroglycerin, pills for erections and ancient antibiotics, central nervous system stimulants, pain relievers. Vials of insulin clogged up the refrigerator's vegetable drawer.

"How is my beauty feeling after her last altercation with Baba Yaga? Cheek all healed?" he asked when she lowered him onto the couch for his favorite reality show, *Masculine/Feminine.*

"Aneta? She doesn't bother me."

"Sure she doesn't."

With the additional incursion of Aneta's name overlaying her worry for Larisska, the mood she had been working hard to preserve was soured. She busied herself with unpacking groceries. The entire place had the smell of rotting food and medicine, the dreaded scent of solitary old age. A new fear struck her—growing old in this foreign country, no husband, no child, no English language. Who did she have here except for Regina and Sasha? She had no idea how to go about putting herself on a waiting list for a plot; headstones seemed to occupy every possible square meter of the local cemeteries.

"What's this?" she cried. Buried under a stack of kitchen towels was an opened pack of cookies, those tasty American ones with cream pressed between two wheels of chocolate. She flourished them as proof of his transgression. "Gregory Markovich. Do I need to remind you that diabetes is a serious disease? My daughter . . ."

"I know, I know. Your daughter suffers from it. But we are different. Mine is Type 2, which is much less serious. And I'm an old man. If I don't have my pleasures, I might as well hang myself."

"There is no need for hyperbole. Just please eat only one or two cookies. I happen to know this is a brand-new purchase."

As she turned away, she felt his hand lightly brushing her behind. Some of her acquaintances worked as home attendants for old ladies who berated them all day, who accused them of stealing worthless family knickknacks or colluding against them with pernicious relatives. She knew that a lonely, good-natured pervert was not the worst assignment in the world and VIP Senior Care was a legitimate company that could prove to the government she was officially, gainfully employed, ready to sponsor her daughter at any time. She removed Grisha's palm from her butt, then theatrically dumped the cookies in the garbage.

"Oh no, that's just unnecessary." Grisha moaned extravagantly. "They are Oreos. Haven't you ever experienced the great American invention that is Oreo?"

"Your blood sugar, Grisha. It's not funny. I keep picking up your insulin at the pharmacy but it's clear you're not taking it. Look how many vials you have lying around in the fridge."

Grisha tossed up his hands, as if to say, I'm beyond all hope! I need the love of a good woman! And turned back to the television. "At least Aneta's off until next week. We are all free from her for a while."

"That's the best news I've heard all month."

On Russian television, a man complained to the reality show host that his wife went at his head with an axe to prevent him from seeing their daughter. He pointed to the center of his scalp where hair gave way to a sutured purple gash. The audience did not look as horrified as one would expect.

"If you're such a poet, why do you sit in front of this lowlife drek instead of perusing Lermontov?" Nadia checked behind the pans, saw a round tin of butter wafers, but decided to leave it.

Grisha didn't respond. He was absorbed in his program, a balloon of deflated belly spilling over his belt. On-screen, the man was
showing the viewers stitches crisscrossing from crown to ear. All
at once, it overwhelmed her, the old pain exploding in her belly.
Hot tears burned her cheeks. She felt herself gulping for air.

"Come here." Grisha turned off the television and the apartment was plunged into darkness. She had not realized that evening was seeping so quickly and the dread of the upcoming night
rattled inside her.

"I don't think I can handle your insinuations tonight, to tell you
the truth."

"That's not what I was going to say."

"I haven't heard from her in weeks, Grish. They say on the news
that bridges are being blown up. No one can leave town. Any minute a shell could hit our apartment building."

"I know. That's terrible." Grisha's eyes were soggy blue is-
lands surrounded by more yellow than white. He was reaching
for her.

"How are they surviving without light or water? They can't
even use the toilet. She's probably not getting our packages."

"A tragedy, your war. 'But man is a fickle and disreputable creature and perhaps, like a chess-player, is interested in the process of
attaining his goal rather than the goal itself.'" Grisha motioned for
her to join him on the sofa. "Look, Nadyenka, there is always a
way to get around a system. Use your connections, write letters,
complain. Do what you have to do. This is America."

"You think I haven't written letters?" she said. She thought of
Regina wordlessly handing over a neatly typed letter, the way she
hugged and kissed her own daughter that day with a sharper
strength than usual. What she really wanted to say to Grisha was
"You think this isn't your war too?" She allowed him to squeeze

her hands for a while, until her politeness gave out. Behind him, she glimpsed the empty vials of insulin scattered across his desk.

"Take the ones in the fridge. There's a cooler under the sink," he said, following her gaze. "Try sending them. It can't hurt right? We can get more next time."

As Grisha slept, she opened Skype. The program was slow in loading but once she was signed in, she had to look twice. Beneath her daughter's picture, there was a green check mark. Slowly, she guided the cursor over that precious square and clicked. The dial, the ring. Her stomach clenched. All the questions of the past weeks were rising in her at once: Is their building safe? How is their health? Is it safe for Larissa to go to her job? Is she getting her insulin? But the screen just rang and rang, and after a few more hopeful taps, she gave up.

It was hard for her to picture Rubizhne now. These years in America had winnowed her memories to a mere snatch of images. Flinging open her fifth-floor apartment window onto the tops of the majestic mast pines, pin-straight as if reaching for the sky. The smell of fresh pine woven through the dry, bracing air, the sight of forest stretching far back toward the horizon. Her soul escaped her throat every time she thought of home. In Rubizhne, she lived beneath birds she never saw in America, the aerial swoop of swallows and swifts.

The wide boulevards planted with rows of roses. Streets lined with busy markets, neighbors selling cuts of pork, fragrant tomatoes, freshly picked eggplant. Over there, everyone had some connection to the soil. Those who worked in the plastics factory bought produce from friends' gardens.

She would never admit this to a single American, but the

pleasures in Rubizhne were more acute than anything she experienced here. How the entire town came together for national celebrations, gathered in the main square for Chemists' Day or Family Day or Victory Day. Wares and talents spilling out from the sidewalks—the seamstresses showing off their caftans, the painters offering portraits on the spot. A karaoke competition breaking out next to the fountain, a children's puppet performance in one corner of the square. And after all that, fireworks, the likes of which she will never see again. Not even the dazzle of Fourth of July over Manhattan came close to the splendor of color against Rubizhne stars.

How lovely it had been to walk just a few paces to the pipe manufacturing factory where she was bookkeeper. The leather ledgers with the numbers in the right boxes, the satisfaction of an anticipated balance. She was respected there—always called Nadezhda Andreevna, the *technolog* stopping by to flirt, to ask if the numbers added up properly or perhaps she had missed a decimal point? The scent of pure spirits on his breath, the hairy manliness of his ropy arms leaning on the edge of her desk. She looked forward to hearing him whistling a Makarevich song as he strode down the hall. That one shattering hour against his cold metal desk that would result in Larisska. The voluminous daisies he left on her chair for Women's Day. Of course he left them on the chairs of the other women in the department, but hers were bundled carefully with hot pink ribbon.

Meeting up with her childhood friend Yulia after work, both of them wearing dresses cut in different styles from identical Soviet fabric. The whole group of school friends piling into Café Avalon, taking turns buying one another mugs of cold kvass.

All that was now gone, her mother had told her before Skype went dark. The factories shut down, the playgrounds and parks deserted. No more Chemists' or Family Day. No more fireworks in the central *ploshchad*. No more markets with watermelons and potatoes and sunflowers straight from a neighbor's garden. Just two weeks ago, on Odnoklassniki, the wife posted in a status update that the bushy-eyebrowed *technolog* of Plastics was killed by stray gunfire back in the spring. He was buried next to his parents, she said, in Moscow.

A week later, on the day after Aneta's return to work, Nadia was determined to arrive extra early. She hauled herself out of bed and dressed, gulped down lukewarm tea and assembled her lunch. The streets were bare apart from parents depositing kids at their schools and the very elderly making their laborious way down the sidewalk or squeezing pears suspiciously at corner markets. It had rained overnight, the streets slick with a thin veneer of damp-ness. Her feet felt light against the concrete and she allowed her-self to linger in the morning sunshine, to notice the way it slipped between the subway tracks above her and dappled the ground.

The day before she had been at Regina's; she and Sasha had had a hilarious time practicing mathematics by counting dogs. How much more pleasant it was to work with Regina and Sasha. When you pushed a child in a stroller, everyone on the street smiled at you, when you pushed an old man, everyone averted their eyes. But children grew up, the nanny faded from the child's life. Somehow it was easier to work where the elderly died than where children forgot you existed.

She turned on Kings Highway and let herself into Grisha's de-ceptively fancy lobby. It was one of those ubiquitous Brooklyn co-ops where all the funds were diverted away from apartment repairs toward an opulent entrance. She had been impressed at first glance:

a mirrored wall, a floor fanned by sea-colored tiles, a tufted velvet bench balanced on gold metal legs. But upstairs was another story, dirt-mottled floors, the intermingling scents of fried dinners, a row of chipped maroon doors. Behind one of them, Aneta was insulting her rather vocally.

"That cow left you alone too, eh? I go away and everything is big mess."

"This is how we like it," she heard Grisha say, a show of solidarity he knew would enrage Aneta further.

"Is that right? Are you a couple now? When's the wedding? Shall we alert VIP that there are some shenanigans going on?"

Nadia quickly turned the knob.

Aneta's hair was loosened from her bun, face glistening from sweaty exertion. Grisha looked unusually dispirited at the dining table. A bowl of unappetizing ricotta cheese with a suspended spoon in it was plopped before his roughly shaven chin. His helplessness was so heightened in that moment that she wondered how Aneta actually treated him when they were alone.

She stared the woman down. "What now, Aneta?"

"That's it. I'm reporting you to VIP. This is last straw."

"What else did I personally do to you? Did I bomb your village or something?"

Aneta hissed, "I told you to speak only English or Ukrainian to me. Is that so hard? And considering what you did to that helicopter in Slovyansk, I don't think it's so very funny, do you? Twelve people dead, maybe more."

"What *I* did? You think I shot it down last night, and that's why I'm late this morning?"

Aneta set her face into a straight line. "I meant your Russki-loving friends of course. They're capable of anything. Or have you conveniently forgotten the 1930s when Russia starved us to death?"

"I just think it's rude in front of Grisha to speak a language he doesn't understand."

"He doesn't need to understand us." Aneta started scrawling something on a sheet of paper. Evidence against her? Lies about her to the VIP offices? "Once they fire your lazy ass, you can go ask your beloved Putin for a pension. But here, we actually work for a living."

She would have to beg to keep her job; there were dozens just like her waiting for an open post. But Nadia couldn't resist the ridiculousness of the image. "When I see my beloved, as you say, I'll be sure to ask a few of his soldier friends to look in on your relatives in Berdychev."

Aneta's eyes almost burst out of her skull, and the sight kept her and Grisha crying with laughter for a full half hour after she was gone.

On the way to the pharmacy, Grisha fell asleep in the wheelchair, allowing her the luxury of being enveloped in her own thoughts. The day was cold, not June-like at all. Every morning, she expected the rush of warmth, but even the afternoons withheld it. A rogue drop of rain sprinkled Grisha's face but she kept pushing him onward.

In the pharmacy, babushki were arguing with the white-coated woman behind the counter. Each had her own demands for the pharmacist: just a few extra pills to send to relatives in Russia or Ukraine or Uzbekistan. Would it kill the woman to throw in just three or four more? An expired prescription was still good, wasn't it? And what do these words on the bottle mean—"This medication can increase the effects of alcohol"? Her vodka-loving husband argued this was a very desirable thing.

The pharmacist was overwhelmed as usual, arguing with the entire horde simultaneously, pushing stapled packets across the counter. "But that's not legal, how many times do I have to say this? Let your cousins get their own medication over there."

"No one trusts those drugs. They look like our pills but they're fakes," one babushka was arguing.

"Can I help you?" The woman was looking toward Nadia for an infusion of sanity. She pushed past the grannies to hand in Grisha's slip for the insulin she would be packing away in a small cooler that would probably never make it to her daughter. But at least it gave her the illusion of taking action. This waiting, this war being translated in her mind, was becoming intolerable.

While the debates at the counter raged, she tested some lotions on her wrist.

"Gregory Melman," the pharmacist finally called. As Nadia paid, they exchanged a look of complicity. They were two mentally sound people among the mad at the sanatorium. The woman even gave her a tight, friendly nod of approval.

Back in the apartment, Nadia flipped on the television and rooted around for any remaining edible potatoes from their recent haul. She hummed as she peeled. "So what do you think? I haven't heard a peep from VIP. Maybe Aneta's all threats after all."

"If they took you away, I would start drafting the most beautifully crafted suicide note they've ever read." Grisha opened a book, leather and gold-embossed, turned a few of its parchment pages. Maybe the Lermontov joke had struck a note with him after all. Even if it was for her benefit, it was nice to see him reading instead of immersed in those nihilistic television programs.

"Why was Aneta gone last week anyway? Was she sick?"

"No, nothing that convenient. Her niece got asylum. She's getting a green card. It seems our friend is nice to her own family. Can you even picture Aneta as a warm and fuzzy auntie?"

"You're kidding, right?" She popped her head up, the back of her skull slamming into an open cabinet door. "Her niece got out of Ukraine? That girl on her phone? How did she manage that? She's barely been on the waiting list a year."

"The girl came here on a student visa and went, 'Oy, oy, oy, I can't go back there. It's a war zone!' So they let her stay."

Nadia lost all interest in the potatoes. A sour acid expanded in her throat. "My daughter's been on the list a total of sixteen years now and they keep telling me to wait our turn. Can you imagine?"

Grisha looked mortified. He probably regretted telling her. "I know, you told me. It's tragically unfair, but that's the seesaw of politics. Maybe these days, the Americans prefer Ukrainians. You know, the Western ones. Who knows?"

At home, a stack of mail awaited her, a spool of messages from her two girlfriends unfurled on her voice mail. She'd missed a party at the salon. Should they all go in on the same house in the Rockaways this summer? What about some night this week for drinks? Her creaky heart lifted once more. She had made friends here at least, friends who checked on her, missed her, who noted that she existed. If she squirreled away a bit of money she didn't send home, she could even allow herself a new dress that could transition from summer to fall, a white dress in which she would greet her daughter at the airport. The girls—yes, at around fifty years old, they were still girls—could go dancing in one of the nightclubs she and Grisha keep passing on one of their strolls. There must be a man there for her, most likely Russian. Not as dashing as the *technolog* or as dully stable as her old neighbor Pyotor, but fiercely loyal, and they would combine the rest of their lives once Larisska came. This was still a country where things like that happened.

She flipped through the pile of catalogs, for a modern Italian furniture store in the neighborhood, a lingerie mail-order company that featured women wearing lace with downturned faces. Smiling at the idea of wearing something like that in front of Grisha. He'd have a heart attack on the spot! Then the letters. Back home, she had enjoyed parsing through the mail, had taken pleasure filing away the queries requiring her answer. A bookkeeper held an important position, and she had received piles of urgent official mail. But here, she preferred the catalogs. Letters were indecipherable, credit card offers and advertisements had to be parsed, word by laborious word.

But then she came across a letter that was no junk mail. It was from the senator's office. She saw the woman's name printed in official blue letters in the upper, left-hand corner. The envelope was too thin to open slowly, too white and bereft of words:

> Dear Ms. Borodinskaya:
>
> I have received your letter requesting assistance with your immigration matter. Each year, the U.S. Department of State receives an enormous number of petitions filed on behalf of foreign nationals who wish to immigrate to the United States. I understand that the immigrant visa application about which you inquired has been assigned the 2B Preference Category and a priority date of November 4, 2008. Currently, visas are only available to 2B Preference Category applicants with priority dates before May 1, 2007.

She didn't bother trying to interpret the rest. By now, the one thing she understood was what "no" looked like. She knew all too well the feeling of helplessness before governments that cared nothing about people like her or her daughter's suffering. For the first time in six years, since arriving in this exquisite miracle of a heartbreaking country, she could identify with Aneta's steady, droning anger. The anger of small, powerless people. Right now, for one moment before the feeling subsided, what she wanted more than a reunion with her daughter was for a vengeful adversary to chasten this country, bring it to its knees, make it humane through a powerful injection of fear.

The next morning, she evaded Grisha's attempts at conversation, her throat dry with bitterness. To avoid explaining her mood, she turned on one of his favorite mind-melting shows. Then she was free to retreat into the galley kitchen and work on salvaging the potatoes, submerging them in a mixture of water and white vinegar. It was easy to keep busy, turning their browned husks over and over in the oily pan, half listening as women complained that their men were unemployed video-game addicts, that they were desperate, emasculated for the lack of work and opportunity. "Who's going to help them?" they said. "They should get off their lazy asses," came protests from the audience. The arguments escalated into insults. She tuned it out, the ugliness on the screen, checking the interiors of the potatoes with the knife tip. As she worked, she could feel Grisha's eyes sliding away from the screen and down her spine.

Something in the caving of her heart made her put the spatula down and turn off the burner.

"Okay, just this one time," she said, and walked over to him. She took his dappled wrist, and drew a trembling hand to her right breast. Neither of them spoke, only listened to the on-air sounds of verbal combat. Grisha allowed his hand to linger where she placed it, but his fingers neither caressed nor squeezed. They rested, like exhausted refugees warmly welcomed into the country of their dreams.

3

After the Mandarins

At first, it was as if nothing had changed. But then Nadia noticed escalating acts of deletion and substitution. At the post office and other government agencies, documents began appearing in the Ukrainian language. Then a few storefronts were altering their signs from Russian to Ukrainian—*odezhda* turned clothes into *odyag*. On television, some of her favorite Russian shows disappeared. Then, the ruble went away and coupons took their place, "transitional currency" that was supposed to be accepted at state stores. Next summer, they promised, the hryvnia would be introduced.

The best course of action, her friend Yulia whispered during their smoking breaks, was to hide rolls of money in your socks, buy everything with cash, avoid the banks. But did that make any sense if one currency was being phased out, another not yet to be trusted? They were always being reminded that the country was finally independent, no longer a part of the Soviet Union. Ukraine had even applied for International Monetary Fund membership! The changes were supposedly a good thing, but few ethnic Russians in the Lugansk region believed anything but misery would ensue from such a drastic, hasty transformation. The eldest of them had seen it all before.

To begin the dreaded wait at the store, Nadia woke early, when the sky was still encrusted with flecks of night. She moved with a stealthy whoosh of her slippers, but from her cot, Larisska heard her and popped up from a tangle of hair and bedclothes.

"Where are you going, Mama?"

"Go back to sleep, *kisa*."

"I'm hungry, Mama."

This was something she was repeating a lot lately. For the past few weeks, just as they were trying to acclimate to the upheaval, Larissa had been inconveniently eating and eating, but also losing an alarming amount of weight. There was no way to keep her in food with the *talonchiki* of bare necessities assigned to them—sugar, margarine, flour, farmer cheese—and now even those were becoming impossible to procure. The prices were so outrageous and arbitrary no one understood what was valuable anymore. The president was saying it was for their own good. "The social protection of the population under the conditions of the liberalization of prices." What in the world did that even mean?

"Baba will take you. I'll see you after school."

Larissa's face crumpled and her lower lip started to quake. Nadia could tell tears were amassing, tears the girl was working hard to contain because she knew her mother didn't like it. "No you won't."

"My darling. I'll be back as soon as I can."

It was strictly verbal comfort. In reality, by the time Nadia finished work, fought for the staples needed that week, and picked up nitroglycerin or something else for her mother, Larisska would already be in bed.

"What if we stayed home again today?" Larisska said, stretching out gangly, dimpled arms. If only there was a way to explain to the child that her mother's absence was necessary for their basic survival, that she was fortunate to be lovingly cared for by her grandmother. That her biological father had not yet provided them with a single ruble, thank you very much, so everything that went into their mouths had to be procured by Nadia's own hands. But her daughter clung to her with a forehead matted with blond baby tufts. It was all Nadia could do to tear herself from the feathery playful pecks of the five-year-old, hoist herself into a wool dress and snagged tights and get out the door.

"Be careful," her mother called after her.

The scene at the store was the usual bewildered chaos she'd come to expect by now. The doors not yet open but the crowd was seething with anticipated rage. Everyone was accusing one another of cutting the line, men were banging their fists against the shuttered glass, babushki berating the most aggressive for their boorish behavior. There was no mayonnaise today, they were being told, a limited amount of sugar and salt. She took her place at the end of a long line but she knew it was useless. They wouldn't make it halfway up this queue; the people waiting since dawn would grab what they could carry, provide for their immediate family first then sell and barter the rest. The doors opened and she was being trampled.

"Take your dirty paws off me," she yelled at some man who was trying, under the camouflage of stampede, to efficiently grope her breasts. He protested innocence—an honest mistake, he was swept off balance—but she was disgusted. It was a relief when the pandemonium stretched far behind her.

At work, almost despite herself, she still listened for the *technolog*'s first whistle of the day. It came exactly at ten thirty, and this time, she was pretty sure it was a popular new song called "Lullaby, 1933," about a mother who goes crazy after her twins die in the Great Famine. Only the *technolog* was capable of repurposing a dirge about Stalin starving his own people into a cheerful Monday-morning musical greeting. He burst into the accounting office, his starched white shirt open at the collarbone, the shoulder pads of his suit enhancing his muscular upper body.

"Good morning, Nadezhda Andreevna."

"Good morning."

"A sunny day for a change."

"An unexpected but welcome development."

"I hope the numbers are adding up correctly. You didn't forget a decimal point, did you?"

She wanted to say, "Oh, they're adding up all right. Too bad they add up to nothing." Instead of actual paychecks, the general director of the factory was now handing out promissory notes. She, like all the employees, had not been paid in three months. Her current task was to calculate the amount owed to each worker, and transfer it onto a thick piece of paper stamped with the company logo.

But she would never articulate a grievance like this in public. They had been trained all too well not to speak their minds. The people in power would do what they wanted anyway—independence or no independence.

Just the other day, she was watching television where a man who had been the most fervent of communists two years ago was transferring his passionate loyalties to an independent Ukraine. And what about this new president tearfully saluting the Ukrainian flag? It wasn't so long ago that he was convincing them all that Ukrainian independence was impossible, that Ukraine continuing as a Soviet entity was the very best thing for the country.

And now the same man was doing an about-face, saying that they were meant to extract their identities from a place they had been aligned with for over seventy years. Easy for the West to say, but what about the ethnic Russians in the East, mere miles from the Russian border? Were they too meant to put themselves in opposition to a country that they were raised to love, whose poetry they had memorized since they were children, whose language flowed like nectar out of their mouths? All while they weren't paid, their bridges and hospitals deteriorating around them? She longed to believe in a truly independent Ukraine, a solid, unified, proud country. But there was no doubt in her mind that as far as their corrupt politicians were concerned, it was business as usual.

"My dearest *technolog,* my accounts have never been this balanced," she answered instead, with what she hoped was a flirtatious lilt to her voice. "These are the most well-rounded numbers I've ever had the pleasure of calculating."

She wanted to hate him. But the *technolog* was fiendishly handsome with his sculpted jaw and veined hands and hazel eyes the color of dying leaves, a lighter version of which Larisska inherited. And even though they had only made love that one fateful time, he still looked at Nadia from beneath those leaflike fronds he had for eyebrows as though she were a wild strawberry sprung up in winter.

"Fear not, my sunshine. I hear we might have a solution coming today."

She looked around. The secretaries were returning from their meetings, displaying a less belligerent look. And no one seemed to pay attention when he called her "my sunshine."

"Is that so?"

"It will be almost as good as money."

She couldn't help but prod the contours of his guilt. "I don't know how we'll go on. We barely make it from day to day. If it weren't for my sister's dacha, her chickens and cucumbers, we would probably starve."

The *technolog* cleared his throat. He had seen her pregnant, had even helped Larisska color at Nadia's desk on a few occasions; he had long ago guessed the truth. "We've all felt the pinch. No one said this would be easy."

She whispered, "Shouldn't someone take a little responsibility?"

At times like these, she wondered why she was still waiting for him to assert his role in her life, even if just between the two of them. Her insinuations were either too subtle for him or he was ignoring them on purpose.

Just then, the loudspeaker was telling them all to gather in the warehouse for a special announcement from the director.

The *technolog* winked. "All is not lost. You'll see." And she felt the foreign shard of hope, an emotion she was sure had been wrung out of her.

They were told to walk in orderly rows but the halls were flooded with every level of employee at the plant. If it were just two years ago, there would have been order to this migration, but the end of the Soviet Union meant no one knew how to enter a room anymore, where to stand, what to recite, whom to respect, how to publicly gather. She saw a glimpse of Yulia in the blue uniform of the line inspector. She was waving to meet up after work; she had some extra potatoes to share.

They were shepherded into the freezing room and directed to form a circle around a covered truck. The *technolog* shimmied next to her, pressing his shoulder against hers. As they waited for the rest to file in, he was rubbing her forearms for warmth, his hands igniting a trail of heat down to her elbows. She allowed herself to cradle the fantasy of the two of them in her mind, a normal couple at work, and when that grew too painful to hold, she let it go.

They were all blowing into their hands, stamping their feet from the cold. Their boss began with an apology about the unfortunate lack of financial remuneration—independence took time, you see. The government needed to get on its feet, then the workers would get paid. A fresh slash of light dappled the room with sudden brightness.

"But while we are waiting for our salaries to resume, the Ukrainian People's Republic is very much sensitive to our temporary difficulties. As you well know, our factory is their very top priority. What is more elemental than directing the flow of natural gas to our nation?" The director was a man who had given many a patriotic speech, but even he seemed to lose confidence in the shape of his own words.

Instead, he climbed onto the back of the truck and lifted the burlap with a flourish. There was a burst of something orange, round, exotic. Nadia moved closer for a better look. Mandarins. It had been a while since Nadia tasted a mandarin, so it took time to adjust to the sight of fragrant, orange balls. *Mandarins,* someone bounced the word down the rows.

"Our good news is that while the country is working hard to establish our independence, it has not forgotten us. We will be paying you in mandarins. We finish so-and-so pipes, you get forty mandarins, and so forth. I don't need to tell you how much a mandarin will fetch at the market."

Watching everyone take in the news, Nadia noted smirks quickly hidden, the stricken deflation of disappointment, the hollow gaze of cynicism. She looked up at the *technolog,* at his red ears, his dashing sideburns, the small terrain of unshaven stubble under his chin. Looking at him so closely was like approaching a painting in a gallery, marveling at the individual strokes that made up the whole. A solitary muscle in his neck was tensing and releasing. He took her hand, and in a single fluid motion, she felt two mandarins being palmed to her.

"Here's some extra. Does your daughter like mandarins?" he whispered. "Mine adores them." Was he making a distinction: your daughter *versus* my daughter? Or was it finally an admission of knowledge, a fusing? Your daughter *and* my daughter? Your daughter *is* my daughter?

After Larisska was born, her mother chided Nadia for neither telling the *technolog*'s wife the truth and snatching him for herself nor actively looking for a husband of her own. There were men, her mother said, who could love a sweet little girl, especially if Nadia were willing to provide him with a child of his own. At twenty-eight, she might still find a businessman who could take her to Europe or America. At thirty, she would have to resign herself to an unpleasant life as a spinster or, in a best-case scenario, a practical arrangement with some downtrodden widower. (And there is no excuse for that, Nadyenka, a girl as beautiful as you. Blond with blue eyes, a pretty, voluptuous figure.)

How could she explain to her mother that it was enough for her, standing next to this man, the vapor of their cold exhales commingling. She could swear to knowing if he was in the building or outside it, feeling an anticipatory shiver when he entered the factory even though the doors were on a separate floor entirely, far from her range of hearing. She could remember every second of their one sexual encounter, how his eyes closed well before his lips reached for hers, how his fingers skimmed the bulb of her neck, his hips gently parting her legs.

She knew little about his life except that he was originally from

Moscow but stayed in Ukraine after being introduced to his future
wife, who had once been a ballerina. He had a teenage daughter
seriously studying the ballet. His Moscow provenance and proximity to culture lent him a romantic air of sophistication, catnip
for the other girls in the office, but that in itself was not the draw
for Nadia. It was an air of nuanced sadness beneath all that bon-
homie and flirtatious crackle. There was an irresistible urge to un-
wrap the layer of fear and self-protection and peer underneath to
what she imagined was a pure, sparkling kernel of truth.

But he showed little indication of allowing her access to the
heavily guarded fortress, so these days, she told herself that their
repartee at work was enough for her. In any case, who needed the
demands of some new husband? She told herself she would have
even less time for Larisska than she already did.

But as everyone shuffled back to their desks, she was spiraling
with joy. He was interested in Larisska's welfare in his own way.
The extra mandarins hidden in her shawl proved that he had been
paying attention to their little family all along.

At home, she opened her satchel and out poured the mandarins. She had taken the tram holding them to her chest, trying to
conceal the telltale bulge behind paper-filled folders. A row of pensioners had suspiciously stared at her during the entire ride. But
once safely indoors, she allowed herself to emit an anticipatory
scream.

"Larisska, Mama, look at this."

Her mother emerged from their bedroom, picking one up and
smelling its surface. "Larisska, look what your mother brought."

Larissa was already tucked into her cot, but she leaped out in
her pajamas. Her eyes widened before the pile of fragrant fruit.

"I will eat them all," she cried. When she was overwhelmed like
this, her torso, from arms to the tips of her fingers, spasmed.

How could she tell them that this fruit *was* money? Her mother clearly thought them an extra gift, a bonus. "You can have two. The rest I will trade for bread and other things."

But oh, the full, full heart of witnessing her girl's bodily excitement. Watching her daughter struggling with the pebbly skin, thirstily sucking out the juice then masticating the slivers and meat of the rinds, her hazel eyes animated with unrestrained joy. She and her mother split one, savoring each sweet segment.

"These two you're eating are a present from the *technolog*." Nadia tucked a juice-dipped strand behind Larisska's ear when she was finished. "He wanted you to know that he got them especially for you."

Of course, her first instinct had been to get an abortion. Every woman she knew was getting them. Yulia had had three already, her mother referenced her own abortions when her father was still alive and she said they simply couldn't afford a third, fourth, or fifth child. The head secretary to the director seemed to have an abortion every couple of months. An abortion was what you got done when your IUD failed or you could not bring yourself to voice a definitive objection when the pivotal moment arrived.

When she became certain of the pregnancy, the first place she went was the gynecological institute. The doctor, a young, stout, Jewish-looking man, took blood samples and wrote out a prescription for all the items she would need to bring to surgery: the optional painkiller for injection, a robe, slippers, rubber gloves. She folded the paper and slipped it into her coat pocket. Suddenly, she felt she was a grown woman. Neither the onset of her period nor sex with her awkward and overly cautious institute boyfriend had given her that impression.

But before she departed, the doctor stayed her by the forearm. "Let me ask you: what are you doing, *devushka*? You are twenty-three years old and this is your first pregnancy. Do you really want to take a chance of never conceiving again? You're not getting any younger. Go home, throw out the prescription in the trash, tell the father the good news."

"Thank you, Doctor," she'd said. The words shadowed her out of the building and all the way home, *Do you really want to take a chance of never conceiving?* and *You're not getting any younger.*

In the end, she did as the doctor said. Except for the part about telling the baby's father. She was sure she told the *technolog* multiple times with her eyes, with a few indirect references to her nausea, but he never acknowledged the hint or their one moment of intimacy. He continued the flow of his flirtation until he saw her protruding belly by August. For a few days after the sighting, he disappeared from her area of the office, busying himself with the chemists on data analysis, assessing cheaper packing materials, generating progress reports to the director or whatever she imagined a technologist did. Then one morning, during a Victory Day ceremony invoking this "glasnost" none of them entirely believed in, making sure the *technolog* was within earshot, she volubly told Yulia that she expected nothing from the father of the child, that in fact, she would find single motherhood a relief.

"Tell the truth, Yul'ka, who's happier among our friends, the single mothers or married mothers?"

The next week, there was the return of his whistle down the hall. It was high, playful, familiar. When she returned from a meeting, a daisy was splayed across her chair.

+ + +

When the baby Larisska was born, she refused the breast. Her mother and sister Olga contorted Nadia's body into a variety of feeding positions. Leaning over the baby, lying next to the baby, plopping the baby's head down onto the breast. But this sickly Larisska cried and cried.

"Oh for heaven's sake." Her sister had her own family across town; she made it clear that she had no time to help correct such elemental impediments. She was constantly in stress mode because her husband had entered them in the lottery to emigrate and their number had just come up. "Let someone more qualified feed her already."

Nadia was horrified. "Have you gone crazy? This shouldn't be so hard."

"Well, what do you think motherhood is, a walk in the park?" her mother said. No women they knew had personal experience with such prolonged rejection. There were difficulties at first, of course, but eventually babies figured it out. You swaddle the baby first, you trick her by shoving the breast at her while she's asleep. When she's hungry, she will give in. Babies don't starve themselves on purpose. But even when Nadia self-expressed the milk and tried to offer it in a cup, Larissa craned her neck and twisted away as if from a vile smell.

There was a formula shortage in the local new mothers' disbursement office. Sour cream, milk, bottles, but only a few cans of formula. They had friends buy up the entire supply but soon they would have to travel to Lugansk. The provisions were waning; how long could they keep it up?

"That baby hates me," Nadia would joke, but inside she knew it was no joke. She had not wanted this baby, and a baby could sense maternal indifference in the womb. To make matters worse, Larisska only slept when in motion, and on most nights, when she could no longer take the crying, Nadia would walk her up and down the hall in her pram.

"She is such an adorably willful little thing," her neighbor Alesia said, flinging open the door to her apartment down the hall, her one-year-old daughter attached to her hip. Even in the full grip of despair, Nadia couldn't help noticing how Alesia's hair blended in with her taupe skin, her coin-shaped blue eyes set too far back into her skull. Hers was worse than a face you overlooked, it was a face that seemed likely to decompose at any moment. When her mother helped her prepare the apartment for the baby's arrival, gathering the hand-me-downs from the women in the building, the only person whose donated baby things they immediately discarded was Alesia's. Just in case. Who knew if radiation was contagious?

"It's been a nightmare," Nadia said. "They tell me she'll grow out of it. I'm going mad. I haven't slept in weeks."

"She will. She'll grow out of it," said Alesia sweetly.

"I didn't get lucky with one of the easy ones."

"Feel free to come and keep us company. I'd be happy to hold a newborn again." Alesia was so thin, she seemed in danger of snapping under the weight of the girl on her arm.

"You must be busy yourself. I wouldn't dream of imposing."

"Not at all. I could actually use the company."

Nadia felt a sharp twinge of guilt; Alesia was a Chernobyl widow. One of the many pregnant women who had stepped off the trolley with the other Belorussian refugees. She was dressed in only a housecoat over pajamas and slippers on her feet like many of the other refugees, her belly huge, holding no bag or purse. Her husband was dead just a month after the *prikaz* came for him and the other conscripted military to neutralize the reactor. Her child was holding her head up but not crawling or trying to stand. Her forehead was also unusually high, which she and her mother ascribed to womb exposure to radiation. Even if most of them knew it was probably nothing more than fear of the unknown, many in the building kept their distance from Alesia as if her body itself were a leaky reactor.

Once in a while, Nadia's mother would shake her head and marvel about that May in 1986 when they finally found out what happened. "How lucky we were, after all, that the wind blew west instead of east."

Alesia shifted her own daughter to the other hip, trying to get a better look at the flushed face in the pram. "She is so sweet. And she will grow up and then we will miss these days when they need us this desperately."

In the pause, Larissa started screaming again, pointing at Alesia, stretching her hands out to her. Instinctively, Nadia pushed the pram out of harm's way.

"I really should keep moving."

"Come by anytime."

She heard the door click shut, and relief flooded her body. But Larisska's desire to reach out to Alesia did give her an idea.

She knocked at Tanya's door on the other side of the hallway. She was a new mother who had no relatives in the area, just a husband who welded pipes in Nadia's factory. They conferred briefly, some money was exchanged, and Tanya agreed to unbutton her housedress. Larisska suckled at another woman's breast even as Nadia's was overflowing. The sight of her hungry baby becoming sated was both heartbreaking and a guilty relief. Larissa was getting what she needed even if the source was not herself. The shame was so strong she told no one, much less her sister, but she would bring Larisska down the hall three times a day, past Alesia's door.

Later, she would believe it was during those daily trips to another woman's breast that she began to really love Larisska. Her red, scrunched face smoothed out into a uniform color, her sweaty twigs of tufted hair became softer and thicker. Once Nadia was allowed to sleep through the night, she understood how lucky she was to have a baby all to herself. Larisska's father was somewhere safe in the city with his family, not dead of a smattering of tumors protruding from the skin. If something happened to her, she was sure the *technolog* could be mobilized to help them financially. She had a secure job at a historic factory highly valued by the Soviet government for connecting a gas pipeline from Russia to its Ukrainian territories. Her mother was strong enough to help with the baby.

Nadia felt a sense of gratitude so profound, it cleared her addled brain. For the first time, she really grasped why everyone called babies miracles. Larisska was no calamity, no curse. Larisska belonged wholly to her, and Nadia would take care of her. She shook with pleasure when her mother made a silly face, her soft digits wrapped around a thumb. She slept on top of a pillow all pursed into herself like a potato dumpling, and Nadia's heart exploded. So what if she drank the milk of another? It was, in the long view of such a wondrous lifetime bond, a small thing.

A new set of mandarin rinds were fanning the table a few weeks later when someone knocked on the apartment door. Nadia was in the bathroom, wiping her mouth with a towel. She had skipped that morning's hunt for provisions. It was simply too cold, the trees shivering and naked. Instead, she would go to the Central Market on Saturday, begin the long string of bartering (mandarins for sugar, sugar for sunflower oil, sunflower oil for flour).

"Come in, come in," her mother was saying, pressing her robe tighter around her chest. Nadia heard the unmistakable voice of the *technolog*. His hat was in his hands and he was spinning and pressing its rim as if sealing down the edges of dough for *vareniki*. Here he was, the square shoulders of him, the easy cowlick of his hair, his uninterrupted eyebrows. He was actually in her home, standing in the middle of her living room. They stared at each other.

Larissa sprang in with a piece of buttered, salted black bread wedged into her mouth, her two pigtails fastened with voluminous white chiffon bows.

"I'm thirsty," she insisted.

The *technolog* bent down on one knee. He revealed from behind his back a box of chocolates wrapped in a shiny red velvet bow. "What a big girl you are. Do you remember me from the office?"

"Let me get changed," Nadia said, her palms suddenly clammy with sweat. "I'll be right back."

Her mother sized up the situation at a glance. "May I make some tea? Let's go, Larisska. Come with me to help. Yes, you can bring the chocolate."

In the bedroom, Nadia dressed slowly, paralyzed before the few nice clothes she'd sewn for herself. There was the red turtleneck, the itchy tweed skirt, the patchwork vest. Her heart was beating too intensely, the reverberations pulsing in her throat. On the first try, she pulled on the turtleneck backward. Her fingers refused to cooperate. He must have finally decided he wanted to help with Larisska. Or to tell Nadia he loved her? Or he was here because his wife found out and he wanted her complicity. An astute secretary or anyone watching them interact at work might have an agenda or just an itch for stirring trouble. She imagined the phone call at the ballet institute, that elfin woman with the frizzy, rust-colored hair picking up the receiver. "I'm listening."

"Your husband has a daughter by a subordinate in the accounting department," the informant might say, then hang up. The expected domestic scene would ensue, the wife exploding with wrath, the *technolog* denying any wrongdoing. (*Nothing happened, I swear to you. Do you want to ask her yourself?*)

She decided to skip the vest, to rely wholly on the impression made by the clinging turtleneck.

"Nadezhda Andreevna." The *technolog* sighed when he saw her.

She had read about these types of scenes in novels, which usually resulted in proposals of unions. In the pre-Soviet variety, an urbane older suitor expressed his love for the inexperienced country girl, or in the Soviet version, a *kolkhoz* brigadier proposed to merge two equally impressive production outputs with his stocky female counterpart in the next town over.

They could see into the kitchen where Larisska was sitting on the counter, swinging her legs. She was eating one chocolate after the next. The longer they stayed quiet, the more magnified the sound of her heels thumping against wood.

"You are very welcome in my home," she said, but it was not at all what she meant to say. "Please have a seat."

The *technolog* did not sit. He was shifting from foot to foot. His sideburns were ridiculously long, she now noticed, practically extending down to the very edge of his jaw. "I'm afraid they are closing the factory."

It took a few seconds to match what he was saying with the pieces in her mind. The factory? The factory that had been around since long before she was born? The factory that played such an important role during World War II that it was listed in textbooks for its contribution to the Soviet Union's victory over the Nazis? The image of the phone call, the domestic rupture, the betrayed wife, all disappeared. What took its place was a picture as cold and black as the winter sky.

"But you said things were looking up. They said the mandarins were temporary."

She wanted to reach for the certificate she had formulated for herself, the one that proved in official, government language how much back pay the company owed her. But of course she'd left it at work.

He was murmuring into the raised collar of his jacket. "It seems they had no plan once the mandarins ran out. We're not getting bailed out. They say there's no other choice but to close."

She was trying to formulate a response when the *technolog* moved closer, lowered his voice. He ran his fingers down her arm and unclasped her hands, "Just think of the bright future. We will band together. This is just a hiccup in our history. In a few years, we will be a great state. Independence can't happen overnight."

"I don't understand. A closed factory doesn't just spring back to life. They'll start taking it apart for valuable metal and that will be that."

She was unsure of whether to allow him dominance over her hand. This particular scene appeared in no novel she had read. But he was fighting for a decent grip, fingertips feeling around for a groove into which he could insert himself. Olga would have probably insisted she agree with anything he said, to extract some confession of his affection. She was aware of breaking some rule of womanhood, one her married sister had grasped intuitively. Or maybe she was supposed to be holding back, displaying the ideal amount of coldness. Machinations like this were foreign to Nadia.

Her favorite character in literature had always been Tatyana in *Eugene Onegin,* a girl armed with no wiles, but whose sincerity turned out to be insufficient for the world-weary Onegin.

"A factory might be closed but there are other opportunities for the resourceful," he said.

"You're just giving up? Can't we all go and put some sense into their heads? Who made this decision? Savchenko? Kulish?"

"It's not giving up. They have a lot to sort out. They can't keep every factory open. But now that we're no longer being economically exploited by Moscow, it's bound to get better. Every week the percentage of coupons will increase. I've opened a savings account. Yes, the interest rate is higher . . ."

"If only we could get out of here," she burst out, thinking of Olga's husband, how crazy his plan to leave had initially seemed. "Even Poland is better than this."

"Emigration? What are you talking about?" He looked taken aback, shocked, even. "Surely you agree that our duty is to stay here, to build our own nation."

"But what is the nation's duty to us in the meantime? Can you tell me that? A paycheck might be a good start. And then food to spend it on."

"Tea," her mother called out. "Whenever you are ready, there is tea. If you would like it. We do need to get going to school."

The *technolog* seemed to be crumpling, receding. "I should get going anyway. In any case, they will announce it on Friday. I wanted you to know first in case you wanted to start making inquiries. Once everyone knows, it's going to be madness."

He looked like anyone else, unremarkable. A man in an ill-fitting leather jacket. She could already hear her mother: *What were you thinking? Once the job's over, you're never going to see him again.*

"Thank you. That was very thoughtful of you. Please excuse me. I was just very upset." She turned her voice soft and spongy as bird's milk candy, and started to edge into the closed circle of his arms. Another inch or two and her cheek would be pressed against his.

But he was swiftly moving toward the door. "I hear there is work in Kharkov. I would set out for there if I could."

Larisska in coat, hat, and gloves brushed against the leather of her father's jacket with one of her chiffon bows. The straps of her nursery backpack were sliding off her shoulders.

"I'm really very, very thirsty," she appealed to him. "Are you going to color with me again?"

The *technolog* reached out as if to pat her head. His hand was suspended like meat in aspic. He produced some muted utterance and disappeared into the elevator.

On her way to work, Nadia took a detour toward Chemists Square, and sat on a bench in front of the giant white marble Lenin. This was her favorite Lenin statue in Rubizhne because of the casual nature of his stance. He had one hand in the pocket of his jacket, and he was holding a leather briefcase with the other. He might as well have been waiting for a metro or tram, on his way to an office position just like hers. As a child, finding herself among all these Lenin statues was so comforting. Wherever you went in town, a kind man stood nearby, protecting you with his benevolent gaze, sympathetic to your flaws but loving you with all his heart. As an adolescent, she had understood deep in the hidden recesses of her soul that she was safe as long as Lenin was around. All he wanted was to pave her path, protect her from enemies. Love her.

Later, of course, she mostly knew this was a fantasy, a girlish fairy tale, though she planned on encouraging Larissa to believe in him too if only to protect the sweet magical thinking of childhood. But now, she sensed he was being physically ripped out of her life. What would she turn into if she were no longer allowed to dream about him?

Usually, cheerful flower bouquets lined the foot of the monument, but today, Nadia noticed something unusual: funeral wreaths.

"Do you notice how thirsty your daughter is? Did she just eat a lot of sugar?" the pediatrician asked that same afternoon. "Because desserts are strictly forbidden. You understand, don't you? She has diabetes."

"She ate mandarins. Many mandarins," Nadia said, with a fresh, panicked glance at her daughter. Her body was numb with guilt or shock, she wasn't sure which.

"And chocolate," Larissa said.

"But my daughter just lost her job and her sister just won the green card lottery and is leaving us for America," her mother moaned. "We will have nothing to eat. How can we afford all this?"

"It's not the end of the world, but your lives will change," the doctor said, ignoring her mother's outburst. "I'll show you how to inject insulin, but you will have to learn to do it yourselves. You will need to draw blood before each meal to measure sugar. You will have to boil the syringes after each use, drastically change her diet to avoid hypoglycemia. Her teachers need to be notified. You will have to be vigilant to make sure she is eating enough."

As Nadia assailed the doctor with questions, Larissa calmly sat with her one-eyed pink bear. She seemed pleased to be in the same room with them all, their attention finally directed at her. Her pleas were finally being taken seriously.

"You see, Mama? I told you I was thirsty."

There was nothing to be done; Nadia would have to leave immediately, seek work in Kharkov before the rest of her coworkers learned the news on Friday. She would have to figure out a treatment plan and then leave it in her mother's hands to execute during weekdays when she was gone. It was too much to take in at once, her mind blank with the enormity of what lay ahead of her.

In the dusk, they passed the city council, and along the park lane on Victory Street, she noticed the Chernobyl memorial, an arch that rose skyward with orderly brick and gave the appearance of crumbling back to earth. She had committed the inscription to memory when it was first erected. It read:

> *To the victims of Chernobyl catastrophe—*
> *to the fallen,*
> *to the living,*
> *and to the never born.*

Three years before, Alesia had left the building with her daughter one night and never returned. Whenever she passed the memorial, Nadia remembered her fearful rejection of Alesia's friendship. Why had she offered nothing to help this woman? Nadia had even pleaded new-mother fatigue when Alesia asked if they could make the trip to the Chernobyl memorial together. She was afraid her neighbor would discern in Nadia's eyes gratitude for the healthy daughter, the brighter future. Now what kind of future did her daughter really have?

The evening was turning cold. Larisska attempted to leap between them as they stopped to pay their respects. She was using their hands as swinging ropes, chattering about the news at school: that new kid Mykhailo from Kiev heartlessly pulled on her pigtails all day, and guess what, Mama, that morning, they were told they might soon be singing a brand-new Ukrainian anthem! Wasn't that exciting?

"What do you think it will sound like?"

Nadia looked down at the foot of the monument, an artistically disorganized pile of rocks. She adjusted Larisska's scarf more firmly to shield her from the bite of wind. "I have no idea," she said.

4

Our Ukrainka

At nine o'clock at night, Lena and Georgina were pounding on her door. She could hear them giggling violently on the other side. "Open up, quick."

"*Devushki,* what on earth?" Nadia cried, fumbling with the dead bolt.

Her friends stormed into her dining room. They looked terribly big-city chic to her once, but now she couldn't help but notice their shrunken dresses and absurd heels. Their shoulders were barely covered by the armor of a transparent shawl. Georgina's dyed-red hair was slicked to one side, a greased-down ponytail draped over a single silver shoulder. Her eyelids were smudged in sparkling blue kohl. Lena's highlighted pixie was poking straight into the air, her mouth outlined in thick magenta pencil.

"No excuses this time. We've made an executive decision: you're coming dancing with us," Lena said. She surveyed the situation with an expression of exasperated sadness. Nadia in her floral house robe for the night, remote control in hand. A carton of untouched strawberry ice cream and the debris of butter cookie dinner were spread across the coffee table.

Nadia muted the television. She had been running First Channel continuously for the past hour trying to make sense of a Malaysian plane scattered across the field just hours' drive from her home. Almost three hundred people, eighty of them children, their bodies flung across Hrabove. Villagers trying to contain the fire, tractors keeping flames away from crops. Bodies almost intact, still harnessed into their seats, the sad sight of luggage sprayed across the field. It was unbearable. Naturally fingers of accusation were being pointed across the country. Ukrainians saying it was the separatists, the separatists blaming Ukrainians. The West blaming Russia. Those in power vowing to get to the bottom of who did it and everyone else certain it would never happen again.

She could make no sense of the news coverage here, rebels and militants? Pro-Russian and separatists? Why was the news complicating an already complicated issue? Western Ukrainians have always hated ethnic Russians from Eastern Ukraine, and her people have always distrusted Ukrainians. Russia believed, erroneously, persistently, that Ukraine had always belonged to them, that it was inferior, that it had no right to exist. It was a question of borders, loyalties, grudges, ethnicities, aggressors encroaching on territories they had no right to traverse. Generation after generation of war, acrimony, famine, survival. In between all that were people like her mother and daughter, their loyalties split neatly across political lines, silent witnesses as windows were being blasted out of high-rises, burning metal falling to the ground. None of those worries about the impasse in her homeland heightened a desire to go to some seedy nightclub.

"It's time we got you out of the house. All you do is work and worry about Ukraine. How are you ever going to meet a man?" Georgina was already flinging open her closet and pawing through her few decent dresses. "A sexy *baba* like you shouldn't be sitting at home on a Saturday night spooning ice cream into her maw. Here, this one will do. You look like a movie star in this one."

"I don't want to meet a man. Have you gone mad?"

"But honey," Georgina said. "When was your last boyfriend? That old neighbor of yours back home? Or Larissa's mysterious father?"

"I'm not looking for any boyfriend."

"But who was it really?"

Her friends were not the only ones who wanted to know about her love life in Ukraine. Regina too once asked if she was married or had a partner. It was dangerous terrain, so to deflect the question, she in turn asked Regina how she and her husband met. Americans loved repeating the romance-origin story, she found, because Regina poured them both a disgusting fermented green tea beverage and spilled the whole story.

She and her friends were sipping white wine in an Irish bar in some Manhattan neighborhood when Jake entered with his gang, the two groups merging as the bar filled with an aggressive after-work crowd. Regina found herself flirting with one of the friends, a banker fresh from working in Russia. She tried to keep up with his feverish, impassioned Russian, but when it became clear that Regina had no adult knowledge of the country and couldn't bond with him about politics and slang and Russian music, the friend grew dismissive. Other than a knowledge of traditional food, she seemed to barely be Russian at all, the banker said. She lacked any depth, any authenticity. She knew it was silly to be hurt by the words of a stranger who knew nothing about her childhood struggles assimilating in New Jersey (she didn't even speak English until fourth grade, had no friends, was bullied by peers who called her "commie") but she burst into tears.

"So Jake swooped in to comfort me, and close up, he was much cuter anyway. And we knew some of the same people at Middlebury . . . a university in Vermont. And so I went out with him. I sound like an idiot, don't I? I know, it's a boring story." Regina was apologetic as usual, though it was true that Nadia's attention had been flagging. "Probably not nearly as interesting as your love stories. It seems like everything in the Old Country is more dramatic than here. We met, we dated, we married, we moved to Brooklyn, we procreated. Blah, blah, blah."

What she would give now for Regina's boring story: the ease of fluency in English by age nine, attending an American university, meeting a husband without too much difficulty, conceiving a child, living in a land free of war. A family together. At the very least, she wouldn't be dragged out to some horrible nightclub at almost fifty years old.

Lena and Georgina exchanged a glance that implied a recent conversation on the subject had yielded a fresh approach. "Have you thought that it might look good for the authorities if you had a husband? It might expedite Larisska's application, that there is a stable family waiting for her."

It was a low blow, using Larissa to get her to join them, one that she would have overlooked a week ago. But now it seemed like exactly the kind of maneuver they would make. "She's an adult, it's not like she's a child who needs a new papa. Now leave me alone."

Her voice unnerved them, especially Lena. She looked ready to retreat. But Georgina was doubling down.

"So what? It's not what she needs but the kind of front you want to present to the people that matter. You don't know how they think in Immigration." She was unfolding Nadia's comfortable working blouses and striped cotton crewnecks and shoving them back into drawers with disgust. "Don't you have a single sexy thing in this wardrobe?"

"A married couple always looks good to authorities. It's more proper," Lena said. But she hovered at the door. Lena was a better reader of people, probably because she worked with them all day.

The point, however ridiculous, did latch onto her mind. Her hopelessness was seeping into possibilities that had not even occurred to her. Maybe Lena was right in a way. A married couple probably did look good to authorities. The right sort of married couple actually might speed things up.

She rose. "I'll get dressed." With a single sweep of the hand, crumbs and empty cartons descended into the garbage can and the coffee table was neat again.

Lena and Georgina had expected prolonged resistance, and the shock of her almost immediate compliance was visible on their faces.

"Really?" Lena said.

"Really. But what I wear doesn't matter." She marched past her friends and yanked out the first thing that emerged, a gray cowl-neck sweater and pleated black pants. "This will do just fine."

"This old rag? Are you kidding me?" Georgina started. "At least show a little leg."

But Lena gave her a silent signal that said "Back off."

"You're really coming then?" As if she still didn't believe it herself.

"I'm coming, fine."

The girls looked pleased. They had made many similar efforts in the past, but Nadia usually fended them off. Between her jobs with Grisha and Regina, she worked seven days a week. Even as she admired her friends for their indefatigable energy, she had no time and no extra money to spend on such outings. And what was there to do in clubs at their age? Her friends were both divorced, with grown children, but they dolled themselves up every Friday and hit up Taous or Amnesia in the city. Once, Nadia let them drag her to one of those venues for her birthday, but they were at least twenty years older than everyone there. It was humiliating to witness her friends flirting, huddling together like anemic birds in minuscule skirts. And the whole club shining a chalk-white spotlight on her mottled face while doing a rendition of "Happy Birthday." And there were Georgina and Lena swearing they only went for the music and revelry, for the particular talents of "DJ Pushkin" or "Yanni" or the pleasures of private karaoke. But their aims were transparent: a husband or at least someone who could make their decisions, pay for groceries, rent, or at least the occasional fur coat, be a companion on vacations, perform the role that would allow them to slip back into mainstream, coupled immigrant society. For now, the three of them were peers in solitude, inseparable.

"Let's at least go somewhere local. No Amnesia."

"Fine." Lena quickly arbitrated with Georgina. "Nadia is agreeing to join us. It's only fair."

"Okeydokey, no Amnesia," Georgina said in English.

"At a time like this, with what's going on in my town, it seems wrong to be doing this. I mean, did you see the horror with that plane?" Nadia embarked on the process of dressing, the panty hose that promised sleek enclosure, the pants that slimmed her hips.

"And what good are you doing for Ukraine or those poor Malaysian passengers sitting around here?" Georgina said.

In the past, she never minded that her friends pretended she was their equal in heartbreak. But their biggest problem was a son who kept borrowing money for ill-fated business pursuits (Lena) or severe constipation (Georgina). Sometimes Nadia wondered if there wasn't some inherent Russianness to their complaining, a private certainty of their superiority.

Georgina emerged from her bedroom with the only dressy heels Nadia owned. They were metallic gold, a size too small. They once belonged to Georgina, who had benevolently passed them on. "Perfect. You will kill in this."

Instead of arguing, it was easier to float along friendship's good intentions. She slipped on the heels. The straps instantly sank their teeth into the back of her heels. Discarding them, she slipped on her comfortable rubber flip-flops with a wedge, adorned with a flutter of silver petals. In these, she could walk.

Lena rushed them out. "Wear what you like but hurry up. Ladies get in free before ten o'clock."

Brighton Beach at night was a mixture of festive lights and music on the main thoroughfare, but when you turned off the central street, you were confronted with long stretches of residential darkness. This particular block was lined with shuttered shops, except for a slow-moving line snaking down the sidewalk. Young men in jeans and football shirts checked their cell phones, while women in oversized hoop earrings and turtleneck dresses sashed by leather belts argued with the bouncer at the entrance.

"This is crazy," Nadia said, eyeing the bare collarbones and breasts in line. "What are we doing here? We're not twenty-two."

"Come on, girls." Georgina pushed her way past men in transparent mesh shirts and identical women with their straight, blown-out hair and strapless dresses, and the bouncer (Georgina's nephew!) encircled them, pushing them through the front doors. The air smelled of smoke and incense, a viscous, gummy atmosphere. Two women in leather bikinis were practically licking each other onstage, the music—a pounding remix of a lesser Vera Brezhneva song, "Sexy Bambina"—was thunderous. Everyone was touchingly young. She wanted to be home. Oh, how she wanted to be home.

But she felt her friends gripping onto each arm, as if anticipating a getaway. They led her to the crowded bar. "Hey, Kostya," Georgina managed to yell over the grinding music, waving over the heads of gazelles three kilometers deep. "Three shots for a couple of schoolgirls."

"Shots?" Nadia said. "Are you ladies kidding me?"

Lena shrugged. She looked tired already but was making every effort to brighten her face. She lived for her nights and weekends. At an expensive European-style salon where she worked, she stood on her feet for ten hours a day. She was the only Russian at a place owned by a transplant from Milan. The place drove her crazy. Children running about underfoot while she applied color, the colorist at the next station so chatty and annoying, it made her never want to set foot on Italian soil. The clients were demanding, never quite sure about what they wanted or whether they liked the result. The vacations tightly parsed out, sick days nonexistent. She worked six days a week, handed most of the salary over to her son, who never managed to get a single business idea off the ground but kept promising to repay her.

"Just drink up," she said when the shots arrived. "To happiness, to getting everything you want this year." The three of them clinked and gulped down the cloudy contents of the shot glasses.

Immediately, she felt her brain grow soft. A heaviness lifted. Now she was able to look around the club with her usual anthropologist's curiosity, to smile at the silly young Russian girls in today's Brooklyn. Did they have to show off their bodies so overtly? Did they have to overdo it with the makeup? They all looked alike to her, with their long ironed hair, their shimmer, perfume so strong they gave off the scent of hothouse flowers. She couldn't find a single girl with nuance in this place; all that gold and boobs and high heels. And the men either completely the opposite, in their scraggly jeans and sneakers and sports shirts, or worse, slick and bronzed in pleated black pants and metallic shirts open way too low down their chests. Larissa, when she arrived, would be too sensible for them all.

"To peace at home and in the world," Lena said, and they gulped down another shot. The lights of the strobe shifted from green to hot pink, the club growing more crowded. Nadia took off her jacket. She was blazing hot in the cowl-neck sweater.

"Now you're talking," she heard Georgina cry in approval. A group of young girls darted glances in their direction, then folded back in to one another.

As her friends wove her through the bodies, Nadia thought the right kind of man for this particular goal would feel ill at ease in these surroundings, he might be a little apart from his cohort, visibly bored. He might have a full glass of something pooling a watery circle on the round table in front of him.

"I know," Georgina yelled, lost to a sea of elbows, hips, and sequins. "There are some seriously raunchy *babas* here and we've got to keep up, ladies."

"Another?" Lena asked them, which was not like her at all. She hated being hungover, hated applying color with a pulsating head to chatty clients. The smoke smelled sickeningly of orange peel. A man in an iridescent purple shirt was raking her over, cocking an eyebrow in her direction. He was at least forty, way too old for what she was planning. She grabbed the girls to escape the invisible net of his desire.

"Come back," he called after her. "I love blondes!"

"See, Nadyush?" Lena said loudly into her ear. Right now it felt like she would never hear again. "Jewish men love a real Ukrainian woman. Not enough natural blondes in this country for them. You should think about it. I know there aren't too many Jews where you come from, but let me tell you: Jewish men make the best husbands."

Georgina was at her other side. "Go up to someone. Anyone. Just smile. Introduce yourself."

"Be confident, but not too self-sufficient," Lena advised.

"Pretend you're interested in their boring jobs."

"But don't start out thinking they're boring. Just find the right questions to make them sound interesting."

Georgina found a vial of perfume in her bag, and she spritzed their hair with it. "They're boring, Lena, for fuck's sake. Let's not kid ourselves."

"It's all in the attitude you take. And whose job is exciting in your opinion?"

The light shifted to accommodate the tempo of a slower song. The gauzy pinks and maroons gave way to a stark, foggy white. It was finally possible to see. Young men were all bunched in guffawing groups with their shellacked chins, their collars raised up to their ears. A few feet in the air, a solitary dancer swayed indifferently inside a birdcage. It all looked about as far from Regina's normal Irish-bar story as possible.

But there was a man conducting a quiet conversation near the bar. He was no older than thirty, sporting neither chest rug nor luminescent shirt. His hair was longer than she would like for a man, a feathered layer of rock-star tresses. His stubble looked orchestrated with great intention, but there was something in his posture she liked and the way he held a wineglass, rather than a glass of vodka or cognac or some other stubby goblet clinking with ice cubes.

"What about that one? The one with the mop on his head and protruding ears?" Georgina was referring to the man's friend, an older man in his fifties. He stood on his heels as if to accommodate his orb of a stomach. That he was hairy everywhere was evident even in this light, from this distance. He was the type of man Georgina believed was good enough for her, the kind she should be grateful to land.

"Okay. I'll be right back," she said, parking her shot glass on the nearby banquette.

"Wait, where are you going?" Lena asked. To Nadia's ear, she sounded incredulous. "Maybe it's getting late." She was blocking her path, clearly imagining that all that business with Nadia finding a man at the club was concocted to lend their night dramatic diversion. It wasn't actually supposed to happen. "Maybe we should take you home."

"*Ty shto?* I'm just getting started."

"Good for you." Georgina gave her a tiny push into the swell of her lower back. "We'll be right here. Good luck with Cheburashka."

The way she said it was so dripping with doubt and haughtiness that there was no other choice but to go.

Georgina, Lena, and Nadia met almost six years ago in an English-language night class at a synagogue on Avenue F. It was apparent they were the only single women of a certain age in a room full of adrift recent immigrants with only a vague desire to learn English: pink young things just sprung free from their former Soviet republics, middle-aged *babas* who'd been recently laid off from cushy jobs that did not require the English language, and a handful of ambitious older ladies who said they wanted to communicate with their American-born grandchildren.

She still remembered how they looked fresh off the plane, Georgina in itchy acrylic sweaters, her eyelids smeared with dark purple shadow, Lena in her rotation of corduroy skirts, wearing an experimental hairstyle to every class. And herself in the cheap, practical blouses she scoured at Rainbow, always late because of job interviews in every conceivable corner of New York City. She was the only one from their circle who was not from Russia or one of its big cities, Moscow or Peter, who was neither a Jew (Georgina) nor had been married to a Jew (Lena). But they embraced her anyway, inviting her for outings to the beach or theater, holiday dinners or a weekend trip to the hardware store. They took turns calling her when she was sick and brought over bouillon or took over in the kitchen, heating up salt in a pan to press to her congested face. They had keys to her apartment in case of emergency.

Even if they spoke about her as a Ukrainka, it was in the affectionate tone of "*Our* Ukrainka" and back then she thought nothing of it. She knew they spent time alone together and discussed her. They had agreed to consider her the one to be pitied but how could she blame them? Unlike them, she was truly, authentically alone. If pity was threaded through their attention, she gladly accepted it.

It was only last March that everything changed. It was the tail end of the annual Women's Day party in Georgina's apartment, Nadia running in from a long day with Sasha. To leave work, where you feel diminished in your humanity, and join your equals was a great blessing. How wonderful it was to meet friends after a frustrating commute with stalled trains, sick passengers, and sardined cars. It was warm in there, the sound of female voices and bottles clinked against the mouths of glasses. She was taking off her cold, damp coat in the foyer, unzipping her high boots, when she heard, "I don't think her daughter ever calls her. She gets all the news of Larissa from her mother. It's actually a sad situation. She even sends her daughter refrigerated insulin, and not even a thank-you. Can you imagine not being in touch with your own daughter? I mean, we have no idea what happened, but you can't help but think it was her fault." Nadia felt her entire body go still, arms at her sides. Her heart was pounding with sick dread. To turn around and leave without drawing attention to herself felt impossible. But she felt glad she never told them how it happened, that she had kept private the memory fluttering inside her all these years.

In July of 2008, the U.S. embassy in Kiev was decorated with the celebratory markers of a holiday. Everyone was handed a flag upon arrival, which created a festive atmosphere in the waiting room. The symbolism of finalizing documents to leave Ukraine on American Independence Day was not lost on Nadia.

"I know, I was thinking the exact same thing," her daughter said, sitting beside her in the waiting room. Numbers flashed on the board and everyone checked the match to their tickets. She was amazed at the orderliness on display. No one was pushing in front of anyone else, but waiting, docile, in their seats until their number flashed on a screen. She overheard some of the interviews in the windows. They were in Ukrainian, not Russian, but simple enough that she could communicate. Her heart was an unpredictable thing, speeding up and slowing at will.

"I was worried about the test results, that the diabetes might be a problem," Nadia said, by way of passing the time. She took out the results of the medical exams. "But they look fine."

"It's starting to feel real now. Maybe they would want my embroidery there," Larissa said, dreamy. She was working on one as they waited, her needle expertly gliding through the holes of the waxed canvas. A scene was starting to emerge, the tufted heads of sheep, the silver fence glistening in the sun. She removed the American flag from the stick and was incorporating it into the scene. "I could even make pillows or duvet covers. It would be a way to make some money while I figure out what to do."

"I bet they would. Ukrainian folk arts are very desirable and rare."

"I could make the traditional ones, or the dresses with the diamond shapes for fertility. I bet American women would like that."

It was still odd to discuss fertility with her own daughter so she just murmured assent. The room was grand, intimidating. She had to go to the bathroom, but she was afraid. It all looked so fancy. When she finally pushed open the door, she found no woman collecting money in a plastic tray; it was apparently free of charge. A free public bathroom? In Ukraine? It was all so exotic, she was almost too shy to go.

On her way back out, she spied water in actual glasses and they too were free of charge. She was told she was welcome to take some, but she brought one to her daughter, in case there was a cap of one glass of water per family. The entire operation was all so organized, so un-Ukrainian. A velvet rope contained a peaceful check-in line, no one was insulting anyone else. When they were asked to turn in any computers or phones, it was as a polite question, not a commanding bark. The tip of her tongue was fiery and weak with excitement and fear. The idea that had been fermenting in her head all these years was finally coming true. They were leaving.

Their number was called and they approached the window. The woman behind the bars was young, barely older than Larissa. She greeted them in Ukrainian with the same inexplicable politeness exhibited by the other employees. They were to stretch out their hands for fingerprints, and that too was done with gentleness, the young woman's cold fingers tapping hers and then Larissa's against paper.

"Are you from Kiev?" She was taking them through the bureaucratic steps with easy small talk.

"Rubizhne. It's in the east."

"Oh, that's nice. I've never been but I hear it's a beautiful city. Peaceful, relaxing."

Fingerprints concluded, she said she would need their identification and some pictures from home to prove their identities. "And it says here on your form that you were sponsored by your sister?"

"Yes, she is in Cleveland, but we will start off in New York."

"Not eager to be so close to your sister?"

Nadia smiled. "Exactly. Anyway, I hear there are many Russian speakers in New York."

"But expensive too, no?"

Not as much as here, she wanted to say. Where anything worth buying would have cost her a month's rent, where this entire process of leaving the country was equivalent to almost a year's paycheck. But she did not want to break the mesmerizing spell of politeness. Instead, she focused on the woman's features, the face bottom-heavy and wide, like a slice of watermelon.

For a minute, the watermelon face looked confused. She looked at their identifications, and the pictures they provided. The top one was of the two of them on vacation in Crimea, Larissa's face hidden behind a safe, floppy hat. She consulted the pages of a bound manual.

"I just have to check with my manager. I'll be right back."

"Is everything fine?" Nadia asked, gathering the photographs back into her wallet.

"I'm sure it is. I just have to speak to my boss."

Larissa's brow was glistening, the tendrils of her hair spackled to her face. She looked so tiny in that moment, so like the six-year-old who would not let go of her hand on the first day or second or third day of school, so like the twelve-year-old who showed her bloody panties and asked if it was the normal color, the right color. Who asked her how long this womanhood thing would last. She couldn't help but kiss her on the top of her head, and Larissa snuggled into her side, smelling of herb shampoo. Mother and daughter as one creature, one being. When the joy struck her, it just exploded with spontaneous, exhilarating spark.

The young employee returned with her boss, a man with a protruding stomach and a toothpick on one side of his mouth. He stood silent, the young woman taking it as a cue that it was her responsibility to talk.

"My boss here is wondering if your daughter is in fact twenty-one. Is the birthday on this identification correct?"

Nadia felt a blast of ice course through her entire body, from throat to the very extremities of her toes. "Yes. Is that a problem?"

"So she is twenty-one right now?"

"As of last week only. But we've been on the waiting list as a family unit since she was nine years old."

There was an exchange of whispers, the man with the belly stabbing a manual page with his index finger. Larissa was gripping her wrist, a tight squeeze of a claw. Sentences floated back at them—"aged out" "as soon as you get there, you fill out the application" "reunion list" "as a parent who is sponsoring her, it might take no time at all." The words were spoken apologetically, but Nadia was too agitated to appreciate the exceptional rarity of empathy.

Larissa's grip on her arm tightened. She was saying something like "I guess we can't go. Calm down, Mama."

"But this doesn't make sense. Shouldn't they take into consideration the age at the time of application?"

"I'm afraid that's not how it works," the woman said, nervously checking in with her boss. He nodded, his look of frustration and annoyance the first familiarly Ukrainian gesture of the whole embassy experience.

Nadia's head was filling with the kind of sound that drowned out everything in its path, a trapped thing ramming against walls, searching for a way out. It was unfair, she continued. Her daughter was nine years old when they applied. How was it her fault the process took eleven years? Why should they be punished for the ridiculously slow bureaucracy?

"Do you want to go ahead and put in the application just for you?" the woman asked her. Her boss, satisfied the conflict had been resolved, moved to the next window, staring over the shoulder of a young man taking fingerprints from a lucky family with two small children.

She felt Larissa pulling her away, the suction of them still united. An entire lifetime rolled before her eyes, album after album. Their future in Ukraine. Her mind felt capable of seeing months, years into the future. The paltry checks, the struggle to find Larissa's medication, how to heat the apartment. And then she conjured something else, a stubborn desire, an illogical pull from within.

"I will go," she decided. "As soon as I get there, I will put you on the list. You'll follow."

Her daughter's face snapped in her direction. Her eyes were wide, panicked. "You would go without me?" She was so horrified, so dripping with shock and disbelief. Nadia could not bear to look. At the next window, the family was eavesdropping, the smug parents who fulfilled a basic duty of never leaving their children behind. They were probably not the only ones; the acoustics amplified every word.

"It's the only way, Larisska. If I don't go, neither of us leaves."

"So neither of us leaves," Larissa said.

"I want us to leave. We need to leave. Don't you think I'm doing this for you?" she said firmly, but with a pang.

"You're always doing things for me. But did you ever think to ask if I wanted these things in the first place?"

The transformation in her daughter was playing out everywhere, the eyes, mouth, the delicate rims of her eyebrows. Don't look at her, Nadia told herself. Look forward. But she could not help it. Her daughter's eyes went hard right in front of her, as if a gate had fallen. The softness, the need, the warmth of those blue eyes was dimmed. Finally, the hand was removed from her wrist. "I don't believe it. You are really doing this," she said. "It's like I can't trust you anymore. You promised . . ."

"What did I promise?"

"I don't know. It's just I took it for granted, I guess. That you'd never leave me."

Larissa turned around and walked out of the embassy, passing back through security and gliding into the shadows of the front hallway. Nadia ran after her across the lacquered lobby, the too-quiet orderly lobby with free glasses of water and free bathrooms. "Larissa, come back," she called, drawing unpleasant stares and whispers. Her entire torso was soaked in perspiration. "Larissa!"

"Are you canceling?" the young officer said into her microphone.

She stopped, frozen, not breathing.

"Or should we draw up your documents?"

"Yes," she finally said. It was the most impossible word she'd ever uttered. It was like plunging a knife into her body over and over again. *Yes, yes, yes.*

At the Women's Day party, Georgina must have heard the movement at the door, the indecisive sound of her halted steps, because she interrupted her own story, raising her voice for Nadia's benefit. "But you know what? She's our Ukrainka, she'll be fine."

This time "our Ukrainka" sounded ominous. Nadia had wanted to leave, to never speak with these friends again. But she managed to emerge from that hallway, pretending she'd heard nothing. Shaking her hair from the light sheen of snow, a wide, celebratory smile on her face. She never told them that she heard their judgment, and what was encrusted within "our Ukrainka" were remnants of ancient Russian imperialism. Even in the Soviet "Union," there was never a doubt that Russians were all that mattered, Ukrainians always in second place. And the thing that cut her down to her very sinews, more wounding than their condescending nickname for her, was the fact that her friends believed she was a terrible mother.

It was a small triumph then to leave Lena and Georgina huddled near the too-high bar stools at this ridiculous nightclub as she made her way toward the long-haired wine drinker. Upon closer inspection, he was a little too pretty for the real job she had in mind, a man who was probably weighed down by a messy tangle of romantic prospects. In her mind, she'd pictured a misshapen type whose gratitude would be the driving force of the transaction, someone who would take one look and wonder how he could help bring their plan to fruition. In any case, it was too late to turn back. The man was looking at her in the disinterested way all young men appraised her now that she was close to fifty. They slightly raised their eyebrows as if the only thing she could possibly want from them was directions or perhaps to find out the exact time.

"May I talk with you a moment?" she asked in Russian.

"You are speaking to me?" He had a thick accent, from someplace mysterious and sexy like Tashkent. He nodded to his friend, an older man around her age, who reluctantly moved away.

She could see Lena and Georgina, their skin paved with blue neon light. That she picked the younger, more attractive man was clearly shocking to them.

"Shall we have a seat?" She pointed to the nearest empty love seat, a velvet tufted thing.

The befuddled man sat at one end. He was wearing cheap-looking leather pants, the material bunching at his thighs. He was confused, polite wonder giving way to suspicion. Was she perhaps a dirty old lady? Was she one of those former rural beauties who were not aware that their peak had long ago crested?

"If you don't mind," she said. "I'd like to show you some pictures."

Her purse appeared on her knees and she fumbled with its clasp, a silver button that refused to be pushed through the loop. When it finally opened, her hand gratefully landed on the phone. Across the room, there were her friends, astonished, barely able to mask the serrated edges of their envy.

"What kind of pictures?"

"Trust me, you will not be disappointed."

The man's neck was tensed but he bent his head down next to hers. This close to a young man for the first time aroused no distinct desire in Nadia. His scent was not masculine at all, but a decadent swirl of citrus and cinnamon and hair pomade.

The first image of Larissa she could find was the one where she was seventeen years old and leaning against a pine tree, the light behind her blond hair plaited down the length of one arm, making her hair bright, incandescent. Her gaze was unusually open, relaxed, eyes directly meeting the camera. It was a stunning photo because it conveyed a face of fierce, unquestioning love. "Our Larisska," her mother had written with the attachment. "Found these in boxes under bed."

She continued to scroll. Larisska bathed by the light of a computer screen. Larisska standing in front of one of her most beautiful embroidered tapestries, where peasant women danced in bright red caftans. Standing with the other teachers and her first-grade class in a blouse she bought for her in Rainbow on Kings Highway. That famous old picture of the two of them on a blanket in Yalta, white chairs and Crimean mountain ranges in the background.

"Do you like her? Do you think she's pretty?"

"Sure, I guess so." The man shrugged. "Your daughter, I presume?"

"She's even better looking in person, I promise you. And a heart like you won't find here, with these painted harlots." Nadia waved around the room, realizing she was encompassing Lena and Georgina in the designation. "She will heal a mouse with a broken leg, that's how bighearted she is. She works with the sweetest children in school. And funny too. She repeats anecdotes perfectly, gets the punch lines just right."

His face was furrowed, but then it suddenly cleared up.

"Oh. I understand. You want me to go out with her. This is you trying to set her up, right? She's having trouble finding a date?"

The very idea, Nadia thought. Her daughter could date actors and models if she wanted to, that's how pretty she was. But Sergei, the last love interest Nadia knew about, turned into a disappointment. Her mother told her never to bring his name up in front of her daughter. But now six years had passed and Nadia realized she had no idea what her daughter had been up to during that time, whose company she was keeping. "Oh please, Mama," was her only response when she broached the topic.

"Not just date. I have a proposition for you."

"What's that?" He seemed to be entertained by their exchange, patient enough to hear her out. The volume on the music reached a new decibel, accompanied by screams of recognition.

"There's a visa called K-1. You heard of it? It is for fiancés."

"A visa? What do you mean for fiancés? What's this got to do with me?"

"You're not engaged already, are you?"

"No." He laughed, looking around him as if for rescue. He met a friend's gaze and made a theatrical show of shrugging.

"She's in Lugansk region right now. You know what's going on there, a senseless war. I've tried lawyers and immigration agencies. It seems living in a war zone won't speed up her case. But you won't regret it, I promise you. She will make you a fine wife, and if you are unhappy, you can always divorce, yes?"

The man emitted something between a laugh and an exhale. "Here all this time I had no idea what you were getting at. And it's just that you want me to marry your daughter for a green card."

"There's the K-1 visa. I read about it," she said, pleased to finally be understood even if his reiteration of her reasonable request sounded crass and illicit. She could feel the flush leaving her face and neck, a flush that rarely went away these days. The music changed to a wordless, robotic beat and the dancers out on the floor were embodying its soulless rhythm.

"You know, don't you, that this costs, *babki*? A buddy of mine did it. I think the going rate is twenty thousand, am I right? Not that I'm agreeing."

"But you will love her. And she will love you. You and I will go to Moscow to meet her—they need that, the K-1 people. They'll

want proof you've met—and you will see that I did not exagger-
ate. She is as beautiful as the photos. She is a real innocent girl. I
will be nearby to help you set up your home. She is a modest girl
but also very smart. I can see you are a man who prizes intelligence
in a woman."

"Let me stop you right there." The man was rising, the neon
light imprinting multiple shadows across his torso.

"Wait." She followed him to the bar, her phone flashing photo
after photo. Larissa at ten showing off new sneakers. Larissa at
twelve in her school uniform. Larissa in bed, the day she left, blankets at her chin, a scowling face pointing at the wall. Her back
pointed at the camera. *Go away, just leave already.*

"I've been polite so far because you're my mother's age, but
enough is enough." The man was gesturing to his friend, slinking
between bodies with that ridiculous glass of red wine still in hand.
The chase was garnering some attention.

Behind her, she could feel her friends moving toward her in
protective concern, swooping in for their rescue. What on earth
was she doing following this young guy around? She could see
them agreeing that she was embarrassing herself, that she needed
to be removed before someone recognized her from the neighborhood.

She caught up to the man anyway, scrawled her cell phone number on a napkin and pushed it in the pocket of his jacket. "In case
you hear of someone," she quickly added in response to his panicked look. "You might know a man who is interested."

He moved closer. An unpleasant mix of alcohol and garlic was
being breathed upon her. "I don't know a man who is interested.
Unless you are willing to pay. Are you willing to pay?"

That was when she felt Georgina's hand at her elbow.
"Nadyen'ka, come with us. Excuse us." They were guiding her

away from the man and his older friend to the exit of the club. The room was now clogged with gyrating bodies, anonymous forms sparkling in the sinister blue of the overhead flares.

"What was he talking about, paying? What kind of woman did he take you for? None of us are that desperate yet, thank goodness." Georgina was talking nervously, a whole stream of nonsense about older women and younger men, and how it was a real shame how little dignity was accorded to women over thirty-five. Her insistence that Nadia not take it personally was only making Nadia refuse to be led. She dug in her heels and drew out the squeeze to the front doors as long as she could.

Outside, an even longer line stretched around the corner obscured by cigarette smoke. Already inebriated women bolstered one another up, laughing and punching at their phones.

Georgina described to Lena her version of what she'd witnessed, full of indignation about his offensive treatment of Nadia. "You better believe I told him what's what. He had no right to treat my friend like that. He was not nearly as nice-looking up close. A horse face, am I right?"

"What a *basran*." Lena squeezed Nadia's arm in solidarity.

Georgina said, with what she imagined was tact, "Of course when I said you should go out there and introduce yourself, it's a matter of delicacy. Strictly speaking, we should really wait for them to come to us. Even here, men like to be the aggressor."

"I thought you were after the friend," Lena said. "The friend seemed like a better fit. He seemed so disappointed when you walked away."

"That other one was still a baby, wasn't he? No older than my son."

The three of them started away. They managed to free themselves from the frenzied cluster around the entrance to the club, all those young people begging for loopholes, why they should be allowed in ahead of other people. The women turned onto quiet, dangerous streets. From time to time, they heard ambulance sirens. It was that hour of the night—cars packed with men from lawless, tormented countries in search of trouble. It was the time of night women stuck together, called each other when they were safely at home, doors tightly bolted.

"What were you showing him on your phone?" Lena asked. They slipped onto larger avenues, navigated all those drunk young people colonizing the sidewalks.

"Pictures of Sasha, the little girl I nanny. He wanted to know about my job, and when I told him what I do, he said he liked kids. I don't know what you ladies are worried about. He was the one who asked for my number." She said this lie easily, proudly.

"Is that right?"

"What about the friend?"

"What friend? The hairy guy? Oh, I was heading for him at first, but you know, close up, this guy was cuter, so I went straight for him. He swooped in before I could even consider the older guy."

Her friends exchanged a glance. In channeling Regina, she was clearly not sounding like herself, but what did that matter? At some point, Larisska would make it here. At some point, Larisska would have to forgive her. At some point, she would need Lena and Georgina less. At some point, after twenty more years in this country, she would have more of what Regina has obtained so easily. She would become a boring American mother with a boring American story. In the meantime, she would stop at nothing until it happened.

"I'm sorry what I said about him. I must have misread the situation. And to think I dragged you away," Georgina murmured. "I'd have killed you if you did that to me."

"That's fine. We'd already exchanged numbers. I'll probably go on a date with him next week."

"Of course you will, honey."

They continued on in a flurry of laughter. Lena started telling them about the infamous Italian owner of her exclusive salon, how he charged his rich American clients arbitrary fees depending on his mood. Because the salon was booked months in advance, they never complained or asked about what they'd received for those exorbitant prices.

"Once he billed a woman a hundred and fifty dollars for a crappy blow-dry and she didn't make a peep about it. Just handed over her credit card like it was normal."

"Are you serious? I can't believe it!" Nadia said.

She acted shocked, the naïve, sheltered Ukrainka astounded by the sophisticated deceptions being carried out in the big cosmopolitan city. It was her role in their group and she finally learned how to play it.

5

To New Happiness

Outside the synagogue, the mothers and nannies were lined up with strollers. It was a few minutes to three, the metal gates of Sasha's preschool still shut. A sideways wind of unenthusiastic snow was enveloping Nadia, and she clustered with all the others under the awning of the construction project next door, a sleek apartment building of windows dwarfing the brick town houses.

Feverish one-sided cell phone conversations in assorted languages made Nadia check her own phone for any word from Larisska. She had just written her after hearing about the Donetsk airport under siege again, the poor Donetsk airport! The same place she would sometimes greet her university boyfriend, her dental technician sweetheart, after his trips delivering black market forged teeth to post-Soviet patients willing to pay for them under the table. She remembered his rosy-cheeked paleness as he alighted from the plane with flowers, waving before even glimpsing her face. It was once a place of expansiveness and hope, this airport, a Ukraine connected to the world. Now there were men trapped inside, some with limbs exploded, bleeding to death. "The Ukies deserved it," the very same dentist sweetheart had recently posted on Odnoklassniki before she could block him.

"Get the hell off our land." Of course she had written none of this to her daughter. Just the usual check-in, the need to make sure Larisska was healthy, whole.

Larissa hadn't written back. The doors opened, the mothers and nannies filtering inside. She followed them down the corridor past an explosion of wall art, watercolors of paired animals signed by children in what she learned was Hebrew, multicolored nine-pronged candelabras affixed to paper. In the classroom, Sasha was holding her own creation, a flat, wooden candleholder that seemed like an imminent fire hazard.

"A menorah!" she corrected, annoyed, when Nadia gushed over the lantern's beauty.

"Menorah," Nadia obediently repeated.

The teacher appeared younger than Larisska, and made sure to address each mother. Her eyes glazed over the nannies. "Happy holidays. Don't forget . . ." And Nadia lost the rest. The woman spoke tentatively as if expecting something, waiting for something she was not allowed to name. This reminded Nadia that Regina had slipped her envelopes for the teachers that morning, cards that contained gift cards in amounts Regina could barely afford.

"But they work so hard," Regina said in that vaguely empathetic way of hers, as if her mind could not possibly grasp the rounded nature of another's daily life. "I can't imagine being a teacher. The toughest job in the world."

Of course, Regina had no idea about the toughest job in the world. This teacher was probably spending her time off on a family vacation or enjoying holidays in the city. Compare this to teachers in Ukraine, the winter breaks of her own mother or Larisska. While the students were out, they were to spend their own breaks and summers spackling and painting the school walls, changing dead light bulbs, fixing toilets and sinks at the school despite a lack of plumbing experience. If they were lucky, teachers received an appreciative basket of potatoes from a student's garden. They were not getting gift certificates for frothy coffee drinks, that's for sure. *Toughest job in the world.* But she handed over an envelope like everyone else, smiled her thanks, and started layering Sasha up for the outdoors.

Her phone rang, the unexpected sound of it ricocheting against her thoughts. It was a number unknown to her, the area code local.

"Allo," she said.

"Is this Nadezhda? Nadia? I'm sorry but you didn't write down your last name."

The man spoke accented Russian; the gruffness of the syllables and delivery pointed to a Georgian provenance. When the phone rang and it wasn't her nannying job or her friends, it was most likely her on-the-books employer. VIP Senior Care called at irregular hours for her to fill sudden vacancies or remind her to enroll in certification courses. They rotated through staff regularly. The owners of the company were engaging in some kind of Medicare fraud or immigration fraud or embezzlement, and employees too close to the company's business operations were quickly swapped out for new ones.

"Speaking." Nadia was half listening; Sasha was stalled in her progress, one arm tangled in her fleece sweater, a flash of exasperation coloring her cheeks.

"This is a strange phone call to make."

"Yes, well, I'm busy right now. Can I help you?"

"I got your number from Boris."

Nadia tugged at Sasha's second arm, and stuffed it inside her sleeve. "Boris? Which Boris?"

"You . . . um . . . came up to him at a nightclub this past summer. He said, pardon me, you were too old for him, but that you

were nice-looking. You probably don't remember the guy standing next to him. Well, with work and all, I'm only calling you now."

Sasha's zipper was snagged on a butterfly appliqué, and for some
reason Nadia could not pry it loose. The girl's arms were helpless
at her sides as Nadia tugged. She seemed incapable of dressing herself, as if dragging out babyhood as long as the adults in her life
would allow her. "There must be some misunderstanding. You see,
I was not looking for a companion for myself but a husband for
my daughter."

"I thought you were nice-looking. Why don't we have coffee
sometime? You will like me, I promise. I'm not unattractive, I work
very hard."

It was hard to hear him. Around her were the effusive greet-
ings, kisses, murmurs of women. She tried to conjure the man
standing next to that nightclub Romeo but the whole incident was
buried so far deep inside her that she could picture only a giant
ball of hair on legs. Sasha was now in full rebellion on the floor,
unzipped, a furry boot pulled onto the wrong foot. Nadia transferred the receiver to her other ear and switched the boot to the
proper side. "I'm very busy, excuse me, I don't know your name."

"Boris. I'm actually Boris too, believe it or not."

"Boris. I have a very busy schedule. I work seven days a week
these days. I don't know where your young friend got the idea I
was even interested in meeting gentlemen."

"Did you not find me attractive or what?"

"I don't even remember you. This was back in the summer,
right? If we're talking about the same night even." She shimmied
Sasha into her fashionable but thinly lined coat.

"Look, how about you give me a day and time you are free. Any
day you are off work."

Her heart pulsed painfully, relentlessly. It took all her effort to breathe. The man had a nice, educated voice with a gravelly undercurrent of normality. His directness was refreshing, flattering. When you pushed the thought of men out of your life and replaced them with work and worry, it was easy to forget that romance existed, that it was in any way desirable. She recalled it all in a flash, the way the kisses of the *technolog* and the dental technician before him made her insides collapse, like overheated fruit. Even her old neighbor Pyotor was able to summon a few pleasurable tremors.

"New Year's Eve. That and New Year's Day are my only days off, I'm afraid."

"Perfect. I've been looking for a Snegurochka for New Year's Eve." He named a café, "Rendezvous on Avenue Z. Perfect for us, no?"

She was speechless, having lost the thread of his associations. New Year's Eve? Snegurochka? Rendezvous?

"Get it? Because we are having a rendezvous," he prompted with a laugh. "Let's say twelve o'clock."

She hung up. Sasha was lingering by her cubby with other similarly adorned children with their own impatient nannies. Two women were trying to engage Nadia in silent sympathy in the vein of: Why is it so hard to get these children out of this chaotic Jewish school? But her own mind was riding the rough wave of anxieties.

She had no idea how the mechanics of dating worked here, even among émigrés who brought with them the scaffolding of its former rules. Back home, it was simple: men boiled with masculinity, chivalry, anger. They presumed themselves kings, most competent of rulers. Women folded themselves up into smaller and smaller squares to accommodate them. In exchange, wives received grateful flowers on birthdays and International Women's Day, they experienced the freedom of complaining about their husbands to girlfriends. She had escaped this dynamic by retreating into a duet with her daughter, but for that she had become the object of pity. Romance was like reading novels, an indulgence she had had time for when she was young. What was the point of traditional relationships now?

Suddenly Sasha was next to her, a firm hand pulling her own. For a second, she thought it was Larisska's until she heard a confident little voice say, "Shall we go, Nadia? I'm ready."

Rendezvous Café was one of the newer establishments in Sheepshead Bay, its exterior a long panel of modern glass and steel. She passed the entrance, stole a quick glance through the front doors, and kept moving. Unfortunately, Nadia was on time, and a woman never arrives on time for a date. At least that used to be one of the fundamental rules of Soviet and post-Soviet dating. It was imperative to make the man wait as long as humanly possible.

Across the street, Nadia spotted a CVS pharmacy and ducked inside to pass the minutes until she could respectably materialize at Rendezvous. She wandered past the long line of shampoos she would never apply to her splitting, middle-aged ash-blond ends. Still, she enjoyed testing her English vocabulary to figure out what miracle each bottle promised. Moisturizing? Clarifying? Texturizing? She took a photo with her phone and sent it to her daughter. There was no immediate response back, not even a smiley face.

"Did you get my last message? Are you OK?" she texted. Sometimes, on a lucky day, her daughter answered the occasional text.

In the makeup aisle, she checked her appearance again. Her hair was carefully curled, her tiger-printed scarf complemented her hair (thanks to L'Oréal Elseve, the buttermilk Belorussian shampoos her local pharmacy stocked). The shoulder pads in her coat gave her a more regal height. She had chosen her lipstick as matte precisely for its ability to cling to her lips despite pressing them to beverage rims. The cold air gave her cheeks a pinched rose color. Her mother used to tell her that a first date was no time to assess a man. How would it matter if she liked him but he wasn't interested? A woman's task at the very onset was to enrapture the prey; what she would do with him afterward would then be up to her. Nadia crossed the street.

The young woman behind the counter of Rendezvous Café had the phone pressed to her ear despite being faced with a line of impatient customers. "*Nu,* pull him out of that school then," she was saying in loud Russian. "If he hates it so much. Let him feel the consequences of his actions." She looked to be in her mid-twenties, but she spoke with the practiced cynicism of someone much older. Her brows were thin, dyed a reddish black and arched high, the severely pulled-back ponytail stretching them back even farther. The woman was dunking a tea bag in time to her nods.

In front of Nadia stood two clearly American women who were being ignored. "Excuse me," one of them kept trying to interrupt. Back home, the employee would have been excoriated immediately, and there would be a colorful exchange that ended in the gruff handing over of a pastry. That people attempted polite avenues of interaction first was one of this country's more civilized qualities.

Nadia peeked into the interior of the café. It was empty except for a big group of women, a guy in a Ded Moroz outfit, and an old man keeping aloft with the help of a walker. She hoped that was not Boris. She glanced at her watch. Thirty minutes late was a respectable time for men to wait for a desirable date. So where was he?

The young women finally received their baked goods, unhappily brushing past her. At the counter, the employee was continuing in the same vein. "Did you talk to his teachers? *Nu,* what did they say about his lisp?" The doors flung open and a woman and child came in, settling in line behind her. Nadia hesitated, her mother's voice reverberating: *Buying your own overpriced pastry would send a gentleman the wrong message.*

"Look, there's Santa!" the child was saying in English, pointing to Ded Moroz. "But Christmas is over. Why is he here?"

She looked up from the assortment behind the display case to find the Ded Moroz at her side. He pulled down his fake white moustache and beard so it dangled around his neck by a rubber band. "You're Nadezhda, yes?" he said. He turned to the employee. "Are you going to serve your customers or are you going to chat on the phone all day? What your friend is doing with her kid is no business of yours anyway. Why don't you put that phone down and work a little for a change?"

The young woman was stunned into silence. "What's it to you, Ded Moroz? Why are you in such a bad mood this holiday season?"

He pulled up a red sleeve with its fleece lining. "We are all busy people here. Let's start with you doing what you are paid to do. How's that?" He took off the hat with the drooping white pompom to reveal a full head of brown hair eroded by gray.

The woman sighed into the phone—"I'll call you later"—cocked one hand on her hip. "So what can I do for you, Your Winter Majesty?"

Ded Moroz turned to Nadia, and she managed, "That little cake over there. And a cappuccino."

"Just the coffee to go. Let's get the hell out of here." He parted his burgundy tunic and dug in his pants pockets for a wallet. Her stomach was starting to announce its hunger. But he was stretching out a hand.

"Boris."

"Nadia."

"Very pleased to meet you in the daylight," he said. "May I?"

A paper bag with coffee was handed to her. Before she understood what she was agreeing to, a sweep of his hand produced a tiara and veil. The teeth of the tiara were being inserted into her carefully spritzed and Belorussian-swept hair.

"I told you on the phone. You will be my Snegurochka for the day."

"I guess I didn't fully understand what you were talking about." The transparent mesh of the veil was painting the café a surreal arctic white. She was regretting this entire excursion. "Sounds like not much of a day off for me."

"Oh, you'll love it. This date will be better than dinner and a movie. I promise."

Dating was more complicated than the old scaffolding made it out to be, not to mention in a phase of life where your personality was fossilized into something certain and inflexible. The abstract prospect of men, with their inflated conceptions of themselves, and their excreting bodies, called up little enthusiasm in her. But one was obligated to keep that option open, and anyway, a simple method of escape from this episode was not easily presenting itself.

The car parked outside was a scraped black Buick, the entire passenger's side streaked with some charcoal substance. Boris gallantly opened the door. She stood staring at the interior. Empty Chinese food containers were gathered into a neat pile on the floor in the back, a pile of newspapers sat on the seat as though for protective lining. Under her fingers, the brown bag was starting to leak coffee.

"You are right not to jump in. It's not wise for a woman to get into a car with a stranger," Boris said. He dug into his pockets again and emerged with his driver's license. The picture showed a round-faced man with small ears, high forehead, and a buzzed haircut. The birthday put him at fifty-three. "Here, take a picture and text it to a friend of yours. That way they know who you're with. That is the smart thing to do on all dates. You have no idea the crazies walking around here."

He strapped the beard back on and waited.

She did as she was told, sending Georgina (and her daughter, while she was at it, if only to involve her somehow in her daily life) the image of Boris's driver's license. The passenger seat was still open, the seat's center indented by the shape of its former inhabitants. She thought of Grisha's apartment building and the crumpled souls dispersed inside. She thought of the cruel and unexpected clang of the Dumpster cover. The car's interior smelled of many competing scents, of meat and cologne and cinnamon. And it was warm where the air was biting.

Boris heaved himself inside and adjusted his rearview mirror. "Believe it or not, I make a lot of money doing this every December."

"Dressing as Ded Moroz?"

"And why not? People want to relive their old lives. The way they were back there. It's normal." He started the car, shimmied it from the cage of its parking spot.

Grisha's depressing apartment building resurfaced in her mind, all those apartments cluttered with porcelain elephants and Palekh boxes as if each inhabitant were running their own personal souvenir shop. "I don't."

"Really? I find that hard to believe. I bet you used to hire a Ded Moroz for New Year's."

She admitted that she had. Of course she had.

By the time Larisska was six, she'd learned to expect Ded Moroz during the New Year's season. The mothers in the building convened weeks before to hire the cheapest Ded Moroz they could find, along with his granddaughter Snegurochka. When the two characters arrived, the mothers gathered downstairs, passing the hired actors the gifts they'd bought for their children. The gifts themselves didn't matter. What measly items did she buy: a pencil, a map, a stuffed bear? Nadia knew that for a child, a visitor who arrived expressly for them was a bigger treat than any present. Knowing that at any moment, the person at the door would ring the bell and inquire with the utmost importance, "Is there a Larissa Borodinskaya at home, please? My granddaughter and I would very much like to see her."

And Snegurochka would waft in, in her soft blue gown imprinted with snowflakes, her two white braids, hands submerged inside a white muff, her cheeks touched with its residue of pink. The snow maiden of a little girl's dreams. Larissa would sit by the young woman the entire time, fingering the fabric of her gown, asking Snegurochka to bend down so she could touch her headdress. Snegurochka, a character plucked out of children's storybooks and refashioned as a symbol of Soviet New Year. Snegurochka, that great invention for female identification, the eternal snowgirl on the brink of womanhood who never had to grow up, get married, or be anything other than daughter or granddaughter. Nadia felt envy for the entire myth of her innocent time-frozen beauty, the way it pulled herself, her daughter, and all Soviet little girls into its orbit. She captured that fleeting, oozing moment of youth's peak lushness. To see Snegurochka before you as an adult was to realize that you were now on the other side of the fantasy.

As Boris directed the wheel onto Ocean Parkway, he explained how the Ded Moroz business worked in present-day America. The parents clicked their wish lists on Amazon, shared the lists with him on an app, and Boris purchased the items more cheaply from his contacts at toy distributors and tacked a service fee on top.

"I can get items in bulk even cheaper. You'd be surprised how many people buy exact same present each year. Imagine! In Soviet Union we all had same things because we had no choice and here, people want same things on purpose."

"Amazing," Nadia said, watching the familiar blocks blur as they moved north. Avenue U turned to T, then to P.

Along the narrow strip between highway lanes, despite the biting cold, chess players huddled over their boards. Orthodox Jewish boys kicked a soccer ball around. The palatial houses of the Persian Jews gleamed with their beveled gold front doors.

Boris talked and talked. A long string of jobs ensured he was never bored. He worked simultaneously as limousine driver, car salesman, vitamin importer. As she had assumed, he emigrated from Tbilisi in 1992. He was Jewish. His relations with his ex-wife were warily friendly, but his thirty-year-old daughter was a constant source of disappointment. She came here with them at the age of twelve, had learned English fairly quickly, so her lack of professional and personal success was mystifying to him. He blamed it on his ex-wife, who endorsed mediocrity in others to feel better about her own paltry achievements. Don't get him started on his brother, who called him three times a day asking for money. His brother seemed intellectually and constitutionally incapable of turning one dollar into two.

She nodded. An entire, exhausting life was unspooling before her. She had only signed on for a quick coffee but was discovering a full cast of characters: a "dull-witted nephew who stopped by unannounced to devour the contents of the fridge," a *"lesbianka*

cousin, if you can believe such a thing even exists," a gaggle of un-
trustworthy acquaintances. Entering into a relationship at this
age was like being handed all of Tolstoy and being casually told
to familiarize yourself with the man's work. What was the point
of starting now? Either you'd read him already or you hadn't; after
a certain age, it was better not to even begin. By now, she should
have thanked this Boris politely and returned to her apartment to
call her mother and Larisska and get the news on the Donetsk airport, the latest location of the fighting. Then she would get ready
for Georgina's New Year's party. What the hell was she doing on
Ocean Parkway in a car with a red-suited man so easily disappointed by a child who committed the crime of not becoming a
millionaire? The car stopped.

"Here we are," Boris said, planting the Ded Moroz hat back
on his head. They pulled up alongside parked cars, the hazard
lights turned on. She climbed out, relieved at least that the journey would be quick, the car not even ensconced in a legal parking
spot. Boris unlocked his trunk. Inside were two black garbage bags,
the very kind that Grisha's neighbors threw out every night. But
poking through the corners of the plastic were the outlines of toys.

"I think I should go home," she said.

"Don't be ridiculous. We are about to have better grub than
anything inside that overpriced café. Don't forget your coffee."

The apartment building they were entering resembled Grisha's and
so many that lined Ocean Parkway. They were all like a gaggle of
Sasha's kindergarten friends you couldn't tell apart. This one was
yet another brick high-rise of middling height, a hyperbolic name
stenciled into cement over the front archway: THE POSEIDON. The
lobby was decorated in a cheap simulacrum of luxury, tufted

benches peeling fabric, the gold mailboxes overseen by a uniformed man lost inside the world of his cell phone. She and Boris stuffed themselves into the mirror-paneled elevator, the two of them and the bags taking up the entire space. Boris adjusted the pillow that served as his stomach, grinned a flash of tightly wedged gold teeth, and despite herself, she could imagine reaching toward the sturdy wall of chest underneath all those layers, sliding her fingers inside the white fur of his collar. He reached over and folded the veil back over her eyes until she could see him in gauze, his brown eyes turning a less precise color.

How long had it been since a day took an unexpected turn?

"The thinking mysterious woman," he said, watching her.

"Don't be ridiculous." She had always found men invoking the mystery of women a lazy shortcut for the hard work of understanding them. But the silky delivery—mysterious woman—slipped neatly into her pores. The door swung open to the third floor and, flushed, she followed him down the hall.

He rapped on a door at the very end of the corridor, in a cool pattern of threes with the back of his knuckle.

"Look, it's Ded Moroz," said a young mother, in a mock-surprise voice meant for a child. "Look who's here, Andreas and Anastasia. Welcome, welcome."

Nadia heard the familiar cheer of children kept inside too long, the anticipatory patter of tiny feet. Boris was in full Ded Moroz mode now, tickling the twins under their chins and asking them if they'd behaved this year. He was pretending he had no idea about any gifts, that his visit was no more than a rest stop on his way to other little children.

"I don't believe you," the little girl pouted in English. "Where are my toys?"

On the table, cookies were fanned out, oblong purple grapes

clustered inside an orange bowl. The apartment itself was sparsely furnished, its tan walls bare of art or photographs. The one decorative item was the New Year's *yelka,* propped against a corner. It was lushly outfitted in silver ornaments and porcelain figurines, drizzled with tinsel, so tall that its point curled into the ceiling. Nadia approached it, felt a few fir leaves prickle between her fingers. They were real.

In Ukraine, as in Russia, New Year's had been the most important of holidays, a single day that contained within it all of one's hopes for the future. Their own plastic *yelka* was more like a bush, but each branch was lovingly draped with ornaments. She would pool her money and her mother's meager pension to buy caviar and other appetizers for the spread, then Larissa would be bundled for a trip to the main square for fireworks. On television, they would watch *The Irony of Fate or Enjoy the Sauna* for the thousandth time, then the president's New Year's address. At midnight, she and her mother uncorked Soviet champagne. Even after the end of the Soviet Union, it was not truly New Year's without Soviet champagne.

In this country, Nadia never bothered with the entire spectacle, but this one was reminding her of all the faith and optimism an ordinary *yelka* had to shoulder. The tree itself was a kind of prayer. In Ukraine, they had always hoped for the simplest of necessities, food and clothes and good health. Peace during wartime would never have occurred to them as a New Year's wish. They thought that was all in the past.

The girl twin was screeching over a braided blond doll draped in a blue Snegurochka-like dress. *Elsa's beautiful, she's perfect,* she was screeching. The boy unwrapped a fire truck and set off a siren that could wake the dead. If she had dared to gift Sasha with a plastic screeching toy, her mother would have pursed her lips and the next day it would be purged. And she would be right. There was not a single thank-you, no recognition of gratitude. Nadia watched as the spoiled kids retreated to their own areas with their toys.

This mother did not seem to know what was expected of her now that the presents were dispersed. She was pretty and small-boned but with a bit of disarray about her, the buttons on her shirt off by a single hole. She ushered them toward the table of desserts already decimated by the children. She squinted at Nadia but addressed Boris.

"She's a bit . . . how to say this politely . . . mature for your Snegurochka, no?"

Boris laid a protective hand on the lower curve of Nadia's back, "Now, now, my Snegurochka here is the perfect age. I had my children young. Who are my children anyway, eh? Didn't you ever wonder how the Soviet state invented a Ded Moroz with a grand-daughter but no daughter?"

"Magic," Nadia said, warmed by his defense of her. She decided this mother got the gratitude she deserved. "You were a lonely old man, and you made Snegurochka out of the snow in your back-yard. Isn't that right, Borya?"

"That's right. And she stayed with me out of sheer duty."

"I actually think I'm the ideal age for Snegurochka." Nadia sniffed. She took the cold cappuccino out of its bag and began sipping it regally.

"I didn't mean to offend you, quite the opposite," the mother began, uncertain of whether Nadia was truly offended. "You are just different, and that's very admirable."

"Ladies, ladies, who wants to toast?" Without asking, Boris opened the glass cabinet and brought down a swan-necked bottle.

"Help yourselves," the mother said, glancing toward the

bedroom where the toy fire sirens were matching real fire sirens for noise level. Boris added a generous splash of liquor to Nadia's coffee, they clinked, and he flung back the contents of his glass.

She drank so infrequently that almost immediately, even as the alcohol burned the back of her throat, it felt as though she were shape-shifting into a lighter person, someone who dwelled only behind a veil. Behind a veil, there was no such thing as war, not to mention day 317 of a war, not to mention a war that seemed indifferent to the comforting peace of cease-fires. The "Day of Silence" in Ukraine was turning out to be a joke as usual, a smiling face hiding a gun behind its back. Poroshenko's idea of uniting the land was warning that if the airport fell to the separatists so would the entire country.

"Have a cookie," Boris prodded her.

The mother was visibly looking at her watch. "Thank you, Ded Moroz, come back next year," she said loudly, even though the children were out of earshot. "And of course Snegurochka too."

She shut the door behind them.

"I never got the cookie," Nadia said, which prompted Boris to wrap her into a sympathetic full-body hug.

They rode the elevator to the next assignment, a girl who would be receiving the same blond-haired doll in a blue dress dotted with snowflakes (it seemed two others would be getting an identical doll, a doll Regina refused to buy for Sasha for a reason that was not clear to Nadia, something about "the Disney capitalist machine"), a pony with a rainbow mane, a mermaid puzzle.

"Look who's here," said the next mother in the exact same upbeat tone, although she was older, her appearance more polished. This apartment was decorated in a sleek modernist style. A black leather couch and chairs with squiggly lines for feet stood on top of a rug splashed with jagged geographic shapes. The New

Year's tree was placed next to the television. The adornments here were restrained: no tinsel, the ornaments clay animals that looked like children's art projects. The sight of those sloppily painted, one-legged horses and blotchy cows made Nadia ache even more. Larissa spent weeks before New Year's weaving little animals out of wheat, firebirds and angels and horses, and they would drape them over the plastic fingers of the *yelka*.

On the red-lacquered coffee table were the remnants of *zakuski*: the marinated mushrooms, the pickles and pumpernickel bread, but they were swept aside by slices of poppy-seed cake, *priyaniki*, chocolate-covered *zephyr*. In front of them stood a four-year-old with bangs and a bowl cut, fingers and chin smeared with chocolate. She used to love just gazing at her daughter at this age; her eyes were two almonds under a pair of disheveled little eyebrows. She loved watching her busy with a sewing project, her intense gaze so fully on the picture forming in front of her. Or climbing into bed with her in the middle of the night, a little body adjusting itself to the adult shape. Or watching her eat wild strawberries with ravenous pleasure, popping one after the other into her mouth until it expanded like a chipmunk's.

You have no idea that the all-consuming baby love for you is temporary, that as children age, the love stretches, becomes distracted by lesser things. She was starting to see the first signs of it in the relationship between Regina and Sasha, the way Sasha no longer ran into her mother's arms when she came home, satisfied in the cocooned elixir of her own private play. Pain moved through her with steady deliberation. The kid looked nothing like Sasha or even Larisska with her sleek bob of brown hair; she was happily spreading chocolate tracks on the face of the new doll handed over by her red-suited date.

The father emerged from one of the bedrooms. He was buttoning the top of a striped business shirt, headpiece still attached to his ear. "Drink, Ded Moroz?"

"I won't say no," Boris said, settling onto one of the squiggly chairs. "Don't forget to take care of my granddaughter here."

The man grinned and uncorked a Hennessey cognac. "Ded Moroz got lucky this year, eh? Just tell me when to stop pouring."

"Just a little in my coffee," she said, holding out the Rendez-vous Café cup. The by-now familiar burn of the alcohol settled on the melancholy, scorching it.

They consumed half the poppy-seed cake and a few *zephyrs*. The man seemed to have settled into his role as host, bursting open a cantaloupe with a knife handle and handing them dripping pieces. He substituted her coffee cup for a real glass and poured them another round.

"To new happiness, yes?"

His wife reminded him, did he forget they were late to Lev and Oksana's party? They still had to stop by the drugstore to get the card. The man waved her away. Ded Moroz and Snegurochka were much more fun than those desiccated corpses she called friends. You tell them that to their faces, the woman shot back. *I dare you.*

Nadia's temples were starting to vibrate. Did her daughter's resentment go further back than she thought? Of course Nadia might have better hidden her sacrifices from Larisska over the years. "It's not like you have a father to discipline you. It's just me here," she remembered yelling in frustration after some misbehavior. Or once even on New Year's, when Larisska complained about her gift of a world map not being laminated, "you must have turned into an ungrateful *tvar'* because you have no father at home to guide you." In hindsight, the absent father was probably used too often as a threatening disciplinary tool.

On the way to the elevator, Boris watched Nadia fumble with the wobbly tiara. "I like it falling off your head like that."

"I'm getting tired. How many to go?"

Boris grimaced. "One more visit. They get these godawful ugly dolls and then we're done."

"Okay."

"And then let's find somewhere more private to celebrate, shall we?" Boris's face was damp, his eyes glistening with what she imagined was desire and what the hell? It's not like she had virginity to lose. It's not like she could blame Larissa for her lack of a sex life anymore. She pulled aside the front of her coat.

"We could go to my place," she said with what she hoped was a seductive lilt. There was a hesitation in his eyes, as if he had expected resistance or at least modest demurral. What was the point of saying no anymore? she reasoned. What was the point of all those absurd rules her mother concocted about reeling in men like trout? The elevator was stuffy, filled with the air of their cognac breath, the aftertaste of chocolate. He stabbed some upper-floor button and she closed her jacket.

"Do you have anything salty? A pickle or *vobla* or something?" Boris asked when the next woman opened the door. "I've been eating nothing but sugar all day."

The woman blocked the door, hands folded over her stomach. She was wearing a ribbed black turtleneck, a gold Star of David poking out around a scrawny neck. "I thought you were working today. We weren't expecting you."

"Just a little herring? Some salad and bread? Where's the spread? Is it a holiday or not?" Boris gripped two young boys around their waists and spun them into a constellation.

The woman held the door open for Nadia, scrutinizing her the way you do with a not entirely well-executed painting at a random gallery.

"You're wondering why I look too old to be his granddaughter," Nadia said. It was probably the alcohol, but it suddenly seemed important not to be intimidated again. "If you must know, he had my mother very young. Now I am fated to keep Ded Moroz company in his old age."

"Is that right." This was not a question, but the hard-faced woman moved to the side and allowed Nadia entrance.

"Where are the toys?" a five-year-old cried. He and his little brother were in desperate need of a haircut. The older one's ringlets scaled down the small of his back.

"I thought you said they were girls," she said, before realizing he only mentioned that the gifts would be dolls. Here you were not supposed to make assumptions about gender and the toys children preferred. Regina corrected her alarm more than once when one of Sasha's friends, Oliver, showed up to a playdate in a princess dress and she had volunteered for him to change into a costume more appropriate, like that of a pirate or sailor. "You are being old-fashioned," Regina would say, her tone a high-minded replica of her daughter's. "Besides, people get very offended about that here, so please don't say anything, and let the boys wear whatever they want."

This woman didn't hear her exclamation anyway. She was fingering the strand of her necklace with knobby fingers. Hers was a face that struggled: almost nonexistent lips, cadaverous skin, narrow brown eyes. The apartment displayed no masculine presence, and Nadia knew better than anyone what a fatherless home looked like.

The garbage bag of gifts was splayed open, the two boys digging inside. The dolls with snowflake dresses were burst open from their boxes. "That's what you got your grandsons?" the woman said. "*Frozen* dolls? Is it because they were on discount or something?"

Boris pretended at shock. "How could you accuse me of this? In fact, they are very popular this year, Anyush, and hard to get. Girls, boys, they all go crazy for them." The kids ran over with their dolls, each settling on a Boris knee. The younger one dropped the doll, fascinated with pulling the rubber elastic of Boris's beard and then snapping it back into place.

Grandsons. Nadia gradually took that in.

This Anya returned from the kitchen with a bowl of Salad Olivier, slices of bread circling the rim like sunflower petals. She raked Nadia over with a long vertical glance. "Another year, another Snegurochka. At least this one is in the vicinity of your age, Papa. I'm impressed. You're growing."

"Hey, hey. What are you doing to me here? Can't you see she and I are on a date?"

A lump formed in Nadia's throat. She could picture the Snegurochka of the year before, a woman like the one behind the counter at Rendezvous Café, young and elongated, a messy shock of brown hair, whose eyes and tiny waist were her best features. Why was she even surprised? But despite herself, Nadia's heart radiated outward toward Boris, for the particular narcissism of children. How little time children spent envisioning the daily longings of their parents.

"You know what, Anyush?" Nadia said. "Your father has told me a lot about you. He said you work very hard, that you are a special, loving person. He's very proud of you, you know."

On the couch, Boris's expression was hard to read. He was pretending not to be listening, but his bouncing leg slowed. The boys loudly protested when the game stopped.

"Even if you are his age, I don't plan on liking you," Anya said.

"I don't expect you to."

She shrugged. "In any case, you'll be gone before February."

"Let's toast to a happier new year ahead," Boris interrupted, peeling the children off him. "Where is the Soviet champagne? It's not New Year's without Soviet champagne."

Anya bent over the refrigerator, slipped out a bottle with a black-and-gold label, and handed it to him to open. Boris worked the cork with his thumbs, pointing it away from the children, until it arced. Froth dribbled over the rim of the bottle.

"Anyush, bring Snegurochka here a real glass, something better than that measly coffee cup."

She was slow about it, but she did bring down three mismatched glasses from behind the glass cabinet. Nadia could see an entire row of glass figurines, hedgehog, moose, and porcupine, its quills tinged a vibrant blue.

They settled to eat in front of the tree. This *yelka* had a giant Star of David on top and candy for ornaments. Chili-pepper lights were strung across its middle, flashing a soft pale red. So this was her first Jewish New Year's even though there was nothing, apart from a single loaf of delicious-looking challah, to distinguish it as Jewish. There was the familiar caviar, the salads, the herring smothered by onions and sunflower oil. But maybe that was the whole point of a Soviet New Year's, a vague holiday stripped of religion, of history, of anything but unsubstantiated, untainted faith in a better future.

Boris winked. "You know, now that I'm seeing you in this light, you actually look like one of those dolls all the kids got. You do, you know, blond hair and all."

"Thank you," she said, her face vibrating with heat. For the life of her, she would not meet Anya's eyes, but she could also sense that Anya wasn't looking at her, that her true thoughts were far from this room.

Outside, evening sloped down without warning. What lay beyond the window was a pervasive inky haze. The near future presented itself to her in a series of wispy thoughts. She was missing Georgina's party, but felt no urgency about making it. Her sister Olga was coming to New York in a week and she would have to steel herself for that. Nothing beyond today felt tangible.

The garbage bag of presents lay empty like a deflated balloon. Boris clicked on a few lamps. The boys were rushed off to bed, the unloved dolls splayed across the couch. Their clothes had been removed, and they lay there in unnatural poses with twisted torsos and braids, hands raised over their heads in astonishment.

She took out her phone to write Georgina she'd be late and saw two missed texts. From Georgina: "He looks like a criminal. Call me later so I know he didn't boil you alive." And from Larisska, just a few blessed words. "Nice beard. Send pic?" She could have levitated right there with happiness, high above the glittering Jewish star of the *yelka*. "*My daughter wrote back!*" she wanted to scream. "My daughter's alive!"

"I'd love to take a picture of you and your daughter before we go," she said instead. "May I? Do you mind?"

They posed, his arm pulling Anya closer, his daughter's torso resisting. Neither of them smiled, but there was no denying they were a pair in the way their faces settled in for the shot. No matter their mutual disappointment, they were still father and daughter, the raw, undiluted fact of it. Nadia saved the photo, swished it over to Larisska with a "Better in person? Happy New Year!" On a whim, she also sent it to Regina.

They rose to go.

In the elevator, she was still wrapped in a cloud of elation. When her daughter wrote her back, it always renewed her hope for the future. A textured, colorful life seemed within her grasp. She started to say, "I hope your car didn't get towed," but Boris gripped the back of her neck in a single swooping motion. The soft pillow of his fake stomach was pressing her against the sharp brass railing lining the mirrored wall. Her lower back was bruising, the rim of her mouth wetter than it needed to be. But from around his head, in the mirror, she caught a glimpse of herself in the sparkling tiara. Her hair was a soft, otherworldly blond, her cheeks swirling with a girlish red. She was pungent with a precise, realized beauty.

She flung her arms around him.

"Kiss me, kiss me," she kept repeating, even though that was exactly what he was already doing.

6

Not Too Young to Know Nothing

✳ **Ukraine, May 2000**

In Ukraine, guests never called ahead, nor were they expressly invited. They simply showed up at your door. Yulia and her husband, Gena, had been sitting around Nadia's table for years. They had all known one another at school, and it was easy between the three of them, free of formality, an enclosed circle of safety and trust. They were always on hand to help Nadia ring in the weekend after a long week of work in Kharkov, but tonight was special; it marked the beginning of a weeklong vacation for Nadia. She was pulling Larisska from school, the two of them booked on a train to Yalta in the morning.

When Larissa returned home with her grandmother, she didn't appear surprised to find her mother with the happy couple ensconced at the kitchen table on their second cup of rose-hip tea.

"My husband is leaving me for a computer, Larisska," Yulia announced by way of greeting. "That's what's going on. If you were wondering how I'm doing."

"Yul'ka! Show some discretion. She's a child!" Nadia protested.

Gena stood up to greet Larissa with a kiss on the cheek. "Every time I see this one she gets older, what is that about? Hard to believe she is already twelve."

"*Only* twelve," Nadia corrected.

"Already thirteen," Larisska said with emphasis. She took off her jacket, patiently waited while her grandmother untied the hat's knot under her chin. She slid into an empty chair, prepared to join the grown-ups. "What kind of computer?"

"That's right, thank you for reminding me, Larisska." Yulia cleared her throat for emphasis. "My husband is leaving me for a computer."

While Yulia was known to make dramatic pronouncements, Nadia secretly thought it bad luck to give voice to something that could possibly materialize. On one hand, it appeared that the institution of marriage was created for people like Yulia and Gena, who parried and griped but always made up with renewed affection. But still, at thirty-seven Yulia should make more of an effort than she did, with her drooping folds of discolored skin under her eyes, those unflattering striped sweaters that enhanced her wide hips. She should really stop talking about her husband leaving her in front of her husband, Nadia believed.

"I can tell her what's going on, can't I tell her? She's very mature for her age. It's time she found out about the real world."

"Go ahead and unburden yourself," Larisska eagerly encouraged, her eyes luminous. "What did Dyadya Gena do now?" She was dipping sugar cubes into the tea and sucking them, a habit Nadia usually abhorred.

"Am I allowed to speak?" Gena tried.

Yulia interrupted. "It's like this, Larisska. My husband is working on a chatterbot. Do you know what that is?"

"Something with computers?"

"Right. A program that talks to you. Why you would need a computer to yammer at you all day, I have no idea. Half the time, this chatterbot's not even telling the truth, lies through his teeth.

But now that Putin is president, my businessman of a husband thinks there will be more money for projects like this over there."

"Software that lies to you?"

"Ridiculous, right? So my husband here wants to move to Peter to snuggle together with his fellow programmers and his chatterbot and use his new technology for good or evil. I wish him the very best."

"And now you see why I never married," Nadia cut in. She heard the slam of a bedroom door, her own mother retorting, "Oh, so that's why you never married."

"You were so right, Nadyush. You know, I almost thought you were very brave to be a spinster, but it wasn't worth it. Men are fucking goats, useless *mudak*."

"Yulia!"

Yulia had no boundaries with her own fifteen-year-old daughter, which was why her Ida was sneaking around at night, enmeshed with young people who, like her father, were restless, unhappy, but were sublimating it into politics. You could not find two more different mothers than Nadia and Yulia. And what was there to be unhappy about? Nadia had a full week off from work and they were going to the seaside. The economy felt like it was on the upswing, there was finally food in the stores. Yana Klochkova won the gold again in the Sydney Olympics. They had a brand-new space heater for the winter, inherited from a neighbor whose wife just committed suicide and was divesting himself of their possessions. Sure, there was a tense hunt for a missing journalist, striking miners, and a military agency dumping toxic waste into the soil. But all this seemed minor compared to a contagious feeling of hope that this volatile country was finally stabilizing.

"Yulia, you're going a little too far rhetorically, are you not?" Gena said. He turned off the computer and switched the radio to the frequency of loud static. "But have you seen anything get better since Ukraine's independence? If anything, our politicians are even more allergic to honesty and state-building and are busy redirecting any profits into their own deep pockets. This is not the place to start a business or do any research. It will just be stolen or shut down." He turned off the radio, his voice switching back to normal. "Shall we make this a real party or what?"

Nadia pointed toward the cabinet, and he slid open the glass doors for the vodka.

"Don't be shocked, Mama," Larisska said in that new haughty tone of hers. "I'm almost thirteen. I know full well that our country is a mess and our men are dogs."

"Do you now? Well, I don't know why I keep sending you to school then."

"Don't be mad."

Larissa moved her chair closer, her cheek resting against Nadia's arm. At the sight of this, Ida rolled her eyes. It was these moments Nadia cherished, happy that unlike her contemporary, Larissa was still in many ways a little girl who needed the comfort of her mama.

"Of course I'm not mad." But what would her girl say if she knew that three years ago her aunt Olga put in the paperwork to sponsor them to emigrate to the United States, that Nadia had packed both of their bags and hidden them in the far reaches of her bedroom closet? Would Larisska be upset at not being told? In any case, it was beginning to look like she had nothing to worry about. Their turn seemed like it would never come.

"Men are dogs, eh? Those are great lessons you are imparting to a young, impressionable girl, ladies. Nicely done," Gena said, pouring them a round.

Yulia pulled him in for an apologetic kiss on the cheek. "You're not a useless *mudak*."

Nadia kissed him on the other cheek. "And as you can imagine, I told her none of those things. And as far as I'm concerned, we are all perfect right where we are."

And she meant it. They could hear her mother shifting about in the cot in her room, the sound of Prokofiev emanating from her old record player. Outside the window, there was the purple silhouette of pines. The new space heater was keeping the room exceptionally warm.

Suddenly, Yulia shot up. "Larissa, you can actually help us. The chatterbot is supposed to be a thirteen-year-old boy from Odessa, but Gena is helpless with slang. He has enlisted a few thirteen-year-olds, Ida's friends, to help him make the program sound more realistic. But we need more. Maybe you could tell us a few phrases the kids are using."

"That sounds so fun," Larissa said, running to their room. "I'll make a list."

"What words can the kids be using?" said Nadia. "Leave her alone, we're going to Crimea tomorrow."

"You're being a little unreasonable. Let the girl help if she wants to. It's perfectly harmless."

Before she could remind Yul'ka of a fact that she may have forgotten, that Larissa was sick and therefore not a typical girl her age, a meek knock on the door announced Artem. He was a classmate of Larisska's who lived one flight above them, and he followed her daughter around like an embedded piece of lint. Nadia considered letting him believe they were out, but then the knock returned.

"Is Larissa home?" came his beleaguered, plaintive voice.

Everything he said took the form of a question. It is cold out? Larissa at school already? His was a quiet but ominous persistence, a lurking outline with nothing filled in. Nadia rose to open the door, and there he was; his body looked like it was filled with stuffing instead of coursing with blood.

"Artem, why don't you ever call first? Can't you see we have guests," she said, not that he could take a hint. He continued to stare at her daughter with those watery eyes of his, rubbing his thumb and pinkie finger together. He looked like her vision of the Underground Man, not that she'd read Dostoevsky since grade school.

"I just wanted to say hello?" Each word was protracted, mechanical.

"Hello," Larissa said, running up and peeking her head out the door, notebook under her arm. They stood murmuring in the hall until the boy finally left.

"What did he want?" Nadia asked.

"Nothing." And Larissa proceeded to scrawl on the page with her pencil.

As parents of children on the cusp of adolescence, she and Yulia exchanged knowing looks. They knew they were entering a new realm of secrets, of private, unspoken thoughts. Of longings they would not be able to access or resolve. Years of heartache, rejection, and hope awaited their girls but there was no slowing it all down, no denying the kids were getting older. What was a mother to do?

November was a perfect month for a Crimean vacation. The foreign tourists had scattered, the air with just the right kiss of warmth and humidity. Strolling the wide paved streets of Yalta's embankment, past the markets and open-air restaurants, Nadia decided she had no need for Europe or America, not when all this belonged to Ukraine. She looked at Larissa, the sleeves of her shirt and jacket rolled up to expose her arms to the sun. They were both inhaling the sea air with giant hungry gulps.

Larissa's voice penetrated her thoughts. "Do you want to hear my words for Tyotya Yulia?"

"What words?"

"The things kids say. For the chatterbot. We use a lot of American words, for example, and twist them into Russian."

Nadia smiled. "It's not just the young people who do that, you know."

She recognized an old coworker from the pipe factory who was strolling with her husband, and waved. The woman paused to remark on how lovely Larissa was, how slender and elegant, how fast she was growing. A budding beauty! But Nadia switched the topic to the weather. The warm breeze was refreshing, was it not, especially compared to the almost-winter nonsense of back home?

They had barely moved on when Larissa continued. "'Jokery' is one. We have two guys that are always called that because they are smart-asses. Here's another one. One kid in my class said after school that our coal miners being out of work was an act of 'Kuchism.' That's pretty clever, right? Kuchma's name but Americanized."

Nadia gripped her daughter's arm. "Look, it's one thing to joke around at home but I hope you're being careful. You don't know who's listening. It's not your business to say anything bad about Kuchma. Do you understand?"

"But everyone makes fun of him. And for your information, Artem doesn't like Kuchma either."

"Lower your voice, please. Well, you should definitely stay away from Artem. I mean, do you even like him? He follows you around like an abandoned puppy dog. Doesn't his mother ever brush his hair?"

"No, as a matter of fact she doesn't. And it's really sad."

Larissa grew quiet, her skin burnished with a rosy glow. Through childhood, she had been the easiest of children, clingy and shy but eager to please Nadia. The former was just now shedding but a difficult age was looming, when you could visibly see the closing of the gates, your child's mind shutting itself off from you, growing impenetrable. Just in the last few months, Nadia watched a new, defiant personality that was pushing against the safe borders carefully crafted for her.

Nadia broke the silence. "You feel like something sweet? Should we find the ladies with the buckets of baklava or *trubochki*? Let's check that you can have a bite or two."

"Yes, Mama."

The prospect of a little sugar treat turned Larissa into a child again. Nadia took out a needle and the little green blood sugar meter that Olga sent them from the United States and decided it was worth the sacrifice of the last of the precious strips. On a nearby bench, she pricked her daughter's middle finger and pressed the strip to the seeping blood. But what a reward not long afterward to watch Larisska push the flaky pastry into her mouth with a hungry eagerness of deprivation. The backdrop of mountains seemed to rise up as if to shield her daughter from the ominous curiosity of strangers slowing down to watch a young girl in the middle of devouring.

As the days passed, she was startled at how much Yalta had changed. How it failed to click with the Yalta of her childhood memories. She remembered it as a luxurious getaway, her mother in glamorous languor posing on the beach, one freckled arm shielding her eyes from the sun. How beautiful she looked in her one-piece bathing suit, how trim and girlish. Nadia could still see her so vividly calling Olga and herself back from the depths of the water. They'd barely waded in higher than their hips when they would hear, "What do you want, for my heart to break? Get back closer to the shore."

She and Olga would be roaming the seashore, gawking at the hotels and health spas built into the coastline. At their own *pensionat,* she still remembered the meals: soup, cutlet, and the magical *kompot,* a drink brewed from dried fruit. As a special treat, her mother would buy them lemonade. The mysterious lushness of the wooded vista, the romance of the sanatoria on the green slopes, palm trees, the villas and dachas, the magic of the never-ending promenade. Men walking in white suits and hats, the women in fashionable trench coats, under the shade of umbrellas. Professional photographers snapping coquettish pictures of the couples, women posed prettily beside rosebushes, men peeking at them from behind the leaves.

They would be signed up for excursions during the day, museums and cave tours. And at night, going to the philharmonic concert in the fanciest of their sewn dresses, looking up at the boxes where the most important Soviet dignitaries sat. She could still remember the hush of the dimming lights, the first notes of the music. Everyone around her listening with the same breathless rapture. For those few days in Yalta, before all that ocean and the proximity of greatness, she had felt like a movie star, a head pioneer, everything that was important, visible.

She wanted Larisska to feel the same way about Crimea, and her daughter did seem to be enjoying the beauty of the scenery.

They took turns posing before the shoreline and in front of the museums and churches. They packed picnics and ate in restaurants and signed up for bus excursions. But the girl was not experiencing the Yalta of her youth. The buildings were crumbling, large gashes disfiguring their façades. The tourists were thinned, the souvenirs gaudy. The men were dressed like football players with long necklaces and shaved heads. Babushki in doorways were begging for change, "for bread, for bread." And that same afternoon, while picnicking on the beach, she once again heard the buoyant sound of Prokofiev. It was the very same orchestra she had seen as a child, now playing for spare change on the beach. She gave Larisska a few hryvnias and watched her clamber over the rocks to drop them into the conductor's hat.

The next day, on the trolley, Larissa's face was glued to the window toward the stretch of the indigo Black Sea. They were climbing up the mountain, the pull of the copper rails above them tugging them onward. "It's beautiful here, just breathtaking."

"Isn't it?"

Nadia drew her daughter closer. The limestone undulations on the southern shore near Alushta were coming into view. This was how she remembered the otherworldly landscape, the dip of the valleys, the craggy beauty of the volcano deposits. "This is stunning, right? But the city has changed. You should have seen it in the Soviet days. Now that was beauty. I wish they kept this place up better."

The guide up front was pointing out Byzantine monasteries, warning them not to miss the bust of Tolstoy tucked between foliage. It was her perfect vacation, someone droning facts at you while you closed your eyes. She felt herself sinking into the passivity of being a helpless passenger, a lovely, foreign feeling of ceding control.

"Now that I think about it, so much of our slang is crude or foreign. When we want to say 'awesome,' we say '*kaif*,' but that's mostly Ukrainian," Larissa was saying. She was a girl who did not stop talking, even as Nadia was always warning her to rein it in. No boy liked a girl who talked too much, not to mention that talking was always dangerous. She wished Larissa had a better instinct for silence.

"Hm-hm."

"We say 'cool' or 'sweet,' we also say '*krutoy*' if we call someone arrogant."

"Interesting."

"I was called a 'chick' once."

Nadia's eyes popped open. "Who called you that?"

She could see Larissa blink, recalibrate. Pull something back inside of her. "Nobody. I think it was about someone else actually. Or I saw it in a movie."

Nadia sighed by way of making it clear that she knew perfectly well what Larissa was trying to do but transferred her attention back to the window. They were reaching the highest altitude, which meant they would soon be dipping down, the trolleybus pointing its nose downward. The initial descent always made her throat go soft.

"Forget the slang nonsense," she said. "Just look out the window. You know Chekhov lived here, Gorky. Remember that story 'Lady with a Lapdog'? Remember the first line? 'It was said that a new person had appeared on the sea-front: a lady with a little dog.' It was set in Yalta."

"I didn't read it. You told me it was too racy."

"That's right. I forgot." At the highest point, the Angarsky Pass, the majesty of the cliffs shimmered in bright resolution before them.

"I wonder why you didn't take me sooner, Mama."

"How could we? After 1991, it was all chaos. No one had any money for vacations."

"I've seen the pictures of Yalta when you were a kid and I've always been so jealous. But isn't it amazing that all this belongs to Ukraine? Artem says . . ." All the talking was starting to drill inside Nadia's head, calling up a vague nausea. She frowned.

"I don't want to hear about Artem. Larisska, you need to have your own mind and don't be influenced by the pessimism of others. He's a strange kid anyway."

"That's right," a woman interrupted behind them. She had been muttering loudly the entire time, a droning insect adding to the irritation in Nadia's ear. The lady pulled herself forward, her cleavage hanging over their seat. "The story was set here because Chekhov was Russian. And Crimea is Russian. Not Ukrainian, Russian."

Larissa looked confused then crumpled. "But I thought . . ."

The woman was not old enough to be this rude. She was around sixty, her white shirt cut too low, a giant cross gleaming bronze on her chest. "Young girl, Khrushchev gave it to you as a present in 1954. Some present, am I right? You want to know what happened? One night, he was drunk and sentimental. Some Ukie must have whispered in his ear and slipped a document under his pen. Can you imagine, little girl? He just signed away Russia's precious territory on a whim. Don't you worry. We will get it back."

"If you please, I would appreciate it if you let my daughter be. Thank you," Nadia said. She was trying to be as polite as possible, ignoring the "Ukie" slur. She was going to say that Khrushchev did not sign over Crimea to Ukraine on a whim, that the story she heard was that the peninsula was in deep financial trouble, and because of geographic proximity, Khrushchev wanted to pass the expenses onto a country that might better understand Crimea's agricultural climate, but she didn't want any trouble. She just wanted them to be safely ignored.

The guide was telling them that the altitude of the Argansky Pass stood at 752 meters above sea level. They were poised at its tip, marveling at a plaque that offered the same information.

"Mark my words. We'll get it back." The woman returned her entire body to her own seat, grabbing a nearby yellow railing for support as the trolley sloped downward.

"That's what Artem said too." Larissa turned away from the window.

Nadia felt too paralyzed to speak, afraid of the ears sitting behind them. They were passing vineyards in the hollow of valleys, the trolleybus heaving itself down the mountain on its rickety well-trodden rails.

"He is still in a very rudimentary stage," Gena was saying. "It'll be a few years before we can show him to the world."

"Rudimentary stage, eh? Sounds like someone else I know."

"Will you be quiet for one minute, Yul'ka? Would that kill you?"

"Probably."

That was the way it was between Yulia and Genya. She chewed him out like he was an enemy of the people, and the next minute, she would be embracing him in Nadia's kitchen as though they were the luckiest of couples. Nadia always admired that Yulia stuck by this nerdy guy who was decent but unassuming and colorless even back in their school days. His chunky glasses, clothes layered every which way, two eyebrows that threatened to collide in the middle of his face.

"Why did you make the chatterbot thirteen years old anyway?" asked Yulia. She was rolling fish into a spherical shape and taking dainty bites of it. "Who wants to engage in conversation with a thirteen-year-old? Personally, I'd prefer a grown-up chatterbot who is an attractive, *delovoy* man who actually pays attention to his wife. Am I right, Nadia, or what?"

Gena ignored the dig. "We did it on purpose. We wanted him not too old to know everything and not too young to know nothing." He turned to the computer, "Am I right, Eugene?"

"I don't know," the computer replied. "That's an act of Kuchism."

Yulia and Gena broke out in laughter. But what was funny about that? What if they could trace the insult back to her daughter? What if they could arrest her? Just the other day, they discovered the poor Georgian journalist dead, and it appeared that their own president could be to blame. Okay for them to laugh, these activists, but that wasn't Nadia. Let the crooks destroy one another while she stayed quiet, out of harm's way.

"I think that's enough, don't you?" she said, and whispered, "No politics. I don't want Larisska to worry about politics yet, understand?"

"Nadia's always grumpy when her vacation is over," Yulia said as if speaking to a crowd of people who didn't know her.

"Hey, Larisska," Gena called out. "Come hear your influence talking. Come, maybe you'll make him smarter."

Larisska emerged from the bedroom with embroidery she was working on. She ran to the table and said, "Can I talk to him?"

"Of course. His name is now Eugene and he has a pet guinea

pig. Maybe you want to ask about that," Gena said. To Nadia, he mouthed, "*No politics, don't worry.*"

"Hello, Eugene." Larissa looked so serious, as if having a real conversation with a human friend.

"Hello, nice to make your acquaintance," a voice in the computer responded.

"Do you like your pet?"

"He is my friend."

"What is six divided by three?"

"I'm not sure. Three?"

Her friends were right. Nadia was in a wretched mood. The end of vacation lingered sour on her tongue. Tomorrow meant the five-hour train ride back to Kharkov and work. The breathtaking vistas of Yalta, the bracing picnics on the beach, the cool mugs of kvass, were a dream that had abruptly ended. She wished the tour guide could have somehow been transported here, a voice of fact and reason in control of the route.

They heard a knock on the door, the telltale sluggish sound of Artem. He knocked again. Why couldn't he stop the knocking?

"Shall you get rid of him or shall I?" Nadia asked her daughter.

"Aw, let him in," Yulia said, wrapping an arm around Gena. "You can't keep them out in the hall forever."

"You are wrong," Nadia said. "I am the mother and I can."

"I'll just say I'm busy." And Larissa slipped out into the hall, conferring in the same low tone. But then they were back. "Artem wants to meet Eugene."

"Oh, for heaven's sake," Nadia said under her breath.

The kids walked in, Larissa leading Artem to the computer. He squinted into its blue light.

"Hello, Eugene."

"Hello. Are you thirteen too?"

"Yes."

"Wonderful."

To Nadia their two voices sounded exactly the same. The same affectless lack of peaks and emotion. The same flat monotone. It filled Nadia with a panic she could not name.

"Let's ask him some facts about our country. Who is our president?"

"Kuchism."

"No, silly. Leonid Kuchma. Who is our prime minister?"

"That's easy. Victor Yushchenko."

"Very good, Eugene. Does Crimea belong to Ukraine or Russia?" Larisska asked.

"Good question," Eugene said, pausing as if to think. "I don't know."

"Smart kid, eh?" Gena said. "Always better to say you don't know than pretend you know everything. Much safer that way."

"Russia."

"Look, he changed his mind." Gena looked pleased with his creation.

Nadia started clearing the plates from beneath them even though she knew they were not finished. The woman on the bus returned, along with the sour taste. "Of course it belongs to Ukraine, Eugene. Why are you always making up stories? I have a splitting headache."

Yulia rose and started shooing out the guests. She kissed Nadia, encapsulating them both in a hyacinth perfume. Her dear friend always so sensitive to her moods. She waited for Gena to hold out her coat, and she slipped her arms inside. "You too, Artem. It's getting late, your mother is probably looking for you."

Artem's body seemed to rise at the same time, a slow folding in of the limbs. "I doubt it?"

"His mother barely knows he's around. She starts drinking as soon as she gets back from work." Larissa said this as if they should all feel sorry for him now. As if Nadia had the time or any resources really to feel sorry for a kid who was always hanging around where he wasn't wanted.

The end of vacation felt more devastating this time around, Nadia thought, back on the train to Kharkov. She barely had time to savor it. And something else, a sense of foreboding for the future. During the week she rented a room in an apartment of a elderly woman who left food for her on a cold plate under a steel pan lid but otherwise didn't talk to her. This was unbearable in the beginning, but now the only thing Nadia was looking forward to was this silence.

The landscape outside the window was a brown swirl of factories, hills formed out of the melting of metals, communication towers, shuttered coal mines, and the intermittent stretches of beauty. The rivers, sunflower fields, windswept steppes, the mounds of green and yellow. The light was dimming on the place, an instant association with leaving and returning. She arrived in the evenings and made it home in the evenings.

It's not like she minded the work at Turboatom, but the people kept more to themselves than in her bustling Rubizhne plant. These big-city types were operating with an air of superiority at the global importance of the company. No one whistled, the friend groups were impossible to penetrate even after seven years at the company. She barely made an effort to find out more details about why their company was such a world leader or anything about the nuclear turbine construction business; she stuck to her ledgers, the updating of financial records, and that was it.

You would think she'd be used to it by now, but tonight, she had been more reluctant to leave Larissa. These days, her grandmother was powerless to do more than feed her, oversee the preparation for school, verify that Larisska wore enough layers in the cold. And Artem was hovering, with his sluggish disaffection, his snarled and outgrown hair, skin the color of fried dough. Who knew what they talked about when Larissa was way too polite to shake him off? What thoughts did he put in her head? Who knew how often he came by when she was away?

She simply had to remove Larisska from this dangerous climate. She would check in with Olga to see if she could prod the immigration people, move them along. The sky outside sank into night. They had to leave, she realized. It was the only way to save her daughter.

It was another Friday night, another impromptu visit from her friends, but this time, they informed her, it was to be a going-away party. Gena and Yulia sat on opposite sides of the table, her mother was busy refilling little bowls with raspberry jam. It was happening so quickly. Gena was really leaving for Saint Petersburg, Yulia and her daughter Ida moving to Kiev where his family would help them settle in. Ida and Larissa sat strangely silent at the children's table, no giggling or whispering between them.

"Couldn't you wait to move to Kiev for a few months?" Nadia suggested. "You can stay with us. We'll find room."

"No, no, we couldn't," Yulia demurred.

"Didn't you hear that they're protesting the dead journalist over there? It's not safe in Kiev right now."

"But that's what's so exciting." Yulia placed a warm, ringed hand on top of Nadia's. The reality of Gena's leaving was now certain, but she was surprisingly cheerful. Her face was flushed with a new purpose.

"What's so exciting?"

"It's a great place to be right now. All that energy. All those men."

That last part was directed toward Gena, who tossed her a withering look. "Men, eh? Have a good time then."

"I will. What else am I supposed to do? Cry every day while you are whoring around with your computer buddies? Seducing the Russian-model types in the big city?"

"Yes, that's exactly what I plan to be doing. That's why I'm going actually. Eugene was a complete ruse, an elaborate scientific cover for my womanizing."

Yulia turned to him, hands crossed. "You know, that wouldn't surprise me one bit. Ida and I have more important business. Like the future of Ukraine for example."

"I'm sure they will be relieved to have you at the Parliament."

Nadia was too exhausted to censor their bickering in front of the girls. She was imagining how silent the apartment would feel without the spontaneous warmth of friends, the hasty setup for snacks, their overlaying banter going deep into a Saturday morning.

"I'd like to visit. Imagine, in just a few years I'll be able to go all by myself," Larissa said from the children's table. She had been paying attention to the volley of the adults a little too closely, Nadia noticed, her sharp eyes darting from Yulia to Gena as if making sense of a map she would need sometime in the near future. "Can we visit on your next vacation, Mama?"

"Didn't you hear what I said, Larisska? We're not going to Kiev anytime soon. There are protests now. It's very dangerous."

Out of the corner of her eye, she caught an eye roll between Yulia and Larisska and felt herself growing hot, blurry with anger. Yulia and Gena thought they were so superior, so flush with optimism, but they didn't take the train to and from Kharkov every week! They didn't see the ramshackle thatched-roof huts along the way. The people who lived in them were not the same people as at this table. They didn't hear the hatred in the voice of the woman behind them on the trolleybus. They were fooling themselves if they weren't afraid for the future!

"Enough with the long faces. Let's drink to Eugene and his success. May he grow up to be the smartest thirteen-year-old chatterbot in the world," Gena said.

They clinked glasses. Nadia swallowed her vodka. She was no drinker; it wasn't settling in her stomach well. But she tried to pantomime genuine merriment. "To Eugene."

She heard the footsteps before she heard the knock on the door.

"That's it." She rose, aware that what she was doing was stomping, and loudly too. She pushed past her mother, who was applying a nervous hand to her neck. Yulia's coat fell off the hook, a damp, wool heap on the floor. Nadia pulled on the doorknob with some violence. Confronting the sad-sack face of Artem, she spoke in an undigested rush. "Ah, I see you're back. This is excellent timing. Congratulations, Artem. This is your wedding day. The priest is on his way. What, why do you look so surprised? In certain regions of this country, kids younger than you two get married."

She heard her daughter rushing up behind her, protesting for her to not be rude or something ridiculous like she didn't have a right to speak to her friends in that manner, but Nadia kept the door cracked open just enough to keep her in. It was the two of them facing off, just her and Artem.

"Well, what do you have to say for yourself? Can't you see we have guests?"

For a moment, it looked like he was going to stand his ground with that insolent mug of his. She thought he would demand to speak directly to Larisska. But then he looked at his hands, examined them closely. And he spun on his heels. Nadia watched him lumbering down the hall, and the only emotion she felt at his retreat was victory.

7

Fondue

The Marriott Times Square hotel was a brass-gilded country of mauve carpet and glass walls. Meeting her sister in a place like this was the equivalent of a reunion at a neutral checkpoint, both sides with their guns lowered. When she materialized from the elevator, Olga walked toward Nadia in petite steps that still managed to traverse the lobby in impressive time.

No one would accuse them of being sisters; there was the seven-year age difference, of course, but Olga was broad and brown-haired, an assortment of body parts attached to a lanky, athletic figure. They both had blue eyes, but her own were watery while Olga's were translucent, ice-sharp. She kissed Nadia on each cheek as if stamping produce with a sticker. A coral shawl was flung across her shoulders.

"Mama told me you are trawling the bars in search of a husband for your daughter."

That was Olga's greeting for you. Nadia regretted not inviting Boris and flaunting a potential new boyfriend in front of her sister. That was a mistake. She had been afraid of her sister's judgment ("What does he do again? A Jew? Isn't he a little . . .

coarse?") but now she realized he could have been useful as armor, a deflection.

"Hello to you too, sister dear. Mama twisted my words as usual. I was not 'trawling.' An opportunity arose. A man was introduced to me, that's all."

"Nadyush, no offense, but Larisska is now twenty-seven years old. And she is living in a war zone. We need to start having more serious thoughts about her future."

Nadia should have been prepared for the first attack. The rush of wanting to be loved and protected by her sister tended to curdle within minutes of interaction. She had to remind herself that Olga believed criticism was a method of helping. It was one interpretation of loving dialogue.

"It's impossible here, so crowded," she deflected. "Where's Vivian?"

"You know what?" Olga stepped back and assessed her appearance. "You look really good. I mean it. Youngish, well put-together."

"What are you talking about? I'm getting older. Can't keep the weight off for the life of me."

"I wouldn't lie to you. When I say you look good, you look good."

The compliment seeped into Nadia, spread pleasantly along the plane of her belly. The certainty that her sister was always right, that her words carried within them an unshakeable authority never dissipated. She immediately regarded herself through the eyes of her sister's praise. Her weight gain was not too serious, and it certainly wasn't hampering her romantically at the moment; after embracing her in the elevator last week, Boris had asked for a second date.

"Here comes Vivchik."

Olga's granddaughter, Vivian, was beside them now, stretching out a pair of arctic arms for a polite, emaciated hug. If she were a young girl in Ukraine, she would be considered homely, with her tiny stature, her shoulders rising almost to her ears, thick snatch of brown hair, and decent gray-blue eyes. Here, she was probably no worse off than her peers, where being skinny was the crucial accomplishment for young women, from what Nadia understood.

"You look so beautiful, my dear, so grown-up." She gave Vivian a warm kiss. Last time she saw her, she was eleven years old, and frankly, much cuter.

"Hello, Tyotya Nadia," Vivian said, tolerating the imprint of lipstick on her cheek. She was clearly adhering to a script spoon-fed to her by Olga. "Nice to see you again."

Olga tucked the flamingo-pink shawl into the cowl of her shearling coat. "Shall we?"

They were swept into a tide of human bodies. Among them, grown men were dressed in orange puppet costumes and families were clogging movement in order to take pictures with these creatures. Shouting hawkers raised tickets overhead, ignoring the sloshing cars flinging mud at their feet. The smell of sickly-sweet peanuts burned the nostrils. Six and a half years in New York City and this was Nadia's first trip to Times Square.

This was turning out to be her least favorite part of Manhattan, a borough she had no use for anyway. Manhattan just did not seem like a serious place. It felt like something young people did before they absorbed the bitter reality of adulthood.

Vivian insists on a trip to New York City, Olga told her on the phone two months back, which was not at all the same thing as, *And naturally, I want to see you.*

They were making little progress down the street but the effort was beginning to feel significant, Olga and Vivian vanishing in a tide of hair and cinched coats, then reappearing. "Over here," Olga directed, as if she were the local and Nadia the tourist from Cleveland. She took Nadia's elbow, wound her arm through its noose. The act of it was so fluid, as though they were often conjoined like this. In fact, they linked arms only for the rare reunion pictures they emailed their mother.

They vaulted themselves through the front doors of the museum. She had taken the whole day off in anticipation of their staying with her. She scrubbed the surfaces of her apartment so it would pass Olga's inspection. But a few days before the visit, Nadia was informed that an alternate itinerary was cemented: Marriott, wax museum, early dinner, then the family would see a Broadway show on their own. It would be a short trip, a jaunt from Cleveland, everyone returning to their responsibilities at home. Shortness of trip aside, they were very much looking forward to spending some time with Nadia.

Vivian tottered in behind them in her high-heeled leather boots, her oval face bathed in the light of her phone.

"Is this any way to act?" Olga berated her. "Can't you look up for a change? You'll fall into one of these grates."

"Oh Baba, it's fine. Quit your yapping."

Olga turned to Nadia, with defeated face. "Do you see how she treats me?"

But Nadia was impressed with the girl, with the insouciant way she brushed Olga's rigid expectations aside. She and Olga had been raised under a strict regimen of social interactions, a road map you dared not veer from. A young girl doted on her elders, anticipated their every need, expressed the proper gratitude. In exchange, she was lavished with affection, with gifts and treats and compliments. The young girl was favored, spoken well of among the adults. She was "good," positively contrasted with someone else's daughter who was "bad." It was clear that Vivian had skimmed the rulebook, but then tossed it. If only she herself had been that brave.

On the board above the front desk, a confusing array of prices was posted: "Ultimate Experience ticket, $44.99" or "Extreme value. Museum + Wax Hand, from $36.99."

She assumed she'd read that correctly: wax hand? Some extreme value; the three tickets were the equivalent of a full day of work with Sasha. But the museum was a nonnegotiable attraction and it would have to be her treat according to the mystical yet unbendable laws of Ukrainian hospitality. Olga would weakly fight with her over who paid, but after the expected three efforts, would graciously accept.

"Three wax hand value, please," she told the cashier when it was their turn.

Olga reached into her pocketbook for her wallet and even began to list through the bills.

"Absolutely not," Nadia said firmly. "I'm paying."

"It's too expensive."

"Please, it really is my treat," Nadia insisted. "Put that purse away." They went through the motions the requisite three times, at the appropriate deescalating levels of impassioned intensity.

The goateed teenager ripping their tickets sleepily eyed the exchange. ("Let me." "No, I will not allow it." "You are being ridiculous." "Your stubbornness is ridiculous.")

"You may collect your hand on the way out," he said when a resolution was reached.

"Thank you, Nadyush," Olga said, putting her wallet away, and the pleasant seeping sensation returned. She was so rarely the beneficiary of Olga's appreciation. To be thanked meant that someone was in your debt, and what was a more powerful feeling than that?

They entered the museum, moving with the warm torrent of bodies. They wandered among Michael Jackson and that British princess, the president of the United States, Frank Sinatra, the blond waves of what was probably Marilyn Monroe. She did not recognize many of the others, the faces exuding the appearance of fame but not clicking to anyone she cared about. Where was Lyubov Orlova, the classic Soviet movie actress and singer so beautiful and accomplished that even Stalin didn't dare execute her, so famous that ships were named after her? These figurines in motion seemed trapped in the amber of time, faces twisted into demonic smiles. Living people that looked dead, dead people meant to look alive. Everyone here, the visitors and figurines, looked equally shellacked and happy.

"Perk up, my dear, or we won't be able to tell you apart from the statues." For a minute Nadia thought Olga was talking to her. But she saw Vivian unfold her pipe-cleaner body and take a blinking look around. "Baba! Quit it already."

"You were the one who wanted to come here. And now here we are." Olga took out her own phone and snapped a picture of Marilyn Monroe. A tour group colonized the room, enfolding its tentacles around them.

Nadia heard Vivian pressed against her, whispering, "Baba said you wanted to hook cousin Larissa up with an American husband. I meet men all the time on the computer." Without the phone in her hand, she looked unprotected and doelike, her Russian as charming as a foreign student's.

"Is that a good idea, meeting strange men on the internet? You're only sixteen!"

"I just mess with them. You wouldn't believe how easy it is," Vivian confided. She moved aside for a group of Korean tourists.

"I don't know." Nadia frowned. "I don't think it's safe."

"Not all of them are losers. By the time you meet them, you've already vetted them. Don't worry."

"Vivchik, it seems like a bad idea."

"I'll set you up with a profile if you want. It's easy and you can delete it if you want. Just don't tell Baba."

Nadia thought of her failure at the nightclub. What was wrong with the plan was her own involvement. What if there was no mediation between the man and Larissa? "Maybe I'm being old-fashioned. Would you do it? If it's not too complicated."

"Oh my God. It'll be done in five minutes. At school, I can tell them that I helped bring over my cousin from Ukraine. Cool, no?"

"Thank you, Vivchik, really."

It occurred to her that Vivian was the first person she encountered in America who initiated any assistance. For six years, she'd been pushing and pushing, making appointments at immigration agencies, law offices, embassies, begging senators to pay attention to a daughter caught between sniper fire. She had been asking everyone for favors but no one volunteered first: *You look like you're in distress, why don't I help you?*

Marilyn Monroe was preening in a glittering blood-colored dress, the scoop of the décolletage revealing waxy breasts. Looking at her, you would never know that halfway across the world, men were losing their precious lives for an airport in Donetsk. Just that morning, Ukrainian forces announced their control of the airport, the week before, the separatists flew their flag over the terminal. In between, the images on television were tank fire, helicopters shelling, trapped soldiers, the plume of black smoke, men dragging dripping bodies across the tarmac. On the balconies of bombed-out high-rises of Donetsk, women her mother's age were weeping. "What did we do to deserve this?" A year ago, when the unfathomable schism began, she was screaming in her head. Now she watched in a kind of trance, numbed to the helplessness of watching her bleeding country from an apartment in Brooklyn.

Olga was emerging between sleek wax actresses in sequined evening gowns. "I'm falling off my feet, girls. Yasha says he's got us a restaurant. Let's get out of here."

She and Vivian shook on the deal with the wax hands that were handed to them at the exit.

There was no elegant way to traverse slushy New York City streets. Olga was gingerly tiptoeing around puddles in her suede pumps, and even Nadia in her practical furry boots assessed each step for safety. Even when they broke free from the Times Square tussle, the city stretched before them gray and insurmountable. The windows of restaurants were fogged over in an unwelcoming way, the snarl of car traffic made it impossible to weave from block to block.

"Yasha's picked us a French restaurant, but it's a bit of a trek," Olga said.

Nadia instantly agreed. "I love French food," even though the closest she'd come to French food was spying the contents of the plates on bistro tables of Regina's neighborhood restaurants. She recalled the least edible parts of a salad and French fries, egg pies in phyllo dough. People sipped out of miniature wineglasses filled to the rim with pale wine. The more she thought about it, the less appealing it was, but with Olga you had no choice but to agree.

"French is my favorite," Olga said, in a way that made Nadia want to insist on any other cuisine.

They passed a string of perfectly good options—Indian and

Irish and something with a Buddha in front—but Olga plunged
on, nose in scarf, wax hand tucked under her arm, burgundy
leather gloves readjusting a wool hat. Nadia was impressed with
Vivian, who seemed to float on the sharp instincts of a phone
addict, her peripheral vision like antennae, slipping through the
flow of the crowd.

For a moment, she mentally deleted Vivian's body and inserted
Larisska's. After a year in America, this would be her and Larisska,
and there would finally be a good excuse to go to Manhattan.
They would see a Broadway show, eat at French restaurants anytime
they wanted to.

Through a neon smudge, they saw Yakov waving to them from
the street corner. On his head was some kind of ridiculous chinchilla, his moustache was almost entirely gray, and his coat was the
wrong cut for such a square man, the sleeves wide and long. Nadia
always felt a sympathetic affinity for Yakov. In Ukraine, he had been
too weak to stand up to Olga in any area of their lives except when
he put his foot down about changing his name to something less
Jewish like Yuri. Of course, in the end, that had been the very
thing that allowed them easier emigration. When they were picking the Jews to save from Ukraine, how could they overlook a man
named Yakov? How could a Yakov not have suffered in a place
like Ukraine?

He kissed her on both cheeks. "Nadyen'ka, you are not a year
older, not even a minute."

She wished she could say the same, but she came up with: "And
you are quite stylish, very dashing."

"Okay, okay, Don Juan, we are freezing out here," Olga said.

Yakov waved them toward a place named Caquelon, opened
the door and ushered them inside. It was like being pressed to a
warm bosom, the warm air embracing them. Their coats were

shrugged off and they were seated next to a fireplace. Nadia expected to be intimidated by waiters in crisp tuxedoes, but the tablecloths looked like Ukrainian kerchiefs and the plates looked like Regina's, a heavy porcelain with charming red borders.

Olga unwrapped a napkin on her lap. "I could eat a cow, an entire cow."

"In French places, you can do just that." Yakov scooped Nadia and Vivian up into the same warm smile. "I did a lot of research and this one had the most stars."

"In the future, you should really let me pick," Vivian said. She'd clearly decided she did not like the place, filled as it was with people their age and older, an entire circular table of ladies lifting glasses in a toast.

As Yakov and Olga engaged in a tussle over the expense of garage parking, Vivian whispered, "Here, while we were walking, I've set up a very basic profile, which means we can browse the options for Tyotya Larissa. I gathered you wanted a Russian-language site."

She had pulled up the Russian website VKontakte and was flipping through pictures of American men. Man after middle-aged man, like a display of shoes, like the spinning fruits of a slot machine.

"How in the world do you know about VKontakte?"

"Here's one. He seems okay." The one Vivian was pointing to had the look of a contented panda. He was posed in some banquet hall, a skewer of meat suspended between two index fingers like a rubber band. "'I have been employed by Citizen's Bank for over twelve years,'" Nadia read slowly, then skimmed his profile for relevant details. "Forget it, he lives in someplace named Nevada. He must live near here."

A woman in a peasant blouse pinned back by suspenders placed before them heavy leather tomes. She was not at all what Nadia pictured a real French restaurant would employ. It reminded her of the Russian restaurants aimed at tourists, the waitresses dressed to resemble rural prostitutes.

"Let's eat. Yasha, you look at the menu and pick for us. I want my usual steak," Olga said.

"Excellent."

Vivian rolled her eyes as if to say, *Is this how old married people behave?* but Nadia found it touching, the way her sister and husband had clearly heaved and shifted over the years, making small adjustments and concessions. In Ukraine, Yakov had been beaten down by Olga, flayed of his masculinity. He was a lowly medical student at a second-tier university on a Jewish quota, in the wrong specialty, with the poorest and most insignificant of patients. Olga had taken every opportunity to remind him of his smallness, his distance from any hope of power. Here in America, Yakov was a gastroenterologist with his own practice, finally accorded the kind of respect that assumed dominance over restaurant and meal selection.

"This seems like a special place. There are very few choices. I like restaurants that know what they do well and don't make you pick from a million options." He pointed at the page, asked about Pinot somethings, and closed shut the leather encyclopedia.

"How about this American?" Vivian's black-painted nail was directed at a "Chris." She translated: "'I like that Eastern European women are old-fashioned and domestic. I am looking to start a family right away.' He lives in Staten Island. That's in New York, isn't it?"

"He's better than the first one."

"Who's better? What are you two conspiring about over there?" Olga wanted to know.

Nadia decided to come clean. "Vivka is helping me find Larisska a fiancé. I'm not 'trawling' now. You have to admit that a fiancé visa might be faster than this endless wait. Even the immigration lawyer said so. They don't consider the regular citizens as war victims here. They only see evil Russians and evil separatists. But every day Larisska can't get out is a day she can get killed."

Olga and Yakov exchanged a look. Nadia was not in the mood for what it might entail. The seeping sensation was fading, replaced by a queasy resentment.

"It's just a way to get her here faster. I know it sounds crazy but I don't expect her to stay with him. They will live nearby and then see if they like each other. But at least her life can begin. She will be safe."

"Of course, that makes sense," Yakov said, looking into his lap at the folded napkin. A glass was brought to him, a splash poured. He sloshed it between his teeth, then nodded.

The women at the next table were rising, helping one another with their coats. They smelled of dry flowers and vegetable oil. If I get to be their age, I only want peace, Nadia thought with some envy. They had an unrushed posture of women who belonged nowhere else, who were expected nowhere else. Outside on the sidewalk, they orchestrated an elaborate round of farewells.

"Maybe you shouldn't narrow the geographic possibilities for Larisska," Olga said.

"What do you mean?"

"Not now, Olyechka," Yasha interrupted. "Try the wine. Is it right? I can't tell if it's been corked."

"Oh Yash, you know I can't tell the difference. All the wine here tastes sour to me. I like sweet wine, Georgian wine."

"But French wine is the best. Everyone says so."

"You're welcome to listen to others if you like, count up as many stars as you like. You probably have one of your wine guides in your pocket. Me? I know what I like."

A cast-iron tureen of burbling orange was placed between them by the waitress in the strange corset layered over her blouse. They were each handed elongated silver forks with mahogany handles. The woman smiled, red everywhere, cheeks and lips and flared skirt.

"What on earth is this? Yash?" Olga scrunched her nose.

"I have no idea." For a minute, a flash of the old Yakov appeared on his face, the panicked look of the diminished outsider.

A bowl of white bread chunks was being passed around. They were clearly supposed to do something with the forks, the squares of bread, the enflamed soup of cheese in a cauldron.

"It's fondue." Vivian demonstrated. She speared bread and submerged it in the cheese.

"It's fondue," Yakov repeated, regaining his swagger, as if he was aware of the delicacy all along and it had been his pleasure to insert it into their lives. "As a matter of fact, I believe it is actually Swiss."

"Where's the cow?" Olga wailed, not entirely joking. "I want my cow."

Nadia was following Vivian's lead. What was not to like about this entire situation? The cheesy bread, Olga's shock, poor Yakov's swift cover-up. Where's the cow? her sister was repeating. The day was finally looking up.

Nadia started cheerfully plunging and rescuing the bread, her fork a powerful weapon. She pretended the first piece was Olga, she decided, and down her sister went into the cauldron. For some reason, she found the act of drowning her sister in cheese very pleasurable. Olga was immediately followed by Aneta. Regina deserved just a tiny dip in the cheese for her benign cluelessness, Sasha only when she was disobedient. Who else? Grisha for all those bad sexual innuendos, for being diagnosed with stomach cancer and refusing to do anything about it. Her girlfriends here for imagining themselves superior to her. The idiots for shelling one another at the Donetsk airport and then moving on to Kievsky, Kirovsky, and other residential neighborhoods. Chris from Staten Island, it was his turn. This would be his fate if he did not bring Larisska to her place for dinner every Sunday. In you go, Chris.

The cheese was bubbling, spooling, the sides of the cauldron smeared with its drippings.

"Can you pour me a little more of that delicious wine?" she asked Yakov, tucking her own smile out of sight as Olga sat there with an unused spoon, not realizing that she had long ago been devoured.

Now that early dinner was over, what was there to do on a New York afternoon that splattered snow in your face? After the bill was paid ("Let me get this too." "Don't be crazy, you got the museum."), they had to decide what was next. Art gallery, said Olga. A crisp walk in the park, Yakov said, knowing he would never get his way. Shopping, Vivian chimed in. Nadia wanted to go home. Being anywhere but near the phone and in front of the television that was broadcasting from Donetsk was an act of treason. The Ukrainian forces might have regained the terminal, for all she knew.

But it was agreed that shopping it was.

At Bloomingdale's while everyone else shopped, Nadia was scrolling down romantic prospects for Larissa on VKontakte. She had been afraid of dangerous creeps, but if the pictures were correct, the men merely suffered from an excess of optimism. All those innocent grins, light-calibrated backdrops of beaches and suburban expanses, those eager little eyes reflecting projections of Eastern European women. Larisska could easily slip into their musings. She photographed like an angel, the flash sparking the reddish streaks in her blond hair. What would she say about herself?

As Olga and Vivian disappeared behind the racks in earnest, Nadia began to construct a profile for Larisska. *Ukrainian beauty in her mid-twenties seeks New York–based American for serious commitment.* Among the dresses, Olga was heard vetoing each of Vivian's selections. "Too itchy." "Dry clean only." "Your mother will kill me."

Upon rereading her sentence, Nadia thought it odd and malformed. She tried again. *You will not be disappointed! I am a very fun-loving but also domestic young lady looking for a man who wants to take care of a family.* The phrasing reeked of prostitution or desperation. She clicked on some competition and her heart dropped. Larissa's contemporaries were models, at least from the photos they submitted. They were sleek and seductive and wet-haired and allergic to clothes.

"What do you think? Please tell her it looks good on me." Vivian was standing before her in a scooped-neck cobalt dress. With her collarbone exposed, the girl looked like a store mannequin. Nadia guessed that was the point.

"I think it's pretty," she offered.

"You see?" Vivian turned back to her grandmother. "Tyotya Nadia says so."

Her daughter was smarter than this site, sharper than all these men. But she would never stick out among the pouting, plotting beauties. What man ever picked a woman from Ukraine for her brains? Her last chance was to appeal to a man's protective instinct; the one that craved above all to be a hero. *A piece of shrapnel is flying overhead as I write this, exploding the windows of my neighbors. Any day I go outside, I could die. At night, I sleep in an underground bunker with a single lamp for company. I long for America, for freedom. Save me.*

She uploaded Larissa's photo, the same one she showed the man at the nightclub. In a certain light, from an angle, one could say she was beautiful. She certainly looked more natural than those artificial sex robots.

Vivian appeared again, this time in Lycra: slinky, asymmetrical, red. "What do you think of this one?"

"It looks great on you."

Olga came at her with a cashmere turtleneck in hand. "Have you lost your head? Is Vivian meant to be standing on the street corners of Pepper Pike?"

"She's a lovely young girl. It just doesn't seem like the end of the world."

"Vivian is going to college soon. If we don't set the right limits now, how is she going to turn out? I agree with her parents on this." Olga stretched out her hand with the cashmere. "And this sweater is such a pretty color on you, Vivchik. And so soft."

"You're not listening to me, Baba," Vivian insisted, holding Nadia's gaze for support. She had the lonely eyes of the misunderstood, someone never truly known or heard.

Olga deflated, threw her coat down on the divan and collapsed into it. "Fine. Pick one. I will keep the receipt. Let your mother return it."

A howl of victory and Vivian shot off to the dressing room. Nadia glanced at her phone. A man had written back. She could see only the first sentence and she spelled out the words to see if she could make sense of them without a dictionary. *I was mesmerized by your profile. Would it be.* Under her layers, her body felt moist with agitation. Why hadn't she thought of this option sooner? The visa could be filed as early as next month if the exchanges went smoothly. Once the paperwork was approved, everything happened fast, the act of emigration being nothing more difficult than a trip to the Donetsk airport. Of course, now there was no Donetsk airport. Lugansk airport had been closed since June. Larisska would fly out of Kiev.

Olga was talking. "What I was going to say at the restaurant is that I think we should start thinking about Larissa's future here in this country. Her number could be up any day now."

Nadia looked up at her sister. "I had no idea you were so concerned. This is the first I'm hearing of it. I am working for my daughter's arrival every day. What are you actively doing that you deserve an opinion?"

Olga looked stiffly taken aback. "I've sponsored you, or did you already forget? She's my niece."

This time, the blue eyes did not have the same intimidating power to mute her. "Have you been checking on her every day? To make sure she's still alive, for example? Have you been talking to lawyers? Writing letters to senators? Have you been thinking of her day and night?"

Her sister was still wearing the burgundy gloves. Yet it was so warm in here, the air artificial and cloying. To her surprise, Olga did not appear angry. She took her hand. "I actually spoke with Larisska the other day, right before coming here."

Nadia neither held the hand nor pushed it away. "So she deigned to Skype with you? I'm impressed. I can barely get her to say hello."

Olga nodded. "Nadyush. We need to work together on helping Larisska."

"What is all this about thinking and working together? I've been doing nothing but working since I got here. Thank you for sponsoring us, but if you'd done it sooner, Larisska would have been able to come with me."

Olga dyed her moustache. From this close, Nadia could see the gray roots of them, the silver tufts above the mouth. "That's not fair. As soon as I got my bearings, I filed. Who knew it would take this long?"

Vivian was storming toward them, the blue dress over one arm, her coat over the other.

"I'll say this quickly," Olga said. "The truth is Larissa wants to live with us."

"What?" She heard a ringing sound, like an elevator stuck between floors. "What do you mean, she wants?"

"We have a good university in town, and she wants to be a dental technician. It's cheaper there, the cost of living is more reasonable, not like your crazy New York. You should come too. I never knew why you settled so far away from me."

"That's insane. This is the first I'm hearing of this. Larissa actually told you those very words? That she wants to live with you?"

Vivian was hovering over them. The dinging sound continued. As if a theater loudspeaker was alerting them to the dimming of the lights.

Her sister's blue eyes were unrelenting in their superiority. "Yes, she did. I will repeat exactly what she said, 'Tyotya Olga, when I come to America, I want to live with you.' Of course, we asked her if she was sure, if she wouldn't prefer to be closer to her mother in New York. But you yourself must see how this is a better place to vacation than to live. For God's sake, you can't cross the street in decent shoes. There are crazy puppets attacking you at every corner. The museums cost a million dollars. People eat expensive melted cheese for no reason. It is a zoo here. We live in a peaceful, affordable place, have a car, a nice car that brings us directly to the front door of our nice house."

Yakov materialized, chinchilla hat in hand. It was amazing how puffed up he was by this new American ego. Back in Ukraine, he hovered at the periphery, that tremulous little voice wafting between the weeds of his black moustache. "Olyechka, maybe it is time," or "I hate to interrupt, but . . ." Now he took Olga by the arm, pointed meaningfully at his watch. "It's time to go. Our show is soon." *Good for you, Yasha,* Nadia inwardly cheered.

"Here, you should keep this, you probably need it." She thrust the wax hand at Olga. "I have to go to the bathroom."

"Now?" Olga said, eyebrows raised. A few shoppers paused to look back at what she was holding. "But we're getting ready to go."

"My boyfriend is waiting for me."

"What boyfriend? You never mentioned any boyfriend. Can't you wait just a few minutes and walk us out like a normal person?"

The "normal person" protocol imprinted on her in childhood meant she had to escort visitors out the door, kiss each of them on the cheek, try to convince them to stay at her place for a few more days. Her sister was tormented by not being informed that she was dating. But she was also waiting for the fulfillment of the ritual, the usual exchange of deference and gratitude to the older sister. She might have even packed the family for a longer stay, had privately planned to transfer their bags from the hotel to Nadia's apartment, to phone her daughter and explain Vivian's delayed return home. ("She offered and how could I not spend a little more time with my poor little sister, all alone in New York?") Deep in her soul, Nadia knew every single step of what was expected of her. But now it seemed pointless to be fossilized in time, in service to old-world rites of power and hierarchy. She had to hurry home, to drag out of Larisska what in the world she meant by saying she wanted to live in Cleveland with Olga.

She stood. "His name is Boris. Yes, he is Jewish. Yes, it is serious. No, I can't walk you out like a normal person. I will say good-bye right here."

Nadia delivered an efficient round of kisses, an especially grateful one to Vivian, and told them to have a safe trip home. It was so much lighter to walk to the bathroom without the hand. In the lounge area, a row of women reapplied makeup, pressing their lips together. There was the orchestral sound of toilets flushing. Glancing down, she realized the loudspeaker was in fact her phone pinging. A long string of messages. She could imagine man after man stretching his virile self into the void, expecting the batting, glistening eyes of rescued Ukrainian maidens. Thinking the exact same thing: *Let me be the one to fight, to save you from this war. No sacrifice is too big as long as you will belong to me. As long as you love me. As long as you thank me.*

8

March of the Immortal Regiment

✳ **Moscow, May 2015**

The wood on the furniture was peeling, the television was completely broken, and there was no trace of either towels or toilet paper. The woman from the rental agency noted their grimaces of displeasure. What did they expect for the price—the Ritz Carlton on Red Square? For a decade now, she had been dealing with Moscow tourists just like them, returning émigrés from America. Why were they never, ever happy? She recommended lowering expectations and just enjoying their vacation. Wasn't life too short for bottling up all that dissatisfaction?

As Boris berated the lady ("I'm not bottling up shit. What kind of shady operation are you running without basic amenities? We're going to tell the entire Russian community in New York City to avoid your company like the plague!"), Nadia rummaged in her suitcase for a stack of Grisha's linens, brought in anticipation of exactly this shortage. They were all varying shades of tan like everything else in his apartment, but the scent of him still hovered just above the surface of the bleach. After he died, when VIP Senior Care was dumping out the contents of his apartment on behalf of the landlord, they let her take anything his son and his family didn't want. Other than their mother's jewelry, they had wanted nothing and the apartment remained exactly how he left it. Now the linen was turning out to be a good idea. She fastened her teeth to the fabric, and ripped them into frayed squares.

"*Vot,* here's our toilet paper," she announced, holding up a taupe fitted sheet.

"Very nice," the Realtor approved. She was wearing a powder-pink pantsuit with matching pink earrings. "It's nice to see you haven't lost the old Soviet resilience living in America. Some of these people returning after twenty years, they've gone soft. They expect all sorts of indulgences. They ask about heat or, even more ridiculous, air-conditioning!"

"I've only lived in America for less than seven years. I'm not American yet."

The Realtor looked pleased. "That explains it then. You seem like a good, hardworking person. Are you in for Victory Day?"

"We're here meeting my daughter from Ukraine," she said. It was an idea Nadia had after Olga's visit. She became convinced that seeing her daughter was imperative. She could not afford to let any more time go by before she could ask her face-to-face what was going on with this ridiculous Cleveland plan. For years, she had allowed Larissa to elude her on the phone and Skype. Her daughter refusing to entertain the idea of meeting her in Moscow even if Nadia could scrape up the vast sums of money such a trip entailed. Then the war came. This time though, Nadia pressed her case firmly and Larissa, to her surprise, agreed to make the trip. It was looking like the Minsk agreement was not holding, and the occasional flare-up, the sudden sound of gunfire, was more than she could take. She was happy to get out.

The Realtor swung open the door. "Ah, well. I've got no problems with Ukraine even if it is an ungrateful nation. I hope you take my advice and stop nitpicking, anyway. Enjoy Moscow, the

most beautiful city in the world." On the other side, a blur of suspicious faces peered at them from down the hallway.

"We will," she said, newly filled with excitement.

"Nice work, Nadyen'ka." Boris turned to her when the Realtor's footsteps receded into the closed elevator. "You could have left
out Ukraine."

"And you could have bought us a nice roll of toilet paper instead of yelling at her. Don't forget she has keys to the place."

"And now she hates us because she knows you're from Ukraine."

"It's more likely she hates us because you're a Jew."

Boris examined the contours of her entire face, from forehead
to chin to the crown of hair exploded by a long airplane flight.

"Sorry, dear," she said. "I shouldn't have said that." That Boris
didn't profoundly listen to her, or at least failed to peek at the seamy
underbelly beneath her words, irritated her. She could see the tuning out happening right in the middle of a point she was making,
whether while strolling the boardwalk or over a meal, his irises
losing their focus and gently turning inward.

"We're both exhausted. Let's just take a little rest, before we do
anything else." He was unpacking his suitcase and neatly folding
shirts into dresser drawers. He was whistling a cheerful, unfamiliar tune.

Oh, how much she had looked forward to this trip! When the airplane crew launched into the landing instructions in Russian—
Welcome to Moscow—she felt an immediate quiver that vibrated
through her entire body. The tremor generated the particular peace
of childhood, being softly nestled among those you understood intimately and who intimately understood you. The Cyrillic words,

so dear, so voluptuous to her ears, made sense and required no translation on her part.

But after that initial frisson, once she and Boris set foot on Russian soil, the burst of marvel began to contract. The airport was overflowing with Russians and foreigners traveling in for Victory Day. They could barely squeeze their luggage through the masses, the lines for visitor services stretched kilometers long, and even the air felt insufficient to circulate among all of them. Then at the currency exchange window, just as Nadia was enjoying the triumph of communicating, the woman behind the bars interrupted her by asking about the origin of her accent.

"Are you from Moldova, or what?" she said in this unpleasant manner, her glasses perched far below the bridge of her nose. Nadia always prided herself on the purity of her Russian. Her Russian-language teacher in school had been a professor from Leningrad, and had awarded Nadia a medal for authentic Russian pronunciation three years in a row! She gave the woman a stern lecture about making assumptions about a stranger's identity.

"Why don't you concentrate on doing your job," Boris added, and the woman completed the exchange with a series of jerking counting motions. But as they turned to go, a stranger standing behind them tapped Boris on the shoulder and remarked that his skin was so swarthy he must hail from someplace foreign like Baku. Was he in Moscow from Uzbekistan for the parade?

"Mind your own business, you dimwit," Boris replied. The man backed away, but it was clear to Nadia that they were both jarred by these intrusions. They had become unaccustomed to the pushy Soviet manner, the unsolicited opinions from strangers. They were now used to the complex jumble of cultures, the benign indifference from New Yorkers.

"Whatever you do, don't say the word 'Ukraine,' please. Not here," Boris said.

"But I didn't."

"Well, don't."

"I won't."

The airport was taking on an air of menace, solitary men in leather jackets waiting for something to happen, the chaos of luggage heaped into a pile before a solitary scanner. She imagined a major Moscow airport in this day and age would be gleaming and high-tech, but Sheremetyevo was decrepit, clogged with inefficiency. She held a protective hand over her purse as they flooded into the waiting area, the arrivals and departures crossing paths like exhausted soldiers.

At the car rental desk, they used her name to hold the reservation but the tight-bunned babushka filling out paperwork asked her if she happened to be originally from Poland. Poland? That was just insulting. She knew a Polish accent and it sounded nothing like hers, not to mention that hers was a classic Russian name that meant "hope"!

"Fuckers everywhere," Boris said, scrawling madly across the form.

The woman turned the contract around, scrutinized the print. Her lips were pursed in disapproval. "Is this really how you write your letters, sir? You should take handwriting lessons."

"Unbelievable." Boris yanked the keys out of her hand and pulled Nadia away from the counter. "I might have to turn right around and go home to civilization."

"Calm down, dear," she said, feeling wifely. The first hint of the codependence of marriage, the not entirely unpleasant aftertaste of need.

Upon starting the car, they discovered the gas gauge pointing to empty. They inched toward the city, breaths held for the closest station. When its neon letters finally appeared beyond the massive billboards advertising cell phone services and soda and a chain of cafés, Nadia felt the air filter back into her lungs. She wished she were handling the situation alone. Watching Boris struggle with foreign powerlessness was worse than managing her own fears. Worse still: that Larissa wouldn't be happy to see her, or that after seven years, Nadia might encounter an alien instead of a daughter. Maybe all children were essentially aliens to you if you thought too much about it.

If New York was a city that hid you, generously stirred you into a crowd like milk into coffee, then Moscow hid you, but reminded you of your inability to ever blend in. It was regal, haughty, and had no patience for your smallness. A statue of a famous poet here, a towering cupola there, wide avenues built for armies and their tanks. Archways high enough to shrink in. She was warned by Georgina not to gawk inside the metro with its marble walls, luxurious chandeliers, its glittering gold letters announcing the future stops. It was a favorite spot for pickpockets whose flinty eyes picked out the awed tourists and followed them until the opportunity— a crowded train, the confusion of a connecting station—arrived. Nadia kept her purse pressed against her belly, but her actual money was dispersed between a pouch lining the inside of her pants and a roll inside her socks.

It was easy to understand why the place had such a sentimental hold over anyone who grew up in the Soviet Union, faces pointed toward Moscow and the centralized loyalties it represented. No wonder she read that former Donetsk separatists were resuming prosperous lives here now that the war was simmering down. It was a parent who gave the impression of taking care of you, who reminded you that he was located at the center of what life could be. In any case, it was the most pleasurable train ride of her life; you couldn't compare this reliable smoothness of gliding from one subway station to another to the lurching subway experience in New York, the unpredictability of a train suddenly taking a new route with a mumbled, indecipherable message she never understood.

When she was a little girl, she had once dreamed of moving to Moscow, of being a professional woman in the city of her dreams. Now she understood Rubizhne was sewn inside her. She came from a small city in a country that others have used, divided, abandoned, plundered. The faster she ripped her daughter out of their mother country, the better.

Her daughter! Coming toward her in an impossible tight lavender dress. She was walking with a new sway, a gait Nadia did not recognize. There was too much to take in at once but it was hard not to notice the inappropriate spandex, the top that stretched too tightly across her breasts. Who had bought her that outfit? She wanted to redirect her focus to the changes in her daughter's face, the way it had filled out, grown at once proportional. But it was impossible to move beyond the shock of those clothes, those uncomfortable shoes. Her girl once in flowered blouses and high-waisted jeans and pleated pants was now dressing like all those tartlets on VKontakte. A rapid-fire assessment noticed a tattoo of a snowflake right below the clavicle and above the breast, a hoop piercing the cartilage at the top of her ear. She almost choked on her own disbelief.

"That's her? That's your Larisska?" Boris asked. After all her flowery descriptions, even he seemed not to entirely believe it.

"Baby, come here."

Larissa edged into her arms and Nadia held her close enough to feel the inner workings of her flapping organs, the heart valve, beat and blood and breath. The shape of her recalled some memory but too much was unfamiliar, from the scent, the hairstyle, the stooped posture. "Let me make sure you're in one piece."

"You're strangling me." Larissa was squirming in her arms, trying to break free. Nadia would not let her, and eventually her daughter gave up the struggle.

The idling train was making loud, unnecessary noise among the rushing of coats, the swell of the crowd jostling them. In a station with trains going in opposite directions, the air was damp with confusion. This embrace was blocking a path back into the station, but Nadia refused to move. Seven years of separation were being distilled into this one moment and she wanted to absorb every drop. She wanted to experience all the ages of her daughter, from baby to now, to assert her motherhood again. She couldn't wait until they were back at the grimy apartment, Larisska out of the shower and smelling like herself. She would take care of all her girl's immediate needs right away: a filling dinner, tea on the table, a plate of low-sugar cookies she brought from Brooklyn. The murmur of their voices into the night.

Around them, bodies stirred and buzzed in the panic of mistakenly boarding a train for Nizhny Novgorod or Ukraine, the search for nearby Chkalovskaya metro station.

"Let go of me," Larissa said. There was the coldness of the cheek, the stale smell of food and travel emanating from Larissa's mouth. At one point, Nadia controlled everything Larissa ate, a careful balancing of sugar and carbohydrate. Up until the very day she left, she planned out all of her daughter's meals. The very final plate, chilling in the refrigerator, of stuffed cabbage leaves and a sliced peach. A huge vat of chilled *okroshka* for after she was gone.

She could feel Larissa pushing against her shoulders, the forced unclasping of her own fingers.

A man stood separated from the crowd, watching them. He was young and attractive in a lopsided, disheveled way. A smattering of beard seemed to have not entirely committed to his face. He lingered next to them, short and scrawny and ill at ease in his brown leather jacket hunched over a football jersey. Just in case, Nadia swiveled Larisska's purse closer to their bodies so she could keep her eye on it.

"This is Slavik," Larissa said, waving him over. "Slavik, this is Mama."

"Slavik," she said, an unexpected word filling up her mouth. Larissa had said nothing about any Slavik and neither had her grandmother.

"Mama, if I may," he said, with a dapper bow, stretching out a veined hand she didn't know how to grasp. But then he was pulling her in and he was hugging Boris too. Boris hugged back, game as always.

It was all confusing. The men shook, neither properly identified. Nadia took Larissa's arm by the elbow, hoisted her duffel bag over one shoulder, and guided her toward the exit.

"Who is Slavik?"

"You said you were bringing Boris." Larissa shrugged. Her heels looked uniquely uncomfortable and Nadia saw a slash of red skin barely hidden by a fraying bandage.

"Without Borya there would be no trip. But never mind that. I want to hear all about him and you."

"You'll like him. Everyone likes him. He's an entrepreneur," Larissa said, and Nadia's heart sank. An entrepreneur meant only one thing in post-Soviet parlance: loser. Even worse, a loser who can smell a future émigrée with all the promise she might provide. But you couldn't tack a husband onto an immigration application. If Larissa got married to this Slavik, she would have to fill out a whole new application on his behalf, wait another seven or more years for him to come. Surely by then, Slavik would be history.

And thanks to her niece Vivian, she corresponded with half a dozen men in the New York City area, but found herself drawn to a Dima who she thought would be perfect for Larissa. He was new to online dating, owned his own body shop in Sheepshead Bay. He did not fixate on Larissa's looks, asking her questions about her interests and hobbies. He said he was not opposed to muse-ums or books. Before she left, she pictured their first night in Mos-cow, her calling up the photograph of Dima on her phone and watching Larissa's eyes glitter with her American future. Instead Larissa said, "He's an entrepreneur," which to Nadia meant she loved this shaggy, unpromising, even dangerous Slavik.

"I'm sure I will like him if you like him," she said. Better to keep your enemies close, unsuspecting.

As if on purpose, Slavik made sure there was no opportunity for her to be alone with Larisska. Even inside the fraying apartment, Slavik stood at her daughter's side like a mushroom, rooted and unmoveable. His boasting stories filled up the room with their end-less droning chatter directed mostly at Boris. A laundry list of accomplishments, money wagered, earned, and lost. Taking over his father's sunflower refinery in the south was a bad move—who the hell cared about sunflower oil anymore?—but now during the gas impasse with Russia, he stumbled on a new idea. Nadia tried to peel Larissa away toward the couch but as soon as the separation was accomplished, Slavik followed them, slid right against Larisska.

"So what is it you do then?"

"A few of us guys supply sunflower husk pellets for heating. It's a good business, especially after a winter like we just had."

"Is that so?"

"You were smart to get out when you did but the war's been good for business, and once it's all over, it will be even better."

"Slavik is being modest," Larissa said, which seemed like an exaggeration. "He can't keep them in stock."

"I think of it as doing my part for the war effort. I'm bringing my country back together. Protesters, separatists. Everyone needs heat, right?"

"Now that's thinking on your feet," Boris said. Off they launched about seed money and investors but their voices filled the entire room, and Nadia found herself busying with the transportation of food from kitchen to table, willing Larissa to follow. But her daughter stayed glued to Slavik's side, her hand resting on his upper thigh.

Then as if by some miracle, he excused himself to go to the bathroom. Without the stream of his talk, they were plunged into silence. "Larisska," she began. She smoothed her daughter's hair, pulling it away from a damp forehead. "How is the sugar? How are you feeling?"

"Fine, I'm fine, Mama, no need to worry about me," Larissa said firmly. "Taking care of myself just fine."

"I like your hair just like this, so we can see your face. You want me to try fixing it? I saw a pair of scissors in the kitchen."

Larissa returned her long bangs to their original location. "Actually, I think my hair's perfect."

From inside the toilet, they could hear Slavik wailing. "Larisska! Larisska! There's no toilet paper in here."

Nadia rushed over with squares of ripped-up sheet. They were neatly and uniformly cut. One would never know that Grisha's suffering, dying body was once pressed against them. She placed the squares into her daughter's hand.

Larissa commanded, "Open, will you!" The door was pushed forward a centimeter or two and a hand slipped out. She took the pile of sheets and slid them through the opening to the outstretched fingers. The door slammed shut.

Her daughter stood at the door until the toilet flushed, arms wrapped tightly around her middle. "You never think of bringing toilet paper to Moscow. We imagine they have everything here," she said to no one in particular, her voice as far away as a train already departed.

The next morning, Nadia rose to find her daughter dolled up in a striped shimmying dress that seemed suctioned to her body. She was sitting at the breakfast table, scanning a tourist guide of Moscow, while applying nail polish to her toenails. An oval-shaped earphone was sticking out of each ear. She bopped her head in time to the mute music.

"Did you already take your blood sugar?" Nadia asked.

Larissa lowered one earphone. "I've been doing it by myself for a long time, Mama. Don't you worry."

Nadia felt at a loss. The rhythm between them was off and she was eager to right it. "Of course I know that. Just asking. Are you

listening to that Vera Brezhneva? I liked the song you sent me."
There was no response.

Nadia poured water into the kettle. She inserted herself into
Larissa's field of vision. "So where should we go today? Tretiakov
museum? Pushkin library? Lenin's tomb? There's no rush there.
He's still very much dead."

Larissa looked up. She was in full makeup, lids smothered in
royal blue caked with glitter, lips rimmed in some pink, partially
eaten away, color. Nadia was tempted to run a dish towel under
warm soap and water, wipe the entire palette away. Except they
had no dish towels. Last night, Boris tried to run to a nearby store
for supplies but it was closed.

"I actually did have a plan, speaking of graves. I want to see
my father's."

The kettle exploded. "What for? Really, Larisska? Calling him
your father is an exaggeration by a large measure."

"That's not true. He was my father, wasn't he?"

"He was nobody," she said, searching the cabinets for tea. They
were empty. "Just a *technolog* in the factory where I worked."

"Well, I want to see his grave."

This was ridiculous. This whole business of children wanting
to know the men that provided them with nothing more than their
sperm felt ironically American to her. She remembered Regina saying that some five-year-old classmate of Sasha's was going to meet
her "donor siblings," that the sperm donor had actually agreed to
write the children notes on their birthdays, that mothers actually
encouraged these relationships. She could not understand it. The
men did not give a thought to these children their entire lives, why
should the reverse be any different?

They could hear the sound of Slavik rolling out of bed. He was
humming in a hoarse morning voice.

"We spent some time together after you left. Before the war."

"You did?" Nadia needed a chair beneath her. This was news. The *technolog* and her daughter sharing a nice cup of tea at the café? The *technolog* and her daughter taking strolls past the common grave of the Soviet soldiers? As she toiled away in New York, he was taking her place? No wonder she looked like a prostitute with no one normal to watch over her.

"How did you find him?"

"He found me. I didn't know at first, just thought he was a friend of yours checking in on me as the war started. But he kept calling, then visiting. Then he told me."

"How often? Why didn't you tell me?"

"Then one morning, he was killed. I found it on Odnoklassniki, some people in town reposting his wife. So that was over."

"I'm shocked, Larisska. You should have said something."

"He was a decent man, Mama. He said he wanted to be more involved but he sensed you didn't want him meddling. He called you 'proud' and 'independent.' He said you needed nobody. It's true. You probably don't."

Blinking furiously, Nadia said, "I suppose you think there's something wrong with being independent from a man." She felt the color rising. "Anyway, I don't remember him clamoring to see you."

Slavik peeked his head in. "Good morning, beautiful ladies." He had a magazine rolled under his arm. "See you in twenty minutes." He disappeared into the toilet room.

Nadia felt her polite smile dissolve. "And what kinds of things did you do together? I suppose his wife didn't know who you were."

"Mama, I want to live with Aunt Olga in Cleveland when my number's up." Larissa said this coolly. But how garish her face looked in the freshness of the sunlight. That unblemished skin once as spongy as just-baked ricotta cheese. Those arms that used to curl about her neck, the golden eyebrows that pressed against her collarbone when she was sleepy. Nadia felt a splintering inside, could feel each sharp point.

"We don't have to decide now."

"We should have some plan for the future," Larissa said. "Slavik looked up Cleveland and said it has the Rock 'n' Roll Hall of Fame. That seems cool. Besides, New York is expensive and I need to save money."

"But your own mother will be helping you. You will be saving money on rent."

"I'm twenty-eight years old now. I can make my own decisions. I'm afraid if I live with you . . ." Larissa dipped the wand back into the nail polish but didn't withdraw it.

Nadia felt the air exploding in her lungs. "If you live with me, what? Your so-called plan makes no sense at all. She's your aunt. I'm your mother."

"I know who you are, Mama."

"Let's take it one step at a time. First you come to New York and then . . ."

The toilet flushed. "Success!" Slavik called out.

Larissa sighed, raised her voice. "Congratulations, Comrade Slavik, but there's no need to announce your toilet victories to everyone."

Nadia felt a strange relief that Larisska had snapped at Slavik. Maybe, after all, there was a schism between the couple that would offer an advantage for Dima the mechanic and the life she had so carefully arranged for her daughter in New York. But then the kitchen flooded with the men and their talk overwhelmed everything, as usual.

+ + +

How ordinary the *technolog*'s name looked on a headstone, she thought. A name simply carved with no preceding title, no memory of the kind of respect he used to command at the factory. His family had the bad taste of plastering a photograph of him on the stone and now she could look nowhere but at that unnaturally earnest gaze of his staring at her out of granite. This rock had nothing to do with the way the *technolog* could illuminate the room by his confident occupation of it. And there was no way to hear the exact tenor of his high-pitched whistle, the one that promised everything would turn out all right.

The other half of the headstone was blank, probably in anticipation of the wife. When she thought of her own burial, she imagined doing something similar. Stretching out the earth, making room for her daughter. But how nice it might have been to have a small space on limestone waiting to welcome you when the time came.

She allowed Larisska to set down the bouquet of cheerful carnations they bought at the entrance to the cemetery. Her daughter in that ridiculous dress was barely able to balance on those heels, an outfit completely unfit for the surroundings. But she appeared solemn. Her head bowed, eyes closed. She crossed herself, muttering snippets of prayers. This allowed Nadia to scan her entire profile, to freeze the sight, compare it against the fragments of her memories.

They were alone for the first time, the men wisely bowing out of the trip in favor of a visit to the KGB museum at Lubyanka— Slavik had greased the right palms to allow them access. It was all quite beautiful at the Khovanskoye Cemetery, the lanes wide, the flowers bright, the graves sheltered by a row of birches and firs.

She moved closer to Larisska and slipped an arm around her waist. "You can't imagine how I've missed you. Every day I worry about you. The day you are safe in America will be my happiest day."

"What's so great about it?" Larissa looked up at her. "America? What makes it better than home?" Those familiar eyes were underlined with blue pencil. The mole she had forgotten about, a mole on her neck right below the left earlobe.

She didn't know where to start. Images of Brooklyn flooded her at once. She began to talk. Sasha, Regina, Grisha, Aneta, Boris, and her friends. Stores that sold nothing useful whatsoever. The public bathrooms were free, so was the soap and paper towels. People who said "Watch your step" when you entered their establishment. When you got your blood drawn at the doctor's, you didn't have to bring your own alcohol or cotton. When you called an ambulance they didn't ask for cash first. No one harassed you about your handwriting or accent. The world was designed for comfort.

"That sounds nice." Larissa lingered at the grave with the bundle of carnations at its foot. This time Nadia allowed them both the time, a final look at the *technolog*. He had been nice to her daughter; she had been on his mind all along: *Your daughter is my daughter.*

She laced Larissa's arm through hers and they walked like the old days. There had never been a point to conversation as long as they could walk in step in the same direction. But when she looked her daughter square in the face, she noticed that Larissa's eyes were glistening.

"Stores that sell nothing useful," she said, so quietly Nadia could barely make out the words. "When all this time, we were dying. Our banks are still closed, believe it or not. No one knows if it's safe to leave the house."

"Oh, kitten." She began to cry.

An elderly man walking by them with his cane said, "Women shouldn't cry in public, you know. It's not attractive to look at."

She'd had enough of these people. She could feel an ignited wick burning to the very bottom. "Shut up, old man. Who asked your opinion? Did I wonder out loud what you thought on the subject of crying women?" The man continued on, shaking his head.

"That's not very feminine. That's all I was saying."

"Feminine? I'll show you feminine, you cretin," she called out to his back. He looked behind him a little fearfully, shaking his head.

When she returned to her daughter, Larissa was staring at her. Whether the look was of repulsion or admiration, Nadia couldn't at first be sure. There was nothing to be done. Seven years was seven years. They had both changed. Why didn't she think they would change before they came together again? Why did she assume time would be suspended while she was gone?

"Mama, I had no idea you were such a badass," Larissa said, bursting into the first smile Nadia had seen since that awful day at the Kiev embassy, before everything crumbled for the two of them. "If you'd only stayed and had a few choice words for Poroshenko and Putin, the war would have ended sooner."

"I would have said, 'I'll show you, separatists.'"

"Or, 'I'll show you, Yanukovich. You and your ridiculous palace. Your stupid Steinway piano, your personalized brandy, your cars and motorcycles, your enormous horse statues.'"

"My God, if you told me this was all a bad novel, I'd believe you."

"I don't remember you this assertive. Were you always like this?"

"You don't remember? What about when you were twelve or thirteen years old, shadowed by that skinny, pimpled Artem kid you couldn't stand but were too nice to reject? Remember how you whispered, 'Help me get rid of him, Mama'? How I managed to chase him away?"

"Oh my God, poor Artem! I never said that, you're making it up. Didn't you pull him aside and say something like, 'You're here so often your intentions must be to marry my daughter this afternoon. Shall I call for the priest and you invite your parents?' He couldn't get out the door fast enough." And they both laughed so hard, her stomach felt like it might burst.

Had there ever been a happier place for Nadia than this cemetery right now? It was as though a heavy sentence was lifted and she saw sky for the first time in seven years. She wanted to carefully extract this moment and can it for the winter so she could take it down off the shelf and know that she now had the means to survive until springtime.

The next morning, she and Larissa were eating breakfast together when Slavik burst into the room holding an AK-47. It was long, the distance from his hip to foot, and it was casually slung under his armpit. "Good morning, everyone. I'm starved."

Nadia covered Larisska with her body. "What are you doing? Put that thing down."

Slavik looked confused. "Aren't we going to the parade? I got us tickets to Lenin's Tomb."

"In Gorky Park," Larissa said from behind Nadia's back. They had been having such a lovely time until Slavik came along. Larissa was telling her stories of her grandmother's unironic Putin figurine collection, and she had been describing Aneta in all her bunned glory. Larissa had even allowed her to administer an insulin shot the way she did every morning since Larissa was a little girl. She had been willing both the men to simply disappear. But here was Slavik, interfering as usual, but this time with a gun.

Reaching over, Larissa took the gun, slid it to the back of the counter. "Don't mind him. He's been looking forward to this for weeks, haven't you, little bear?" Into a bowl, she ladled what remained of the oatmeal, added a splash of milk.

"But why do you need to bring a gun into Gorky Park?" Nadia wanted to know.

"He's a huge Kalashnikov fan and they'll be promoting their products for Victory Day," Larissa said. "You know, men are boys. They want to take their pictures with their women and their guns."

Nadia thought this was the most absurd thing she'd ever heard. Those very guns were responsible for the death of that neighbor who went out to drop off bread for his son and was shot by a nearby sniper. Her mother had described the scene in more detail than necessary, his wife dragging the body, trailing blood down the hallway. And what about the *technolog*? But now she could not allow herself to think of him dead, alone, on the street.

"It's fine, Mama. Can you give me a little breathing room, please?" They had had such a lovely morning but now Larisska was drawing away and returning to her Slavik's side.

Slavik shrugged. "You'll see. It's really a rocking time." He buried a spoonful of oatmeal in his mouth.

This Victory Day was the largest yet, the seventieth anniversary of the Nazi defeat. Didn't she know? Slavik was explaining as they walked from the apartment building to the metro, speaking to her as if he were her elder. He'd heard the presidents of Cuba, India,

Vietnam were all going to be here. No United States here of course; they were still waiting for a president who would be a real friend to Putin. Or Germany or England or anyone else still grumpy over the Crimea business. As he spoke, Nadia only thought about how Slavik's stature might have been a problem for him at school. Short Slavik, tiny Slavik, rearing up with his fists to fight anyone who disagreed with his cocky pronouncements.

"The Ukrainian junta will be defeated. I know you're Americans now but with all due respect, surely you can see that we can't just keep bowing to America, am I right or am I right? As it is, everything's in dollars. But you know who doesn't lick America's feet? That's right. Putin is master of his domain, unlike all these weak, goddamn presidents. He was completely right to take Crimea. What else could he do after the Maidan coup?"

Maidan coup? Nadia glanced nervously at Boris. Here was a man who had many opinions of his own, but now he was quietly listening to Slavik's rantings. As they descended into the metro, he might have said, *Akh, it's a complicated situation, isn't it? So much history. One side borders Europe, the other Russia. So many years of enmity, it was only a matter of time.* But mostly he nodded his head, and it occurred to Nadia that he either did it for her, toward some kind of future between their families, or he was tuning Slavik out in the same efficient manner.

The metro was stuffed with the medallioned, the patriotic, the Soviet nostalgics. Kids in Octyabronok hats, old men in their former war uniforms. She didn't like that Slavik pushed his way on the train first, not looking behind to check on Larissa's safety. On the train, Larissa picked up the thread. "Junta, junta, you know how I hate that word. You saw those poor Ukrainian soldiers. They sent them out to our town with nothing. No uniform, no good shoes. Babushka lets a few of them shower at our place once a week."

Slavik rolled his eyes as if in the direction of all the train's men. *Women, am I right?* "I wasn't talking about the soldiers, my dear."

Nadia was nervous. "Please, let's talk about something else," until the train pushed into the station and they were being extracted with the throng.

At Lenin's Tomb, soldiers were waving them into the line. "Show your tickets. No photography, no smoking, no talking, take off all your hats, open your bags for inspection." They were being hustled along by armed guards, the line twisting around the mausoleum's granite mouth. Slavik jumped out of line to buy a bouquet of chrysanthemums from a deluged babushka.

"Why are we here again?" she whispered to Boris. "We should be at a nice museum or something."

"This could be your new son-in-law, Snegurochka." Boris smiled. "You fight it, it only gets worse. Believe me, I know from experience. It ends how it ends with no interference from the *mamasha*."

"Why is he buying flowers? For whom? Certainly not for Larisska."

They were making her jittery, these armed men barking instructions at them as if at soldiers. The tourists from non-Russian-speaking countries, the innocent Italians and Chinese and Germans, didn't seem bothered. That she understood what they were saying only made it more frightening, and she wished they'd gone to the Tretiakov or somewhere pleasant instead of this display of Russian might.

"It is colder than I expected," she said, knotting her scarf tighter.

"We'll be inside soon." And Boris started to whistle.

They ducked inside the mausoleum, beneath the gold letters spelling LENIN, where Slavik and Larissa were clearly continuing their argument.

"You are a simplistic thinker," she was saying. "You're like that about everything. If you look a little closer, you'll see things are not as easy as you're making them out to be."

Nadia was thrust into darkness and she held on to Boris's firm hand guiding her toward a distant light. There he lay, Lenin, like a precious ring in a velvet box. His one fisted hand lying beside him, his face illuminated by a beam of light. She remembered reading somewhere that the embalmer bragged he had made Lenin look better after death. It was exactly like the wax museum in Times Square, except for the hush in the room, people gently placing plastic bouquets of flowers. Slavik moved forward too, adding two chrysanthemums from his bouquet to the pile, receiving smiles of complicity from the other flower-givers. *Those were the good old days, weren't they?* The tourists simply looked confused, and who could blame them? She herself couldn't be sure if the man should be receiving flowers when there were much worthier dead people sprinkled throughout cemeteries all over the former Soviet Union. There were certainly unmarked graves not too far from her hometown, men that might still be indirectly dying because of the embalmed man in front of her lying on his bed of granite.

"Keep walking. No stopping," she heard the orders of the guards. Her stomach felt like it was turning inside out. When they exited into the light, she felt like she might bring up the contents of her breakfast. But they were being directed toward the Necropolis, toward the tombs of Stalin, Dzerzhinsky, Brezhnev. Boris was snapping photographs of Stalin's head, which blasted off from the top of the stone like a rocket. The blocks of Stalin's tomb were heaped with long-stemmed roses and wreaths, many more than had been placed before Lenin. Slavik added the rest of his flowers to Stalin's grave.

"Now that's a man worthy of your mourning," Larissa said sarcastically.

"What are you talking about? You don't know anything. Stalin was good for Ukraine." Slavik was poised. Nadia recognized that fire in his eyes, it was a warning, a prelude to action. She stepped between her daughter and Slavik though a part of her couldn't help noticing Stalin's tremendous face staring down at them all. Good for Ukraine, if you thought starving millions of people on purpose was good for a country, she thought. But there was a time and place for disagreeing and this was not it.

"Let's all calm down here."

Overhead an explosion rang out in the sky. It filled the air with a single terrifying bang. Everyone started, craned their necks upward to the origin of the sound. But Larissa cried out, tears streaming down her face. She was in Nadia's arms now, her shoulders heaving with fright.

"There, there. It's okay. We will be okay."

"Mama," she moaned. "What was that?"

"Okay, we are getting out of here." Nadia was taut with a new clarity. She would cover her daughter's body with her own and move to the sidelines, hide in the crowd and run to safety. She felt ready, as if she had been training for this moment. Another shot rang out, then more. She was surprised to find that no one was running.

"Fireworks, you silly girls," Slavik said, pointing upward. "Some kids are just playing."

"Fireworks," she whispered into her daughter's hair, running her hand up and down her spasming back. After so many years, it was here in her arms. It was not pulling away.

"Come here, little one," Slavik said, and Larisska rolled out of her reluctant arms and into his like a docile puppy.

With the afternoon came warmth, the shedding of scarves and light jackets. They were exposed under the open sun, a sea of heads pointed toward a central marching thrust. The crowd was several rows thick and, if you were not a giant, it was impossible to see the proceedings.

"Look at that T-14 Armata! Not bad at all," Slavik cried. He and Boris pushed aside some bodies so they could glimpse a better view of the tank, its earth-colored Cubist body and saluting cannon. "I heard it can do twelve rounds a minute no problem."

"You can't beat this fire control. It's state-of-the-art," Boris said. The two men were finally sharing a common interest, overlaying words about the tank's machine gun, unmanned turret, electronically controlled engine.

"*Ura,*" everyone screamed as it rolled past them.

She was just on edge, Larissa explained. Waking up every day at four in the morning to the sound of artillery fire would make anyone nervous. Nadia had given her a few slivers of Grisha's sheet and she was dabbing her eyes with them to avoid smudging her makeup.

"Tell me more."

"Babushka loves Slavik, of course," Larissa said so that her words were almost gulped down, lost to the vocal merriment.

"Of course she does. This is the same woman who screamed for Putin to save them."

"That's true."

"And you? How are you?" Nadia took her daughter's hand. It hung heavy like a small dead animal. She squeezed it anyway. "All I thought about was your safety. Your health. There is nothing worse than being separated from your daughter during war."

"You left."

"So you will too. The lawyer tells me they are finally getting around to the 2008 applicants. It could be any day now. You could be flying out within a month."

"You left me," Larissa repeated.

"Twelve-speed automatic gearbox," Slavik was telling Boris, their heads craned at the departed tank. "It's pretty sweet."

Larissa gestured at Slavik. "He's never coming. His dream is to move here."

Nadia tried to hide her deep pleasure at the news. "That's probably for the best. I mean, look at him. Victory Day, your very own grandfather almost died fighting the Nazis, and all he can think about is his precious gun. He put flowers on Stalin's grave. Is this the man you want to spend your life with?"

Larissa's mouth tightened. "I don't see Borya being any better."

"He is, he is, you just don't know him."

"I could say the same about Slavik."

But wait, this was not at all what she wanted to talk about, although it was worrying how the men were salivating over the tanks on a sacred holiday like this. But the military band was drawing closer, removing any possibility for further conversation. It wasn't the perfect time for Dima, for the possibility of sweet, bespectacled Dima, the affable mechanic with a purchased Ocean Avenue apartment that had risen, he boasted, at least four times in value. He was only looking for a serious woman. "What I want for you is to think about a future. All this is the past."

In Nadia's memory, Larissa's eyes were the color of unblemished sky but in person, now, she saw they were even brighter than that. A crystal touched by the palest of blue.

"Why don't you move so we can see something for a change?" she heard.

"Shut up, he has a rifle," someone else said.

The crowd seemed to contract before Nadia's eyes, and she yanked Larissa backward through a parting to the sidewalk. A man was carrying a little girl in a *Masha and the Bear* hat, her tights speckled with some animated creature Nadia didn't recognize. The girl was waving a flag that said KALASHNIKOV.

She tried to pull her daughter as far away as she could but Larissa stood firm. "You left me. You had a choice and you left me alone here."

Nadia's heart turned to ice. "I left so I could save you."

"You think that's how it felt to me? But something good came out of it. I had to grow up a little without you. I only wish it didn't have to be during a war."

Larissa folded her arms, her scarf dangling loosely about her bare shoulders. Nadia could barely rein in her heart but no words were rising to the surface. According to several of Regina's American parenting tomes, a parent needs to acknowledge a child's feelings, to validate them by listening rather than distracting or redirecting. A part of her knew this was right but her mouth was not obeying. It was simply not translating the complex fusion of her emotions.

"Look, why don't I show you something?" Nadia said at last.

She scrolled down her phone to a picture of Dima. It wasn't his best shot, especially around the mouth and eyes; in fact it gave him the appearance of a squirrel. "Handsome, no?"

"Who's that?" Larissa was trying to get a look in the bright sunlight. Nadia was hoping that she was not disappointed, that she understood that this was what passed for apology. It was the best she could do.

"That's Dima. He's your future. Look at what I did for you."

"I don't understand."

Slavik and Boris were walking toward them, their arms wrapped around each other. Slavik was moving his hips like some kind of Norse god. Nadia was growing impatient. Enough was enough. Larisska had barely thrown a glance at the screen. Instead, she seemed mesmerized by Slavik in his white polo shirt speckled with tiny anchors, the navy collar of his shirt raised to the ears.

"Come," he said, taking Larissa by the hand. How it hurt Nadia's heart to see the way he yanked her toward him and how she teetered for a moment on those unnatural, ridiculous heels.

"Wait," she said. "Don't drag her away like that." She felt capable of slapping him, punching him, or worse. Shooting him. She could picture the target so clearly, the surprise on his face. But she and Boris had no choice but to keep them in the field of vision, to push through the obstacle course of the parade. From time to time, Slavik swiveled and reminded them to get their cameras ready.

Helicopters were flying overhead, the music was deafening. Kronstadt Sea Cadet Corps was announced on a loudspeaker that seemed to be attached to Nadia's head. "Over here," Boris said. He was holding on to her arm too tightly, and she sensed he was as uncomfortable here as she, and that his bonding with Slavik had all been an act for her benefit. She squeezed him back, a grateful grasp of the flesh. But it was imperative to not lose sight of her daughter and the *entrepreneur*.

"Wait, Slavik, let her go. I said, let her go!" There was still time for her to say it. But what was it she was going to say?

They were emptied out of one horde only to be plunged into a circle of people standing around an elevated platform. She could see more Kalashnikov flags glimmering white.

"Slavik, don't touch my daughter." She had managed to snatch a piece of Larissa's striped dress in her hand and then it slipped away. No, that wasn't it, exactly. She made a lunge for it again and this time held on to the fabric. Slavik was looking up at her, amused.

"Your mama wants to go, let's give her the first shot," she heard him say. He murmured some words to muscled men in tight T-shirts. She and Larisska were being shoved toward the stage, ahead of an unhappy line. "Why are they getting to go ahead of us? We've been waiting for half an hour."

A rifle was handed to her. It was heavy and smooth and it fit perfectly in her hands. A male arm was hoisting her onto a platform in front of a white background that said KALASHNIKOV. Someone handed her daughter a rifle too. From this vantage point, she could finally see some of the parade. Rows of soldiers in perfect formation, red sashes draped across their chests, holding flags representing the fighters from all the Soviet republics: BELORUSSIAN FRONT, she made out. UKRAINIAN FRONT.

An impatient voice behind the camera brought her back to attention. "A lot of people waiting. Let's go, let's go. Beautiful mama and daughter. Pose sexy-style, like James Bond girls."

The crowd was too thick with anonymous male heads, none of them paying her any attention. She and Larissa posed back to back, one hand on the barrel, the other on the trigger. The photographer was saying to her, "Hey, *mamasha*! It wouldn't kill you to smile."

9

The Center of the Forest

They could ask only girls, but that would discriminate against an entire gender. Regina didn't want the boys to feel left out. So it was decided that even though they could not really afford it, the entire class would have to be invited.

Worries Regina voiced to Nadia in the days leading up to the party: should they send a breezy email or mail cards with a picture of Sasha with a giant quill: *Zdravsvuyte! Best-selling author Sasha McLain invites you to the "Russian Tales Around the Campfire" party at Magic Destinations on Atlantic Avenue.* Or should they perhaps reverse course and stick to the "invite the same amount of guests as the age of the birthday girl" practice, which meant just five girls? Should they encourage parents to mingle or make drop-offs? Would the kids know Sasha well enough to come so early in the school year? Regina's anguish was so raw that Nadia's heart went out to the poor thing.

"Don't worry so much," she advised Regina. "Just stick with something simple. The kids need so little."

Regina would quickly agree, "You're right, of course," but then invariably return to her original worries. Of course she wanted simple in theory, but Nadia didn't comprehend what was at stake. These parties were judged on every level. By the school, and by Sasha and the memories she would harbor for the rest of her life. They would also be dissected by the mothers who held decision-making power on important school-policy matters that would impact their lives for the next eight years. The bar was already set high by the few other birthday parties held in the first two months of school: an Alice in Wonderland party, the 1950s bobby socks party, the party on the actual Nickelodeon set. Those parties were imprinted in Regina's mind, parsed for individual details she could tweak for her own.

Nadia gave up voicing opinions after a while. What could she feel but tenderness for a woman who treated a child's birthday party with this much gravitas? Regina had recently chopped her long hair into a bob with cropped bangs, which gave her the appearance of an oversized child, and Nadia was always tempted to smooth the bangs away from her forehead with a long-nailed finger.

"While Sasha's watching the movie, let's get to work on the gift bags, okay?" Regina said.

"Sure," she gamely agreed.

Gift bags? She'd never heard of such a thing. But here she was at a table laden with red paper bags, shoving tiny Russian-language books, color crayons, beaded bracelets, sidewalk chalk, and marshmallows the size of teeth inside them. One would think the party was for an important dignitary or poet.

Each gift bag was to be attached to a stick, which seemed like a bad idea to hand over to kids, especially the boys. "Camping," Regina explained. "Don't forget that's the setting. But it's more than that. The theme will be 'Russian Fairy Tales Around the Campfire,' which means the kids will collaborate on a giant story, then we get those copied and bound. It will have a cute Russian flair. And we send it to each child as a thank-you card. Original, no?"

Nadia knew novels had themes, movies had themes. She didn't know birthday parties for children had them. "Sounds interesting. And perfect since you're a writer."

"Exactly. And Sasha loves to make up stories. You've seen how she does it."

Was that actually true? To Nadia's eye, Sasha's favorite activities of late were extorting chocolates from weak adults or patiently beading miniature necklaces for her dolls. "She has such an imagination," she said, which fell into the realm of truth.

They worked side by side stuffing tiny plastics into bags and Nadia wondered if Larissa and Slavik were still together. She had been afraid to broach the topic of him over Skype. Their truce felt still too recent to risk straining.

"Nadia, would you mind? I'll need all the hands . . . how do you say . . . help during the party. Would you mind arranging so you could be there?" Regina approached the request with her usual timidity.

Normally she would mind. To switch her hours would be an enormous ordeal. No one wanted Saturdays and the new babushka assigned to Nadia was famous among the VIP attendants for her vitriol. No one could finesse her or quash her fears of being robbed except for Nadia. But this was Regina asking for help, and she needed Nadia.

"Of course Nadia will be there," Sasha said. She ambled over from the program she was watching, with pink winged horses flapping around rainbows, and eyed the progress on the gift bags. Her body was thinning out, stretching like soft clay. Her face was losing its spongy airiness, skin draping over her bones like a skyscraper in progress. She was getting to be of an age where local oldsters on the street were gallantly calling her "beautiful" and "young lady." It felt all too soon to Nadia, too sudden.

"We'll make s'mores, right, Mama?"

"Um, I don't know."

"S'mores. This doesn't sound too Russian-themed." Nadia had no idea what this was, except it was Sasha's most pressing desire and what could be more infectious than a child's anticipation of treats?

"But they're only for children," Sasha reprimanded them. "Not for grown-ups. This is a children's party and grown-ups should keep to themselves. There will be none for you."

"Sasha, that's not a nice thing to say!" Regina said. Then she explained, "If the kids had to eat an actual Russian dessert, there would probably be a mass rebellion on our hands."

Nadia liked Russian desserts, especially the layered cakes with meringue on top. She also liked the sweet ricotta balls covered in chocolate. But she had long lost the sense of the original conflict. Girls or boys? Theme or no theme? Sasha was safe and happy and loved. Why was this not enough here?

On Atlantic Avenue, they unloaded wooden sticks, candy, fruit, jugs of lemonade onto the windswept sidewalk. A striking black woman with long straight hair and thin legs in minuscule lace-fringed shorts greeted them outside the storefront and held the door open as they made multiple trips with the plastic bags. The interior was nothing more than a bare white cube with a door. Regina had complained that the place was almost prohibitively, expensive. Kids were carefully added and culled because of the confines of this space.

"This is it?" she couldn't help asking. In these cases, when you didn't want to be understood, speaking a foreign language was a godsend. "I expected something fancier."

"You'll see," Regina said sideways. "It's going to be amazing. She used to work lighting on Broadway shows."

The woman flicked a switch near the entrance and an image of a dense forest was projected on all four walls. They heard the ambient sounds of distant water flowing and the incessant chirp of crickets and the crunch of leaves underfoot. Light could be adjusted from day to night, the woman explained, the sounds changing accordingly. To illustrate the whole scope of possibilities, the woman kept on clicking through purple palaces and underwater seascapes and jungles and outer space, before settling back into the forest, the birds. A deer ran across the walls, hind legs shaking.

"Does this remind you of Russia?" The owner posed some version of this question to Regina.

"Oh yeah, totally. It's like the dacha where I spent summers with my grandparents. It was such a magical place." It was the first time Nadia heard Regina talk about her Russian childhood. The woman was either fascinated by this information or politely asking follow-up questions. What was a dacha like? Was she fluent in Russian then? What did she remember about the Soviet Union?

"Pretty neat, don't you think, Nadia?" Regina beamed when the lady went to test the lighting in the projection. "The place just opened. Ours will be the first party here."

It was all rather unsettling, Regina's Russian nostalgia, the white cube, the forest, the sky projected on the ceiling. As a child, she had spent entire days wandering a real forest whose edges brushed against the back of her apartment building. The memory should have been a happy one, but now it scraped at her.

Sasha was pointing to the bag of marshmallows, perhaps wondering how they were to be charred, to be transformed into the so-called s'mores. They set about unpacking the treats, setting up the play stations according to Regina's intentions. The night option was still and lovely, the ceiling purple with stars. In daytime mode, the birds were deafening, the volume of them exploding between Nadia's eardrums.

In reality, she didn't remember any birds. To her, the Rubizhne woods during mushroom season was blessed silence. There was only the swish of the wicker basket against the curve of your skirt. The smell of earth and wet soil, and of course, the mushrooms themselves, meaty and pungent. The reverberations of triumphant voices as a group of them wound about the speckled necks of birch trees.

The game was always the same and it was divine in its simplicity. Whoever gathered the most *opiata* won. The only caveat to these rules was if you found the elusive white mushroom, you won even if you walked away with the pair of them—as they tended to grow in pairs—and nothing else in your basket. She'd stumbled upon the white mushrooms only a handful of times in her life but their charred, sautéed taste was always at the tip of her tongue. It was almost an entire meal, the sheer circumference of the cap larger than both of her hands.

In foraging expeditions, no one worked together. It was crucial that each of them relied on their own wits, that they remained solitary and fanned out. To find the clump of *opiata* required concentration and a sharp eye around the roots of trees. After school, Nadia whittled several perfect sticks with a paring knife, shaped to draw foliage apart.

The local kids knew that there was such a thing as poisonous mushrooms masquerading as *opiata*. But poisonous mushrooms didn't scare Nadia; she could tick off each type in her head.
Only an out-of-towner couldn't see the difference right away;
the imposter mushroom had a thinner stem, was wan in color.
She would never be able to describe what made it wrong except
purely by sight and instinct. As a joke, she once placed a poisonous pretender into the basket of one of the local boys, but he got
so angry when he was shaking out his spoils that he hit her shins
with his foot. The pain was so excruciating she didn't try the
trick again.

On the most successful expeditions, they emerged from the
woods with baskets full of them. Then they ran back to their complex where her mother fried them all up with butter and salt and
sometimes onion and they scooped up the sautéed mushrooms
with their fingers. They were so textured, the taste too deep to call
up in her imagination.

When studies ramped up at school and her friends spent
more time with their schoolwork, the groups tended to be younger
kids in the building. They were dull competition, and often
had to be watched so that nobody wandered off or she would
catch hell from their mothers. But once her sister started university, she brought home her new friends, fresh hunters, and
Nadia could surprise them with her prowess. She loved how impressed twenty-year-olds became when a thirteen-year-old beat
them in under an hour. Her basket was almost always the fullest,
because she had patience. She did not get distracted or bored. No
matter what the task, Nadia could see it through. That was her
talent.

+ + +

To her surprise, the arriving kids did not seem awed by their transformed surroundings. They came trudging in with sleeping bags that were immediately dumped by the door. The adults separated themselves into the parents and nannies and they stood against the wall holding plastic cups of seltzer. The fathers drank beer. The owner of the place sprang into action and shepherded the kids toward the fake campfire in the middle of the room, rushed to disperse them among organized activities. She forgot about Sasha, who was sitting by herself next to a superimposed picture of a blinking deer.

Nadia rushed over to crouch next to Sasha. "Join party," she encouraged, but the girl's arms were folded. Any perceived slight could tweak her mood these days. The kids were not paying sufficient attention to her, failing to acknowledge her as guest of honor. They were turning to explore the surroundings laid out for them, the ersatz campfire, the tents, the provisions.

"Smile, say hello to friends," Nadia suggested, even as she knew there was no use. Sasha was even less inclined to smile when the notion was suggested to her. Regina found the characteristic irritating but Nadia admired this about Sasha, that she allowed herself the intractable sense of being right as the injured party. By contrast, Nadia herself had been a pleaser as a child, always assuming any mishap was her fault.

The owner of the place drew Regina closer, their heads bent over a tablet. The time promised on the invitation had barely arrived, but they were both checking their watches, eyeing the door.

The room went dark and the ceiling exploded with stars. One little girl exclaimed, "Ooh," and the rest were temporarily silenced at the surprise of it. The sudden cessation of seeing.

+ + +

There were a few unfamiliar faces on this particular mushroom hunt, two boys and a girl from Olga's university, but they all generously agreed that Nadia was welcome to tag along.

"I'll be quiet, I promise," Nadia yelped. She had been facing one of those endless summer days when friends were indisposed, adults were distracted, and the world was blank of amusement.

"Are you sure we want her underfoot?" Olga sighed to no one and everyone. "She doesn't mind hanging out at home." Nadia's presence was an inconvenient grievance for her, and their mother's insistence that she include her little sister if she lacked playmates only deepened the injustice.

"You don't have to do a thing. I'll explain to everyone how to find them." She dispersed the baskets and walking sticks to all four of them, eager to be seen as unobtrusively helpful.

The two boys admitted they had never gone mushroom hunting before. "I grew up in the city, what do you expect?" one of them said as a basket was handed to him. His name was Andrei, the same name as the father she never knew, the father who died of lung cancer when she was a few months old. To Nadia, the upper body of this Andrei was disproportionately larger than his legs, but she could tell that her sister's and friend's energies were focused on him to the exclusion of the other boy. His face was squinty with an abundance of hair in the front and thick, puckish lips.

"It's not that hard. Avoid the red one with the dots. You'll be fine," Olga said in a way that exuded indifference that Nadia knew to be artificial.

Olga was wearing the strawberry-red dress, the one worn only to special outings like birthday parties. It was a deep, shiny material their mother procured from a woman who returned from a business trip to Finland. In the right light, the color popped along the prism, turning pink and fuschia and magenta, and all her friends—forced to work with the same dreary material available in the state stores—envied her for it.

With scissors and a needle, next to magazines open to models wearing similar styles, her mother constructed that dress for Olga. From the odds and ends of what remained, she presented Nadia with a pair of underwear she was too afraid to wear and ruin. In the dress, Olga looked like a masculine Marilyn Monroe, her wavy wood-colored hair curling under a wide boatneck that only accentuated the muscular width of her upper body. It was not a dress for the woods to Nadia's eye but she decided that she would go ahead and wear her underwear too. Why should her underwear be stowed for special occasions when Olga put on her special dress for no good reason?

"You can't miss the red *mukhamor*," she clarified in case Andrei thought her sister as unwelcoming as she did. "Whatever you do, don't touch it."

"Don't touch the one with the dots," not-Andrei repeated. He was sitting on the couch with his legs spread wide, his jeans an unfashionably light blue streaked with white that rode too high on his hips. Nadia sympathized with this not-Andrei, with his tuft of hair above his lips, eyes slightly crooked over a too-small nose. She tried to signal this by leaving the best stick, the stick she usually employed, for him.

"If you get sick we'll make you drink water and stick a finger down your throat." Olga directed this solely to Andrei, who was leaning against the wall with crossed arms. She walked back and forth in front of him with no clear purpose.

"That doesn't sound as disgusting as it should. I wouldn't mind your finger down my throat," Andrei said.

For a while, they were all forced to watch Olga aligning her hair in the mirror, checking the boundaries of her lipstick. "You're ridiculous," she tossed back at him.

"Am I?" he asked, in a weird way of not being a question. The friend and not-Andrei sat at opposite ends of the couch. When it was time to go, they rose and filed out, one behind the other.

The woods began behind the apartment complex, at the end of a path that led from the playground. Despite it being a warm day, there was just a handful of children pushing one another on the rusted swings. Some were in crocheted hats, pulling themselves along the horizontal bars even though the equipment was long ago made crooked, one leg buried in the grass.

They set out on the path for the woods, Olga and Andrei in the front and the other, lesser couple, Nadia guessed, following behind. From her view at the very rear, Nadia watched the bodies sway toward and away from each other. The second boy, the not-Andrei, seemed to say something unpleasant because after a while Olga's friend abandoned her walking partner and joined the couple at the front. Their formation resembled a kite, clustered with color at the front, a long, lonely string trailing behind.

They were walking too slowly, with not enough passion for the hunt. Nadia was growing impatient. These grown-ups didn't have a chance against her. She knew every inch of the woods here, every brook and branch. By the time they approached the task at hand with any serious attention, her basket would already be full with *opiata*. Maybe she would even glimpse the thick stem and cap of the white mushroom, the rarest and most desirable of them all.

As the birthday party started in earnest, circumscribed factions were forming: at the periphery, the nannies; by the table of food, the parents with siblings; and in the center, the kids. The kids were not allowed to fend for themselves for a minute, Nadia noticed. They were being guided with meticulous detail through one activity after the next. Marshmallow decorating was followed by some complicated woodsy craft project abandoned by half the boys in favor of flattening the tents with their feet. A man dressed in a bear suit sent them into peals of frightened screams: Russian bear! A hopping race inside sleeping bags made at least two girls fall over and cry. Sasha refused to take part in any game where she was not the player of honor, but she recovered when the cake arrived and when they all turned their faces toward her to sing "Happy Birthday."

Next to Nadia, the nannies talked easily with one another, a few of them greeting her with a friendly nod before diving back into some subject of mutual interest. The mothers were making a show of easy camaraderie, some rocking babies in pouches as they stood, others unwinding the arms of toddlers from around their calves. Nadia watched Regina among these women. She had no other children to occupy her and she was making an effort at circulating among all the mothers, touching them on the shoulder as she wove. They were asking her something about the crazy candidate running for the American presidency and his love for Putin. What did she think about that? Nadia couldn't hear the answer, but the mothers nodded over their plates of pizza as if Regina was a special authority on the subject.

At home, Regina seemed to her nothing less than fully American, and yet here, among these smiling, sophisticated women, Nadia understood for the first time that Regina was no native, no insider. Among them, she stuck out, her body tensed, her clothes matched too intentionally by color. The way she was unable to keep still, her own smile more strained at its edges. The other women occupied the space with effortlessness, in roomy shifts and open-toed wedge shoes and long, exposed necks. Even the velvet dress that had seemed so stylish to Nadia earlier that morning now appeared too dressy, inappropriate compared to what the others wore.

The owner of the space clapped her hands. "At last, storytime, storytime." The children were hustled into a circle and the lights were dimmed. Nadia knew that this was Regina's proudest moment, her own personal stamp on the party. She rose before them like a professor at a podium and explained (presumably) that each of the kids were to provide a sentence toward a fairy tale. Then the Russian-themed story would be illustrated by Sasha, and each child would receive a copy as a gift for attending the party. Regina was very excited about this idea. It would be a group story, an insight into the minds of children at a particular point in their lives.

Even a year ago, Nadia would have thought it all the usual Regina lunacy—just let the kids run around and stop torturing them with silly adult activities—but this time, she paused. She could tell that her brain was shifting in its thinking since talking to Larissa last week. She was starting to change, to snap into a new perspective. Maybe Regina was right, and this activity would be cherished, remembered.

Last week, over Skype, Larissa happened to say that some journalist had approached her about telling her story of living through the war. She had her doubts at first, but the journalist promised it would be published in an American newspaper or magazine with her picture to accompany the story, and she decided the publicity might be a good thing for someone in her position. More public sympathy might expedite things, right? In any case, they promised to put it in her own words with minimal interference, just an oral history of the experience. She'd always wanted a picture of herself in a newspaper.

"But what's the point?" Nadia asked, anxious that Larissa was putting herself through yet another wave of trauma. "What happened is in the past now. Isn't it better to just look forward to the future? You'll be here soon, just focus on that."

But she went through with it anyway. "You know what, Mama? It wasn't so bad and she was very nice and seemed really sympathetic. I kind of feel better now that it's over. Who knows why? It is out of my head anyway."

Nadia was about to argue that it was the worst idea she'd ever heard. And what if the publicity did more harm than good? But in the same conversation, Larissa had also shyly announced that she decided she would come to New York instead of Cleveland after all. Her voice was softer, more open than it had been in seven years. No explanations were offered and Nadia was too afraid to ask. All she knew was that it was not the time to push back against any of her daughter's ideas.

Nadia said, "Of course, I can see that. It must have been a relief."

Her daughter's face on the screen was blurry—could it have been an entire year since she saw her in Moscow?—but a mother's mind was able to fill in every detail, from moles to misshapen bottom teeth in the front to the almond shape of the eyes.

"I felt a huge weight off. I got it out of me, you know?"

"Where can I read it?"

It was inside some journal called *Atlantic,* and she was able to find it online without too much difficulty. There was Larissa's photograph, taken just days ago. Her face was bare of makeup except for some mascara and she was in the middle of a sentence, her lips forming a perfect, horizontal *O*. Larissa's account was translated with a dictionary over a period of several days, but she was able to read her daughter's words online.

She was afraid to confront the swirling horrors that had agitated inside her own mind. Would her daughter's pain feel cheaper this way, exposed to the world, open to derision or, even worse, pity? But the words were in print, solid and unassailable.

> We wake up at four in the morning to explosions. Once
> the bombing begins, we might as well get up and start
> the day. The windows, fortified by tape, are rattling
> with enough force to shatter into a million pieces.

To her surprise, her daughter's ordeal felt even more true for being written down.

"And then she pooped in her pants," a redheaded boy proudly announced.

"And she peed in the sink," his friend said, picking up the thread.

"She pooped and peed in her bed," a pigtailed girl added.

A woman looked toward Regina. Would she let this continue? Regina intervened. "Let's take the game seriously, guys." She crawled among the children and tried to pick up the original line of the story. "Once upon a time a little Russian princess named Masha found herself in the middle of the dark, dark woods, and . . . what happened next, Skylar?"

One father made some joke that involved the words "chill" and "drink." The parents were watching Regina's hard work on the floor with a mixture of sympathy and commiseration. Some were squinting at their watches in the dim light, deciding on a second beer.

"She pooped and farted?" Skylar said.

"No, let's play seriously," Regina insisted. "Let's see if we can tell a whole story together. Then I write it down and we have a whole book. A book with your words, imagine that! For you to keep forever and ever. So here we are in the woods, and poor Masha is all alone. This is a dangerous situation. What happened next?"

"She runs," says a girl with pigtails and glasses rimmed with bright pink plastic. Nadia couldn't understand the rest.

She could hear their voices echoing through the rustle of the trees. Once in a while, Olga or her girlfriend called out, "Found one!" "Hooray!" But those feeble pronouncements were nothing compared with the frequency and vigor of her own victories: "Got four." "Found them." *"Opiata!"*

They would give up soon on a hot day like this. The region wasn't known for hot days and big kids Olga's age were limp in this kind of heat. Like Olga herself, her contemporaries seemed listless and unmotivated, all too interested in school gossip and American movies and American fashion. But not Nadia. She was alert and swift and would earn high marks on a communal farm with her unrelenting, ceaseless production. *Opiata* grew around the stump of a tree and this is where she focused her attention, on trees that had been felled. She didn't hear the boy appear around the fringes of her sightline, but bumped up right against him.

"Hey, kid sister."

"We're not supposed to follow each other," she said, annoyed. "The person in front of you would just get all the goods and there'd be nothing for you."

"Come here." Andrei gestured to her in the friendly way of equals. As though he wanted her diagnosis of a condition or some horticultural expertise. It was annoying the way Olga's friends spoke to her, but then she was the one who gave them the permission by setting the tone.

"You're holding me up."

"It won't take long, I promise."

"We don't have much time, you know. We have to take advantage of daytime." But her basket was almost full, *opiata* brimming out of the sides. They could be hunting for hours and she would still win. Olga's friends rarely focused on the task at hand, too busy gossiping and dreaming.

"Like I said, it won't take long." The reverberation of echoes made it seem as though her sister was just meters away, as though she would run in, raise a haughty eyebrow, a hand to the hip. How disappointed she would be that Andrei had chosen Nadia's company. Her familiar grating voice was loose and distant, beyond the shadows of leaves, the sound of scattering animals across tree branches.

Poor Masha the princess was still stuck in the forest. Three wishes had been granted to her by a "fish witch" but now she was paralyzed with indecision. The kids were quickly losing interest even as Regina continued to prompt them, presumably to bring forth the flow of their imaginations. The door swung open and a willowy, handsome man walked in. He seemed unrushed, calm, nattily dressed in tight-fitting slacks, a button-down shirt with his sleeves rolled at the elbows. The only two fathers instantly greeted him, sliding a beer into his hand. Nadia knew this was Jake, but after four years of working for the family, she had met him just a handful of times. Regina attributed his absence to his demanding job, she described his employer as akin to Google and Facebook, but a company that did something with dogs and healthy meals. It entailed trips to Berlin and London and marked the apartment with the heaviness of his recent presence.

"For God's sake, save your wife. She's going down in flames out there," one of the men said to Jake, and he followed the gaze to the middle of the campfire, the children breaking out of the circle and Regina pulling several of them back to their spots.

Jake took a swig of beer. He belonged here more credibly than Regina even if he barely inserted himself into the trenches of neighborhood parenting. It was just that he sank in among the others, his appearance allied with theirs. He scanned the room and his eyes landed on Nadia. For some reason, her heart pounded so loudly, she could feel it thrashing about in her chest. It was a sensation separate from Boris and his benign gaze, a recipient of someone appraising you from all angles. She was glad he had ceded the apartment to the women, that she was never forced into awkward exchanges with him at the end of a long day of nannying.

He smiled and gave a little shake of the head, a recognition or greeting. He walked over to Nadia, pronounced a stream of English-language sentences at her. In the light, his face was nothing more than lines depicting a spherical shape. But he smelled of salt and his neck pulsed and the black chasm of his mouth opened and closed.

"Come here," the boy said, leading her away from the ideal moistness where mushrooms grew. No one had ever held her hand, except for Yulia and another girlfriend or two, so the sensation of being pulled along aroused an unfamiliar passivity. The woods around her were turning strange, all the familiar landmarks curling and shrinking and changing shape. There was only the feel of his hand wholly covering hers, leading her with firm resolve.

Of course there were many hints scattered about her childhood that some trajectory or another would eventually lead her to this particular terrain. She felt a vague haze around the fact that it had come so early in the guise of this schoolmate of Olga's. They walked out of the open space through which light shone into a path where the trees grew thick and firs clumped together against the sky.

"Let me just see something for a moment." He disengaged her basket from her grip and set it on the ground. Next to it, he placed his own. His was empty. He pulled down her skirt and underwear. It was an act of nonchalance, almost mimicking her grandmother yanking her out of wet clothes for fear of catching cold. Her underthings were folded on the flat stump of a tree. He did the same with his own pants and white underwear, briskly efficient. Then he stuck several fingers all the way inside her until pain scissored her vulva. Everything he did with nonchalance, thrust her thighs aside with his knees, balanced his heavy body on top of her ribs. Then with a series of short, stabbing motions, digging inside her. His eyes focused on the patch of grass chafing her cheek, his nostrils flaring soundlessly. She held her breath, took in some air, then held her breath some more, waiting for the hot ache to lessen. It didn't. After a while, he exhaled and peeled himself out of her.

Later, she thought that there must have been a basic truth lurking in her upbringing that encouraged her to obey his instructions without question. To lie shivering on top of a veiny root, curiously observe the descent of swallows overhead. But no other option was presented to her and nothing about the eventual act surprised her. If anything, a part of her felt he had earned it, that it was owed him. He had been temporarily rejected by Olga, and in her heart she knew that the egos of men must not be damaged in any way. Where else could the poor guy turn? What other path was open to him? She was sure this happened to all girls, a normal turn into adulthood, as necessary as vaccination. Hers just happened to take place here, in the forest, mushroom-hunting.

The entire region below her belly throbbed and stung. She was afraid to actually look at the blood crusting her leg or even gingerly feel the damage with her fingers. As she wiped herself with a leaf, pulled on her underwear and skirt, she noticed the telltale thick stem of the rare white mushroom. Pushing aside some mossy undergrowth, she spotted its twin; you'd expect to see them in pairs. It was the first sighting of the entire summer.

"Thank you," he said formally, with an awkward little bow, once he was dressed. "So I guess I'll go find the others."

"Wait." She reached for the two mushrooms—even now, the sight of them gave her so much pleasure, an automatic reaction to the miracle of locating one—and placed them in his basket.

"You'll impress them if you return with these."

The two points at each temple were still red, a bead of perspiration where his moustache should have flourished. "That's great of you, kid."

She heard his whistle, then her sister bellowing, "Oh Andryusha, where are you already?"

"See you back at your mother's." He sauntered away, in no great rush. With light, almost contemplative steps.

But she found she could not make her way back home. She stood planted to the spot, the very trees holding her from movement as if to say, *Not yet*. Her jaw buzzed. Why on earth had she given away those precious white mushrooms? Now he would claim the credit for finding them when the mushrooms belonged to her. She replayed the scene in her mind until it morphed, reshaped according to her will. In her new version, she gave him an identical poisonous mushroom and he ate it right in front of her.

"Thanks, kid," he said. He would eat and eat until that easy grin of his froze. His eyes protruded, and he clutched his neck with both hands. His face grew purple and engorged. He fell to the ground convulsing. Oh, what a terrible and endless death it was, a whole body disintegrating before her eyes. But she didn't move, didn't even attempt to call for help. Just watched him writhe with excruciating pain. Watched him peel apart into bloody shreds. Why, oh why, had she given away those mushrooms?

Evening fell and adult voices were calling her name. It was only when her mother's panicked echoes wound their way through the trees that she remembered where she stood.

"I'm here, I'm fine, I fell asleep," she whispered, her voice finally growing louder. "This way!"

"Thank you," Jake was saying, presumably about the quality of her work or her care of Sasha all those years. She was nodding furiously with that dopey I-can't-understand-you smile.

"I congratulate you. On Sasha's birthday," she offered when the precise words were located.

Behind him, she noted that Regina was not allowing the children to reject her activity. She continued to press crayons into hands—if they illustrated first, maybe the narrative would explode out of them, was probably her thinking. A few of the children were openly rebelling, busy decimating unopened bags of marshmallows. A stick fight broke out, the mothers involving themselves in a separation. More than one girl was sobbing. Out of character, probably out of contrarian perversity, Sasha was the only one following instructions.

Regina's panic at the unfurling disaster was transparent. Yet another birthday party devolving into chaos, another typical and unoriginal celebration. Nadia understood that immigrating from Russia was Regina's unique story. It was the bright color she had splashed her life with, and it was imperative that she transfer the shreds of its uniqueness onto Sasha. But this color was being muted right in front of her by all these indifferent kids and their impatient caregivers. They were all trying to differentiate their own kids as rare beings, to set them apart with their own sparkling stories.

Someone was tinkering with the wall switch and the forest was giving way to a princess palace, voluminous with unicorns and purple tiaras.

"No," the boys protested. The images kept changing, desert to outer space to savannah, none of them seemingly meeting expectations.

The nanny next to Nadia was pulling her charge out of the fray, hoisting her into an uncomfortable snowsuit and buckling her into a stroller (a six-year-old in a stroller!). Nadia wished Jake would rescue the party by reminding Regina that it was better to let the children entertain themselves however they wanted. But he was observing as though one of the guests, just drinking that beer and grinning as if he did not know the frenzied state of his wife's mind.

For God's sake, she would do it herself then, march up to Regina and pull her aside, *Leave them alone!* Nadia was on the balls of her feet, ready to push past the ineffectual Jake. Why couldn't Regina stop herself, pull back from all that control, stop caring what others thought? Why couldn't she apply a little perspective?

Of course, Nadia didn't move. They were all watching, weren't they? The mothers, the fathers, the neighbors, the nannies. Here the community was always on alert, waiting for any little infraction, any crossing of the line between adult and child, boss and employee. Interfering would not help Regina with the women she was trying to impress, the self-selected gatekeepers that forbade entry into a private coven of mothers. Their faces were hard at the unruly happiness of their offspring.

The wall once again took on the image of the forest, awash with the sound of artificial wind and birds, the empty rustle of projected trees. Parents were grabbing their children by the elbows, maneuvering coats, scarves, amidst the screams of siblings. They were reprimanding them all the way toward the exit, but Regina continued to stand alone in the center of the forest with an eager, vulnerable smile: *Come back. Tell me more. Don't be afraid. I'll write it down.*

10

Poppies for the Living

✳ **Ukraine, 2008**

On the riverbank, she watched maidens in white dresses putting the finishing touches on their wreaths. They flitted across the moonlight, light as water nymphs, helping one another hang ribbons and plait hair. Larissa was flitting around everyone in an ornate traditional peasant dress, but Nadia pretended she was not paying special attention to the emotional tremors of her daughter, that she was here like everyone else in Rubizhne, enjoying the holiday.

It was Ivan Kupala, a festival brimming over with too much ripeness. It celebrated the peak of summer, and by some inevitable default, the height of a woman's desirability. Girls lost their minds over these silly pagan rituals and it looked like Larisska was one of them. It was just a week after her twenty-first birthday and Nadia had never seen her daughter so frenzied, yanking her friends toward the bonfires, holding her red-and-white wreath in place with one hand. She had recently gained a little weight and the roundness in her face lent her a fresh spark of health. The dress she had embroidered herself, hunched over it night after night, going over it with complicated cross-stitching.

"Please," Nadia prayed, "let the wreath float directly to him." Or sometimes she rephrased the wish. Let him pluck her wreath out of the water with intent.

Who knew that her daughter's entire happiness, the alleviation of her own guilt, rested in the nimble fingers of one Sergei Zagdansky? From the looks of him, he did not seem up to the task of shouldering so much intergenerational hope. His two front teeth were spread apart like curtains, his hair spiky and bleached blond, a shadow of moustache smeared across his upper lip. A cross was dangling over his Nike T-shirt. He was wearing a tight black swimming suit with a white heart stamped across his upper thigh. It was not at all clear that he was romantically interested in her daughter. In fact, he appeared to be flirting with one of the other girls, one who looked eerily like a young Yulia Tymoshenko, with a white-blond braid woven around the top of her head. But then all the girls looked like the prime minister tonight on the Day of Ivan Kupala. A holiday brought back from Ukraine's pagan past to make them all feel Ukrainian again.

Catch the goddamned wreath, kid. She almost said the words aloud.

"Did you say something, dear one?" Her own date was Pyotor, the widower next door, with whom she had pleasant sex a few Saturdays a month. A longtime coal worker, he was retired with a pension at fifty. He had droopy eyes and a practical hoarder's sensibility. Once, under his bed, she spied a dizzying number of food shopping bags, and another time, an outrageous amount of salt shakers in his kitchen cabinet. When he got drunk, he tended to proudly announce that he belonged to the fourteen percent minority of Donetsk residents who did not vote for Ukrainian independence in 1991.

No one blamed him for his eccentricities because his wife hung herself eight years ago. They were all shocked, of course, that she left herself so flagrantly for Pyotor to find. The women in the building thought it had to do with her temperament and profession—she was a redhead and a regional actress—who had choreographed it this way for ultimate revenge, the final act of dramatic tragedy. On the day it happened, no one could attest to a scream or any other expression of horror—they pictured him entering the apartment, taking in the sight of her, cutting her down, and making the appropriate phone calls for the funeral. He never once raised the topic but Nadia disagreed with her neighbors' assessment. His grief was drilled deep and compartmentalized for the rest of his life. She and his dead wife did not overlap in his speech, and for that she was grateful.

"Did you say something," he patiently repeated.

"Was I talking out loud? Just a mishmash of silly thoughts."

"How was your weekend in Kiev?"

A crucial part of their love entailed telling each other nothing, asking nothing of each other. "We had a lovely time. Larisska bought a new pair of shoes."

"Well, I'm happy you're back." He had drawn his legs closer to his torso. In his mouth was a reed of wheat. He too was looking at the young ladies, who were giggling in their symbolic preparations. The *vinok* they wore around their scalps were voluminous with flowers. They scattered to the water, thick braids twisted over their heads or draped around a single shoulder. On the other side of the bank, the boys started to gather, to ready themselves for the reception of the wreaths. Larissa and her friend were handing out candles for those who were sticklers for tradition.

Nadia jumped up. "I'm going to help distribute." She crawled over the feet of picnickers, some dressed in regular clothes, others costumed in traditional Ukrainian garb. On one blanket, an accordion was playing, on another, a guitar. Despite herself, she looked for the bulky outline of the *technolog*. She heard he was back in town from Severodonetsk, unemployed from the chemical plant there. Her former coworkers said he had put on a lot of weight, making him almost unrecognizable. She scanned the tired faces of older men. He wasn't here, and that was a relief too. One less complication standing in the way of her escape.

The meals dotting the blankets were modest to say the least. Since the pipe factory closed sixteen years ago, the *technolog* and the rest of them had dispersed to new and part-time and uncertain jobs. After fifteen years of going back and forth to Kharkov, she herself was barely holding on to a bookkeeping position at the city museum, a temporary job given to her because the director was Yulia's sister.

She approached Larissa's circle. Her friend, Galya, handed her a pile of candles, but Larissa held her head low, her *vinok* covering eyes and eyebrows. "I'll do it myself," she said.

"Don't be like this," Nadia whispered. "Tell me what you'd rather I did. Do you want to stay here forever?"

"I said I will do it myself."

Larissa's friends circled her, nudging Nadia out of the circle. It was time! It was midnight! The bonfire was finally ablaze. The wreath encircling the dewy head of the Tymoshenko look-alike was a vibrant mix of purple carnations and green herbs; it could not be confused with Larissa's, which was mainly white and red, dandelions and daisies mixed with red poppies. When Sergei saw them floating toward him, there could be no mistaking his choice. If he would only pick Larissa's. Everyone would "celebrate" their wedding, they would take a cleansing swim at dawn, and Nadia could leave knowing her daughter was absorbed in a relationship, happy. But she was worried, so worried. She could glean no public indication of his interest.

On the count of three, a long row of girls in white robes set their wreaths on the water, pushed, and let go. By the distant orange of the fire, Larissa was chameleoned into the group, plunged into its black hole. It was amazing to Nadia that her daughter could still earnestly believe in these pagan rites. That jumping over a bonfire meant good luck or a sunken wreath meant there would be no wedding or wishes would come true if you discovered a budding fern. Shouldn't magical thinking be eradicated by the time you reached twenty-one years of age? Look around, she wanted to yell at all the girls. Barely any of your parents have a decent job here and you are enacting dreamy, medieval peasant rites!

Still, the wreaths as they dappled on calm waves were a beautiful sight. It was as though they were being pushed along by the current, the drooping branches of sturdy oaks, and the gentle exhale of wind. Nadia watched as twisting forms of woven flax floated toward some unknowable destiny. A few of the *vinok* were illuminated by candlelight, which may have sounded like a good idea in medieval times but was simply impractical; candles could set the wreaths on fire or just fall over and be extinguished.

Pyotor's arms were wrapped around her, the grizzle of his beard chafed against her collarbone. "I think our Larisska might find her husband tonight." He was being particularly cuddly tonight, something she wasn't appreciating at the moment.

"You think?"

"I feel the dark forces working on her behalf."

She turned around to face him. "Why does it have to be a husband? Isn't a boyfriend enough? Or maybe instead of either, she could just concentrate on her studies?"

Pyotor didn't have time to take offense. Tanya, an upstairs

neighbor, a widow who had not succeeded in seducing Pyotor away from his grief, drew him away by the elbow for introductions, and Nadia was left alone to marshal her shawl more tightly about her shoulders. Despite the warm day, she shuddered.

It was the summer solstice, the night of vampires and witches and *rusalkas,* murderous spirits whose existence once terrified her as a child. Her mother would murmur to her at night about women who dragged people below the water's surface, witches who took the guise of normal people but damned you with the evil eye. *Domovoi,* the ghosts of dead people who lived in your house and demanded particular food, order, and respect or they would create domestic havoc. There were barn demons, water demons, flying women who kidnapped you to distant places, carrying you away on their backs. They might be invisible during the day, her mother said, but they were waiting for the setting sun when you were left alone and vulnerable. Didn't she ever read Gogol's "Viy"? If you survived the night, you would often be safe from their magic, so the trick was to make it until the morning, when the evil would be dispelled.

Five years ago, as she turned forty, an age that knew better than to distinguish between good and evil, she started to believe that those unclean forces must have kept many people company as they were making sense of the kind of country they lived in. They kept the storytelling going, providing one vital link to the motherland. And to look around now one would assume that even if they slumbered under communism, these spirits were being summoned back to life. Who knows? Maybe now they had legitimate reasons to haunt and kill, reasons living beings could not possibly understand.

+   +   +

Larissa first mentioned the prospect of Sergei a week ago. They were out in the field gathering the raw materials for the wreath. The field was not abundant, probably already plucked of the best flowers, the local girls having covered the terrain just before they got there. It was their little ritual, the gathering of the daisies and fern, then plaiting them together on an old towel. That this would be the last time until they reenacted the tradition in New York filled Nadia with a sweet ache in her abdomen. It was hard to believe that the two of them would be making wreaths in America in a matter of weeks.

Across the square, the remaining plant was spewing fresh black smoke into the air. The sight of chemical fumes over exquisite fields of flowers was a familiar contrast in their lives but Larissa was particularly occupied that afternoon, her freckled nose pointed at the sun. It was Sergei she would miss when they left, she announced. Almost as much as Galya and the rest of her old girlfriends who were always running in and out of the house in their socks and pleated skirts, dragging her out by her arm to some party or picnic.

"Sergei? Who's that?"

"I wasn't going to tell you. What's the point? We're leaving anyway."

"That's true." She had not been particularly receptive of boy talk, redirecting her daughter to her studies, to more important aspects of the future. "There will be so many boys in America. It's better not to waste your time."

"But he is nice, you'd like him. He seems tough on the outside but he really has the biggest heart."

Larissa returned to the stalks of dandelions, plying their tubes into knots. It only recently emerged that she was a talented embroiderer. All Ukrainian girls mastered embroidery, of course, but

Larissa's work was much more elaborate and sophisticated. In the evenings, she spent hours painstakingly weaving scenes of country life onto canvas. The thread was a very specific Czech variety she ordered from catalogs. Sometimes eyes of peasants or cows would be punctuated by glass beads, sometimes gold metallic thread would emphasize the sun.

Now Nadia could read the torment swishing around her daughter's mind and she wished her own wisdom could be implanted inside her, enough to dull the pain at such a small thing. She turned instead to their upcoming Kiev trip, the medical tests, the embassy forms. When they returned to Rubizhne they would be free to leave. Wasn't that remarkable?

"Excited?"

"Scared," Larissa admitted. "Should have taken English instead of German."

"Who knew our number would ever come up? Eleven years? Forget it, after five years, I gave up hope. Why make you switch languages for something that will never happen?"

Behind Larissa, the chemical plant with its steel grid and yawning exhaust pipes continued propelling its vapor into the clouds. It's funny; all this time and she never stopped to think of the implications of what was being made inside, the industrial explosives, the insides of bullets.

"He's the best in languages. Far smarter than me. He speaks perfect Italian," Larissa said.

"Sergei?" Nadia smiled. How easily youth fell in love. She was passing her daughter the next daisy in the arrangement. "Italian is a beautiful language."

"He knows everything about our politics, medieval history."

"Is that what he's studying?"

"He's going for his specialist's degree but he hasn't ruled out a

master's yet. Their class is working on this ten-volume project,
'Memory Book of Ukraine. Lugansk Region.' After volume two
was published, he was asked to join the project and he was only a
first-year. His research is called 'Relations of the East and the West
of Ukraine: Search for Historical Compromise.' To have your own
chapter is very rare."

"That sounds very impressive," Nadia said. Not to discount
Larissa's enthusiasm, but if only women could be as proud of their
own accomplishments as they were about their men's. "I hope he
hasn't asked you for your hand in marriage just yet. Do you want
me to have a chat with him like I did with that Artem?"

Larissa turned a deep raspberry color.

"Mama, I was thirteen. That was a little different. It's not like
I'm a child anymore." The wreath in her hands was starting to take
shape. Daisies, connoting peace and tenderness, were well represented. A few dandelions were interspersed. They represented innocence. Cornflowers meant modesty. But where were the field
bells, the heathers, the flowers that were about strength, success,
independence? Those were the ones Nadia always gravitated to.
Instead, her daughter wove in a red poppy for a burst of color, a
classic Ukrainian symbol of sorrow.

"You are a child because you are always my child."

"Anyway, I don't think he likes me that way. We're friends."

"That's good." Nadia did not mean to sound relieved. "I mean
there will be so many boys, right?"

Larissa began working on the ribbons, attaching the brown
one, the one of soil, of Ukraine, of nativity, to the center of the
wreath. "But they don't like me. Everyone always thinks of me as
the sick one."

"It's just diabetes, Larissa. Do you know how many people in
the world have it?"

The ribbons were emerging from her daughter's purse at once, yellow for sun, green for youth and beauty, orange for bread, red for truth, purple for wisdom. She sped up the braiding as if she wanted the conversation to end as soon as possible.

"It's hard to feel deprived. I want treats like everyone else. I feel like my whole life is about depriving myself."

"You get a treat every now and then."

"But I want to not think about what I can't have, you know? Tea with sugar, a cookie. Every day I have to stop myself from wanting."

"It's just a daily shot, there's no reason to make it out to be more dramatic than it is. You're not missing much with the baked goods. This is no Paris, you know."

"I haven't had much luck with boys."

"In America, treats will be cheap and plentiful. In America, Olga says you can't tell the sugar-free cookies from regular cookies."

"It's not just the cookies."

Hiding her irritation was proving difficult. Why was her daughter so incessantly negative? Why was she acting like she didn't want to go? "Fine. Let's just not be dramatic, all right?"

Larissa was silent. The chemical plant was puffing with more energy this morning, which was always suspicious. The last time it was this active was after the Orange Revolution when it felt like the country was either finally righting itself from a dangerous fall or some calamity would punish them for insisting on elections that did not tamper with their ballots. Nadia was getting out before the collapse and Larissa would just have to appreciate the decision later.

She noticed her daughter had taken out a blue ribbon and was inserting it with a blade of grass. "What are you doing? That's for orphans."

"I know. It's for my father, whoever he is. There's no ribbon for a parent whose identity I don't know."

So that was her daughter's calm revenge, that was how she punished her mother. "Your father? What father? This is your gratitude for everything I've done for you?"

Nadia rose, flower parts cascading from her lap. From this vantage point, she could see only the top of a head, the center part, a braid. Plaiting ribbons for a cowardly man, a weak man who disappeared as soon as the factory closed. Who never had the courage to say the words—I'm your father. Your daughter is my daughter—even just between them. Every day she bled for her daughter but instead of appreciation, the girl continued to harp on this one insignificant detail.

She chose her words carefully, with ornate spite. "When you get a boyfriend, then talk to me about fathers. Until then, I suggest you try being a little more grateful to the parent who actually raised you."

Before Larissa could lift her stubborn little head in her direction, Nadia stomped away. She was going to halt after a few paces, wait for the teary apology she was sure to receive—her daughter always regretted her outburst right after it tumbled from her mouth. But she found herself continuing to walk to the tram stop, and glimpsing the headlights of a tram, she simply climbed on. She thought she could hear Larissa running behind her, her sandals clopping against the soft soil of the field, calling out, "Mama, stop." But she didn't turn around. Even as the tram pulled away on its track and Nadia kept her eyes directly forward, she couldn't believe that she was capable of abandoning her daughter so deliberately, with this much unyielding force.

But it was within her, and she was.

+ + +

When she was ten or eleven, her daughter liked to play a game of hypotheticals. She would begin with calling forth horrific scenarios and her mother would have to tell her what she would do in those situations. The two of them trapped in a burning building with the exit closed off? Nadia would lower her down an open window with connected bed sheets. They awaken to a man in camouflage pointing a gun at Larissa's face? Nadia would trip him, bind him, knock the gun out of his hand. She and Larissa would run out of the apartment together, hollering for help.

They both enjoyed the game. It gave Nadia pleasure to work through numerous varieties of the same self-sacrificing impulse, where she would beg the intruder, "Spare her. Kill me." Or push Larissa out of harm's way, only to sink into quicksand herself or direct her to "Run, run!" while burning inside the building.

It was a test that escalated, where the stakes grew. Where her mother had to prove herself as protector, one willing to pay the highest cost.

"What if my heart was failing and I needed an emergency transplant?" her daughter would ask at the very end.

But Nadia always produced the right comforting answer. "I would tell the doctors, 'Cut me open right away. Give my baby the heart.'"

The knock on the door came almost immediately after she returned from the field. Making love with your neighbor was inconvenient when you were in need of privacy. Pyotor knew the sound of her approach and departure, the specific tap her shoes made, the timbre of her key scraping in the lock next door to his. He could probably hear her breath between walls, her fights with her mother, her choice of nighttime television programs. She imagined him alone in the apartment, gluing together one of his tiny building replicas, his ear trained to the sounds she made on the other side of the wall.

"You in there?"

"Not now, Pet'ka."

His voice was floating out of the keyhole. "Your mother is out, no? Your daughter?"

She was agitated, butterflies flapping in her chest. "This is not a good time anyway. I'm waiting for Larissa to come home." Men. Men were so insignificant, why did they have to play such outsized roles in their lives?

"But you're leaving tomorrow. Just five minutes. I can finish in five minutes."

She should tell him she was emigrating and be done with it. Who could tolerate this blubbering? But she remembered his wife, the cheesecakes she used to bring over on holidays, how she would watch Larissa after school when she was running late from work. The way he found this wife dead on a normal weekday evening, swinging from the light fixture.

"I said not now!"

"What is the matter, Nadyen'ka? Why is it so hard to get a minute with you?"

She kept the door closed and conducted the exchange through wood. "It's not hard to get a minute with me. This is not a good time, can you understand that? To have two people want to come together at the exact same time does not happen in every single instance."

"But can it happen a little more often?" was the reply.

"Don't you understand? There are extenuating circumstances right now. I need to be alone."

"Excuse me, Pyotor Ihorovich," she heard. It was Larissa, and the door swung open, and they were plunged in each other's arms, fused cheek to cheek, crying their apologies. The identity of her father didn't matter, Larissa said between breaths, and Nadia assured her daughter that she knew how her daughter suffered with diabetes and how hard it must be and she would find her the best sugar-free treats so she wouldn't even notice the difference.

And Pyotor was watching the whole open-door exchange with a bewildered expression, too hapless to leave them alone to it.

"I'll come over later," she said, shooing him away. She would give him his five minutes, she thought, feeling generous now toward a man who would soon be consigned to her past.

Pyotor was famous in the building for his postretirement hobby, a painstaking miniature replica of their entire city using matchsticks, cardboard, gravel, wood, and shreds of wallpaper he peeled off all their walls. No one understood what drove him to do it, what was the point of the exercise. Couldn't he visit the originals outdoors any time he wanted? The chemical factory with its Lenin monument at the entrance, the city museum that took over the kindergarten building, the Afghan war memorial, the Eternal Flame before the mass grave of Soviet soldiers who fought in World War II, the large, concrete Labor Square. All those landmarks were available to anyone in the mood for a stroll.

"Someday the city will be gone," he explained to Nadia when they were preparing for sex later that evening, folding their clothes on the chair, her hose rolled up into a fist, shoes tucked under the bed. "And my creation will live on."

"Why on earth do you think this will survive if the city's destroyed?"

"I will put it somewhere safe. Store it in a bunker."

She turned away from him to unsnap her bra. Forties were no joke; she gained weight if she even conjured a plate of nice, crispy *khrustiki* in her mind. The flesh around her middle seemed to have materialized overnight. She slipped under his duvet cover.

"I had no idea you possessed such an apocalyptic temperament."

"Who doesn't have one these days? You'd be a fool not to."

"Eh, we're always in apocalypse and we always survive."

He ran his hands over her breasts, which was always the initial step of a highly orchestrated process. It took her a few months to feel comfortable with his coal miner's hands, whose history was impossible to cleanse. She murmured her encouragement to move on to the next step.

The replica of the city stood right by the bed, an eerie reproduction complete with the mosaic on the Ukrtelekom building with its tiny sun surrounded by flapping birds. Say what you will, but his hobby and her daughter's embroidery gave them a common interest that smoothed the way to good relations. They would often ask to see each other's work, taking it seriously where others discounted them.

He was kneading her belly, moving in the direction of her pubic hair. For the first time, she noticed that other residential buildings were included in the panorama but not theirs.

"Where's our pile of bricks?" she wondered.

"I will add it when we marry," Pyotor said. It was time for phase two: lightly tickling the walls of her vagina, she would not allow any fingers inside her. "Larissa will marry and you will move in here and the configuration of the entire building will change. Then I will build it."

The tears so recently near the surface threatened to return. She could not afford to think about Pyotor, to weigh Pyotor in a decision she made eleven years ago. She would miss him, the simple limits of his need. She could see their alternate life as a married couple stretching before her, and it looked just fine, time marked by meals and short outings and quiet evenings with tea and cookies by candlelight.

"Maybe I should hold on to a few of your houses," she said, "in case something happens in the apartment. A fire or flood."

"For safekeeping, yes?" He replaced his finger with the sharp push of him.

She sighed. "For memory."

Pyotor wordlessly finished and she exhaled a satisfied hum that was more empathetic than related to any internal state of gratification.

"Thank you," he said, kissing her shoulder.

"Don't thank me, for God's sake. It's nothing."

"Enjoy Kiev. Hope you and Larisska have a nice vacation."

She tiptoed out of his place holding the mass grave of Soviet soldiers, tiny white squares embedded into faux grass. "A promise," Pyotor said, handing it to her with a wink.

The Kiev doctor was younger than she expected, and good-looking. He reminded her of Anatoly Solonitsyn, the actor from that Tarkovsky film *Andrei Rublev*. The same rusty blond hair, sharp jaw, intense light-eyed gaze. He displayed a melancholy cheerfulness as he examined Larissa, encompassing all three of them in the experience. "We look pretty healthy," and "Can we take a very deep inhale?"

Larissa performed accurately, on command, the way she always did in doctors' offices since she was a little girl where she meekly held out her behind to be bruised by the needle. The doctor's blue eyes had flecks of brown around the iris and Larissa was studiously avoiding them.

"Here is her vaccination record," Nadia said, unfolding the paperwork from their regular Rubizhne pediatrician. The doctor looked newly puzzled. When he asked Larissa to come back with him, Nadia naturally followed. When he asked her about her diabetes, it was Nadia who answered. It was the first time it occurred to Nadia that maybe her daughter should be carrying around her own records, that she might have seen the doctor alone, the way others her age probably did. That she was an adult seemed incomprehensible to her, as if her child was nudged into that stage before any of them were ready.

The doctor turned to Nadia. "You brought the tuberculosis test fee for her?"

"Yes, I gave it all to the secretary."

"Then let's get her X-rayed."

They brought her down the hall to a dark room where the technician handed Larissa a plastic blanket to hold over her waist. In all her other X-rays no one handed out any protective equipment, but this was a hospital the United States trusted and it operated on a higher level.

"What is this for?" Larissa asked into the darkness. Some pieces in her voice crumbled in places.

"Quiet." The technician retreated into her booth.

"I'm here, Larisska, don't worry," Nadia said. "I'm right here."

The doctor's voice floated to them out of the black void. It sounded husky, syrupy. "To protect you reproductively. It's just a precaution, so don't worry about that. This is the West for you, it is extra careful. We want you to have many children."

"Quiet." Then there was the click.

"See?" Nadia said. "Nothing to worry about."

"Nothing to worry about," the doctor repeated. He walked them to the exit. "So you're leaving just as the country's applying to join the EU, huh? You might regret it. Things are about to get a lot better around here."

They emerged from the courtyard onto Antonovycha Street. This checkup cost them three hundred, six months of rent. If they didn't pass the medical exams, if even one vaccination was missing, she would have to come up with the money to redo them.

"Let's walk for a while, find a bite to eat," she said. "How stuffy was it in there? I could barely breathe."

"It wasn't so bad."

The workday was concluding, the narrow streets clogged with rushing workers. It didn't help that cars were parked halfway onto the sidewalks, necessitating a weave around their narrow noses. They passed a salon, a bank, a Thai massage parlor, a fur shop, then a bridal store of some sort, THE WEDDING SHOP stenciled in large, English-language letters.

"The doctor was cute, right?" Larissa said.

"Was he? Cuter even than Sergei?"

"Maybe? Sort of?" Larissa smiled, wove a hand around her elbow.

To an outsider, the two of them must have appeared more like two friends than mother and daughter.

At the Kiev ballet that night, the women sat in one long row. Her best friend Yulia, her daughter, herself, and Larissa. They were all acting as if the outing was a normal one rather than a conclusion to something, the last time they would see one another in a long time unless one of them found the funds for the international trip. Nadia could barely concentrate on the ballet. The story was ridiculous and remote from her concerns: a village boy decides to leave his fiancée to marry a beautiful living doll. She kept peeking down the row at the profiles seated next to her. Her best friend with her long downward-sloped nose and high forehead looked visibly older. Her daughter, Ida, with her dramatic long ink-black hair and purple lipstick, and her own Larisska, sitting up straight and wide-eyed, utterly enraptured with the show.

When the fiancée rescued the lover by destroying his beloved doll, Yulia turned to everyone and whispered, "That's what happens when you try to ditch a Ukrainian woman."

During the intermission, Nadia found herself gawking at the ceiling of the opera house, the crystal chandeliers, carved wooden furniture, the marble floors, the sumptuous coat check window. She had forgotten how beautiful the structure was, how grand it made you feel to be inside it. "Look what you'll be missing in America," Yulia said to her, noticing. She pointed at herself. "They don't have old buildings like this in your new country."

Their eyes met. "Are you implying you're the old building?"

"Ha-ha," Yulia said. "In this case, I was actually referring to the building. But what I really can't believe is you are going to the embassy tomorrow. Imagine. By the end of the day, you girls will have everything you need to be out of here. You'll be almost-Americans."

"I'll miss everything about everything," Larisska said.

Nadia knew her daughter was nervous, unsure about the whole thing. Even the tiniest changes in her life would invoke anxiety. "We'll be citizens of the world, won't we, Larisska?"

"Don't be so sentimental. You can help our cause from New York," Ida said, crackling her gum.

It was hard to believe the girl was Larissa's age, they seemed decades apart. In the evenings, she and Yul'ka spent hours comparing their daughters on schoolwork, obedience, boyfriends or lack thereof. Yulia was worried that Ida was always shuffling around in the nighttime. For all she knew, Ida was either selling her body or protesting government corruption in a café around the corner from Maidan square where she and her pierced university friends met every week. During their comparisons, Nadia always pretended to be impressed by Ida's political convictions, protested that Ida was superior to Larissa in every way, but her heart was always suffused with new appreciation for the self-contained person under her own roof. But now that they were leaving, she wondered if there was indeed something glorious about Ida's contribution to Ukraine's change and if Nadia's own urgency to flee contained a bead of cowardice.

"What's wrong with sentimental?" Yulia stuck her tongue out at Ida. "We are best old friends and this one is leaving us."

Ida shrugged. "We could have used Larisska here in Kiev. There's a lot of work to be done."

They heard the raising of voices, an employee of the opera house screaming at one of the visitors on the ground floor, "Are you stupid? Read the rules of attendance. No weapons allowed in the theater."

They leaned over the railing. A man brandishing a gun was standing among a small group of his buddies. He was circling it in the air with wide, jerky motions. "Relax, lady. It's just a tiny rifle. I'm expected at the *komandirovka* later tonight. Do you want to take this up with the Berkut?"

The friends were shielding him with their bodies, amused. On instinct, theatergoers were slowly edging away from the scene, shrinking closer to the outer walls of the theater.

A woman, probably his grandmother's age, did not seem intimidated. "This is a palace of culture, young person, and the rules are very clearly stated. Have your boss call the National Opera of Ukraine and ask for Vira. I'll be happy to set your boss straight."

"I will do that. We'll see how you like getting no pension."

"Please proceed directly to the coat check. No one is afraid of you."

"Is that so? I'll make you afraid of me."

"Calm down, calm down." His friends were leading him outside and down the front steps. "He's had a few. Don't mind him, lady."

The crowd dispersed for them, shaking its collective head. There was a pause, then a debate broke out that neatly divided among gender lines. The guy was headed to work after the ballet, what could he do? The opposing female view argued that he could have left it in the coat check and skipped the entire scene. Nadia realized she had been numb with fear the entire time, the knuckles holding her purse were turning white, opaque. Larissa was breathing hard beside her, chin pressed against her shoulder.

"We're fine," she said with an oddly calm voice. "Right, everyone?"

"Sure, just some loser." Yulia was already flipping through her program. She was pointing out to Ida the biography of the principal dancer. Her exact age, and look what heights she'd climbed, the lead in *Coppélia*!

"She seems very accomplished," Ida said. "Unlike me, right? Isn't that what you and Tyotya Nadia talk about? That I need a real job?"

"That's not at all what I tell Tyotya Nadia."

"Yeah, right."

"Are we fine?" Larissa whispered, uncertain. She held Nadia's hand, tightly squeezing her palm. "You don't think he'll come back?"

"He's gone, don't worry, baby. Of course these uncultured men bring guns to the ballet. A bunch of idiots getting into trouble." She checked her expression and shifted it into a smooth brave mask. *What if I needed a transplant? What if our building was on fire? What would you do?*

"Ida was right. There really is no need to get sentimental. I have no doubt that *this* you will not miss," Yulia said. The lights flashed in warning, and they returned to their seats. "I'm sure Americans are much more civilized at the theater."

An atmosphere of recent drama lingered in the American embassy waiting room the following day. Larissa was long gone by now, the front door banged shut behind. She could still hear her daughter's disbelief vibrating between her ears. You would go without me? The swish of a mop against wet floor, the murmuring exchanges on either side of a window. It was as if everyone was waiting for her to make a choice.

"Do you want to go ahead and put in the application just for you?" the woman behind the grate repeated.

"Yes. I will bring my daughter over as soon as I get there. As soon as my feet land on the ground."

"Of course you will," the young woman said.

"We'll just be separated for a few months. For God's sake, my daughter is twenty-one. She'll be fine."

"I'm sure she will. She's an adult, isn't she. It's time for her to

figure out how to live life on her own. Please hand over the paperwork then."

"What do you do," Nadia said, reaching inside her bag—she
could have pulled out a mattress, a rabbit, a gun, for all she knew—
"when your child becomes an adult?"

After Nadia returned to Yulia's place from the embassy, she found
Larissa gone. She was with Ida, Yulia assured her, the two of them
tiptoeing in at dawn. Pretending to be asleep, she could hear their
voices in the apartment, the confident sounds of youth condescending to mothers who, in their eyes, knew nothing. It was the first
time Larissa was out all night without telling Nadia where she
would be and when she would return. In the white light of morning, Nadia watched her with one open eye moving about the room.
She was undressing for bed, slipping her nightgown over her
head, and collapsing on her pillow. A few hours later, when she
was woken up, makeup was smudged down her cheeks, makeup
she had never worn before. An adult.

"Let's go," Nadia said, wiping her daughter's face. "We have to
catch the train home."

On the ride back, Larissa sat on the opposite corner, tucked herself into a window nook with a paperback. The fields mottled
with dirty animals flashed by, the clouds a blur of elastic white.
The sounds of the rest of the train were sharp and precise, the footsteps and sliding windows, the distant scrape of forks, plates, and
conversation. The train itself hurtling forward, humming method-
ically on its tracks. A few hours in and Nadia noticed Larissa
gulping water, wiping her mouth from the overflow. She sprinted
between her seat and the bathroom a few times.

"What did you drink last night?" Nadia demanded into the

thick silence. "You know you're not supposed to drink sugary drinks. What did you eat?"

"Mama, I'm twenty-one." That chin was held high. It continued to be pointed to the country view, to the haystacks and barns and the metal pyramids of factories.

"That's no excuse." But what was she supposed to say? The woman at the embassy was right, wasn't she? Nadia watched Larissa blinking, all the signs of high blood sugar. But she denied she wasn't feeling well, and would accept nothing from her mother, not even a cup of juice. Nadia unfurled a *Focus* magazine, tried to concentrate on the article "The 100 Most Influential Women in Ukraine."

Suddenly, she felt a hand gripping her arm. Larissa's eyes were glassy, staring at her as if at a stranger. "I will never forgive you, you know."

"What?"

This was not her daughter's voice. "If you leave, I will not forgive you. Do you hear me?"

"This is how you talk to your mother?"

They did not exchange a word for the remainder of the ride, Nadia pretending to be immersed in a list of influential women, Larissa staring out the window. The countryside was slick with rain, a slimy coating of gray and green. When the train pulled up to the station, Larisska grabbed her overnight bag and shoved her way to the exit. To give her space, Nadia took her time gathering empty plastic pouches with cookie crumbs and Orangina bottles. Children! If she wanted to be petulant, Larisska knew her own way home. Nadia felt a deep exhaustion grip her. She thought of what awaited her in the days before leaving by herself. She could hardly think of what would befall her on the other side.

When she descended, a crowd of onlookers were gathered, a

curious concern in their postures, and she knew. Larissa was sprawled on the ground, her skin the white-yellow color of egg-shell. She was shaking, her knees spasming. Her face was contorted at an unnatural angle.

"Someone help her, she's having a seizure," Nadia screamed, elbowing at the crowd to create a wide berth for her. "We need an ambulance. She has diabetes." She whipped her head around, saw someone drinking a Coca-Cola. She grabbed it from his hands and tried to pour it down Larissa's throat. Her daughter's eyes were fluttering, trying to focus on a single spot.

"I'm right here," she kept saying, dribbling the sweet soda inside Larissa's mouth.

It felt as though there were voices offering advice but no one was bending down to help her with the physical work of revival.

"Is someone calling?" she barked.

"If you call them, you better have cash," some useless interloper warned, and indeed when the ambulance arrived, the first thing they asked was, "You got any cash?"

"Yes, yes, some. I can get more." She would call Pyotor for it at the hospital. She would rob a bank, or steal some old lady's purse. She unfolded a few bills in her wallet. "Here's something. Just take her."

One of the women started to protest that it was not enough, not nearly enough.

"I'll get more to you, for God's sake. Have a conscience. My husband will meet me in the hospital."

"Bring cotton, alcohol, syringes, insulin, water, orange juice." Satisfied, they began hauling out the stretcher from the back of the van. They transferred Larissa into its drooping center. An unabashed crowd had formed, openly staring at the attempt to lift a body off the ground.

Nadia was ready to bite their heads off. "What are you looking at? It's just diabetes."

When they took her away on a stretcher, Larissa spoke, weakly. "I didn't drink anything." Her eyes remained closed, her voice dim and faraway. "I didn't eat anything either. But I didn't check it this morning."

"That's okay, everything will be okay. Lay your head back down." She took her baby's hand, but it slid away from her, and in the ambulance, it remained inert by her side. Her teeth were chattering, forehead clammy with perspiration. Nadia kept smoothing her daughter's hair from her face. She did it so repeatedly, her hand tired and the hair was slicked down, oily and flat. There was nothing worse than this helplessness of not being able to will her daughter to recovery. She felt chewed up, desperate, constantly in motion: checking her pulse, applying the back of the hand to her forehead to ascertain heat.

She leaned into her daughter's ear. "I promise you, Larisska. I will bring you over. I swear it on my life. Do you hear me."

Larisska's eyelids fluttered but there was no response. *How could you ever leave me now,* was what Nadia heard in the silence. What kind of mother leaves a daughter in this condition?

"I promise you. You will not be alone here for long. I will move mountains and you will be in America with me within a year. Darling, dearest, baby, your mama's right here. She's always here."

They arrived at the hospital, Nadia carrying one side of the stretcher herself, tossing what remained of her money at anyone who threatened to separate her from her daughter. She continued to hold her hand as the doctor spoke only to Larisska and said it could have been worse but she would have to better monitor her sugar. It was the first time a doctor didn't address directions to Nadia.

Larissa nodded, sipping her juice. Her skin was approaching its normal blanched-almond shade. She was not entirely her old self nor did she give any indication of remembering *I will not forgive you.* Nadia pressed her hand and kissed her. But the person in the bed was someone other.

Pyotor arrived to hand over the materials and the large stack of cash he must have borrowed from neighbors. His eager presence was a relief for once.

"This must be your husband," the doctor said.

And Pyotor smiled in the relieved, slow manner of a child that didn't fully understand that the adults were talking about him but he was sure it fell into the general category of praise.

The wreaths of the women floated across the water, some moving more erratically than others. Once in a while, one of the girls would be forced to wade in to correct the path of a wreath that wandered off into the tendrils of moss. Several sank, which supposedly meant their owner would never marry, and there would be a general drone of disappointment. Nadia lost track of Larissa's wreath as soon as it settled onto the water, but she kept her eye on Larissa. Her daughter in her painstakingly embroidered dress. Her daughter who had not spoken to her normally in the two days since their trip to Kiev. It was like someone was slowly and painstakingly shredding her heart.

What was the Kupala ritual that meant that your daughter was lost to you? That your daughter was no more? Then she remembered. Of course! The bloodred poppy. The flower of death, of sorrow, the flower they embroidered in their lapels to commemorate the dead of World War II. Who knew that poppies were also for the living?

But now the wreaths were reaching their destinations. Sergei wandered into the water up to his knees and he plucked a wreath from the water. She could see him lifting it in the air. She held in her breath.

"Sergei and Larissa," the girls were screaming. "Sergei and Larissa will marry."

Pyotor murmured into her neck, "Well, didn't I tell you?"

"Are you sure it was really hers?"

"That's what they're saying."

"Congratulations, Mama. When's the wedding?" Her neighbor Tanya encompassed her and Pyotor on the slightly astringent question, as if to imply the question of which wedding would be first.

"Oh, go away with you," she said. "No one is in any rush."

She would never see any of these people again. Not Tanya, who once breast-fed Larissa for extra money but lost her husband in a welding accident soon afterward and had been flirting with Pyotor ever since, not Larissa's friends, whose quirks and talents she knew as intimately as that of her own daughter, definitely not Pyotor. People were starting to pick up their blankets and what remained of their food and turn back up the hill to a flat patch of land where their cars were parked. There was a long row of exhausted good-byes. Ivan Kupala was not a government holiday; they all had to get back to work.

Tanya kissed her good-bye. "Do you by any chance have any salt I could borrow for dinner? I'll bring it back as usual."

"Of course," she said, and thought briefly of Pyotor's hidden salt reserves. "Maybe Pyotor can drop it by later."

"That would be great. At least we didn't see any evil spirits tonight, eh?" With a wave, Tanya joined the exodus.

When the first reeds of sunlight appeared on the horizon, the young and old waded into the water for the final purification swim

until all that was visible from the surface were the silver tips of bob-
bing heads. The bonfires were out, the cleansing concluded. Just a
few young people remained, passing between them a clear bottle
of some brown liquor. That gap-toothed Sergei and Larissa were
not among them, but Yulia Tymoshenko sprawled with her friends
along the riverbank like a group of *rusalkas,* their necks gorgeously
limp and stemlike in the porcelain light.

It took every effort to stop scanning the remains of the festivi-
ties for sight of Larissa, to pack herself up. What if her baby never
came home? What if her blood sugar was still not under control
and she suffered another seizure, a more dangerous seizure?
Her baby needed her. Did the promise she made in the ambulance nullify the basic promise of motherhood? She knew that
children struggled with setting boundaries with their parents, but
what boundaries did a mother dare to set? If she went out to find
Larissa, she would never leave here and her daughter would never
leave here. And whom would that help? She needed to open her
fist, let the precious object drop somewhere soft. And go.

Underfoot, there were empty glasses, charred wood, food wrap-
pers, and the remains of trampled wreaths, once-beautiful flowers now stomped into the earth. She rolled all her belongings into
her towel and folded them into the cart. Her daughter would not
be waiting for her at home, that much she had to accept. Her
daughter might even be angry with her for a few days.

But now Pyotor was beside her, one hand swiveled around her
waist, saying, "A surprise, open it," and holding out a perfect little
replica of their high-rise building. He was staring at her in a mean-
ingful way that gave every indication that when she pulled open
the structure, probed deep inside its windowless hallways, she
would find a plain gold ring that once adorned the finger of his
long-dead wife.

11

Give My Baby the Heart

On the morning of Larissa's arrival, Nadia realized she had forgotten the mangoes. All the other preparations were complete. Boris would bring them home from the airport. Larissa's room was all set up, the closet emptied, the walls decorated with her embroideries. Dinner's main dishes would entail a hearty *shchi* with a floating fish head and stuffed cabbage leaves. Olga would be arriving on the 7:49 train to Penn Station. Everything was perfect except for the mangoes.

Even the weather offered no obstacle. It was an unmarred March sky, warm for the season, iridescent with suffused sunlight. Deep in the front courtyard, the pensioners were already spreading out their rainbow chairs and blankets for the day's vigil. The garbage truck had come and gone. The last of the morning traffic was dissipating, chess players having taken their spots at the boards in the concrete square that called itself a park. Nadia felt a diffused panic that something could always go wrong.

The remaining days that had led up to this one were spent checking off a long list of unpleasant tasks. The most urgent one involved breaking the news to Regina that she had finally received The Letter. The one that said words she had fantasized about for almost eight years. Her baby could join her. Oh, that letter. She would always remember first laying eyes on it. She had held it with trembling fingers, run her fingers over the gold-embossed address, then ripped it open. When the words congealed with the help of a dictionary, she had sobbed as though turning inside out, her organs spilling out of her body. Even afterward, the fit would overtake her at unexpected times, a massive need to cry and laugh at once, a panicked heart at what this meant, a feeling that it couldn't possibly be true. She was afraid she could not contain herself and had postponed saying anything to Regina.

When Regina came home in the evening last week and was busy shoving her gym bag into one of the cluttered cubbies, Nadia pulled her aside so Sasha couldn't hear, placed a hand directly on the woman's shoulder. Regina's blue eyes narrowed with wary concern. Was there a problem with Sasha today? No. Did Nadia want a few extra days off? Not exactly. Her eyes were already filling, she could feel her lips losing muscle control.

"What's wrong?" Regina said, worried. Did she need an advance on her salary? But even as Nadia started to speak, to explain that her daughter would finally be crossing the ocean and this would permanently alter her own schedule, she realized that she had waited too long. The message descended on Regina like a stone.

"What does this mean, Nadia?" Regina asked, a wild nest of panic in her eyes.

"I'm afraid I really should stop," Nadia said, knowing she was handling this terribly, that she was handling everything terribly. "I will be busy getting my daughter settled. You barely need me anyway now that Sasha's in kindergarten."

"You mean not work here at all?"

Nadia nodded, her throat pebbled with something she could not swallow.

"No!" Sasha wailed, clearly listening from the other room. It was an explosive outburst, a primal *I will not allow this*. She was still dressed for school, her outfit accessorized by shimmering bracelets and strands of plastic beads. Her eyelashes were flecked with glitter.

Nadia smoothed the girl's hair out of her face. Freckles had bloomed on it almost overnight, sprinkling the nose and cheeks with tiny brown seeds. Tears were dangling off the ledge of her chin. What a gift it had been to experience a reincarnation of her daughter's youth, to watch this girl flourish while Larisska's ragged childhood had been glimpsed in snatched hours. She bent down. "But Sashenka, you don't need me anymore. You're a big girl who goes to big-girl school."

"I'm not a big girl. I'm still a baby." And Sasha's words could have come out of her mother's mouth as well, because Regina was stricken with a kind of bewildered expression, as if she didn't know where to turn, who would be responsible for telling her what to do. She had a mislaid, unprotected look. Everyone needed a mother, it seemed. She drew them both close into her chest.

"Oh Nadia, I had no idea," Regina despaired, her hands nervously twisting the hem of her cotton T-shirt. "Why don't you tell me anything? A little warning would have helped."

And her own heart was contracting too because as much as she hated the hour-long commute from her Brooklyn to this Brooklyn, the hot days in the too small, unbearably overcrowded playground where at least a handful of kids were declining into screeching meltdown, the long stretches of tedium, she felt as ensconced in this particular home as she ever felt in this country. Even as she told them their lives were about to change, she absorbed all the details she would never see again. The brown, peeling cabinets in the kitchen, the hole in the screen made by a hungry squirrel who made off with a wedge of baguette. The blackout curtains she sewed together, the stickers affixed to the wall of the animals and their initial letters, the plastic drawers that held Sasha's clothes, and how she would refold them each time she came, the little socks, the many adorable pink dresses, the taffeta of the princess outfits. Sasha's nail clippings in the garbage because the girl would allow only Nadia to clip her toenails. On the wall hung a Winnie the Pooh frame she bought on Neptune Avenue, with Sasha at her different ages, the soft pudge of her flesh melting to lean angles. "What'll we do without you?"

"It's not like I live in another state. I live right here in Brooklyn." But they all knew that her Brooklyn was another state, another universe, and only the portal of labor brought the two worlds together. Once there was no pretext of work, she would vanish from their lives like a plume of smoke.

They made a compromise. She would continue, and bring Larissa if necessary, until they found a replacement they liked. "Yes, yes," she agreed.

But that was behind her now and she had been waiting for this one day. The refrigerator was piled with the appropriate aspirational and celebratory foods, the second room was neatly turned out, the cot unfolded and made up with fresh sheets that emitted citrus. A fresh bouquet of sunflowers stood erect in a tall glass vase. But an unnamed hole remained in the center of all these arrangements, terror she didn't understand.

She stabbed at the name Boris on her cell phone.

Boris picked up right away. "Well, good morning, Snegurochka.

What, are you worried I won't be there on time?" His voice was hoarse, newly used for the day.

"Actually, yes. I'm just making sure you didn't forget."

Boris exhaled a theatrical breath of victimhood. "How could I forget? You've been reminding me of only one thing for weeks now. Are you going to keep reminding me of our wedding day?"

"You'll probably be late to that too." She told him repeatedly she did not want a wedding. But Boris, who proposed to her on New Year's Eve, insisted there were too many colleagues to whom he owed an invitation. Plus word of it would make his wife jealous. He would wait until Larissa arrived, but afterward, they were having a wedding and that was that.

"I told you I would be there. Why do you keep checking up on me? Do you not trust me? Is that it?"

"And one other thing. I want to be alone in the terminal. Will you wait for us in the car?"

Was she a teenager ashamed of her parent? Was he a chauffeur? If so, he would bill her at the end of the month. His services were very expensive.

"Borya! Stop this joking around."

"*Nu,* okay. Relax. Have it your way, as usual. It's cheaper not to park."

"You'll be here, right?"

Boris dispensed with humor. She imagined him putting his hand across his heart in a show of earnest sincerity. "Of course I will. I promised, didn't I?'

She hung up. Three hours until she had to leave. She threw a shawl around her shoulders and left the building.

"Good morning, Nadia Andreevna," the pensioners called out as she walked past them. There were half a dozen of them arranged in a semicircle, in their voluminous housecoats, their feet tucked into plastic slippers. They were, as usual, guarding the entrance to the building, monitoring who was coming and going, who was entertaining dangerous or inappropriate visitors. She was the only shiksa they liked, they said. "A rare day off for you, I see."

"My daughter's coming today."

"For good or a visit?"

"For good. To live."

"Ooh la la. Well, that is exciting. Mazel tov."

"It is," she said, smiling uneasily. "It is a great day."

A lady in a coat dotted with turquoise pelicans said, "Well, congratulations, we had to go through this with my niece last year. Your headache now begins. The Social Security cards, the green card, the health insurance. And you'd think the children are grateful? Ha. They're in a bad mood because they miss their friends and their dogs and their jobs and hate it here and hate you. You can't please them. Americans are too slow and fat, the bread doesn't taste right, the buildings lack that classic European elegance they're used to. All you think about is them coming. But what happens after?"

The question struck Nadia in the gut. It hit in the center of that vague terror she couldn't touch.

"Have a nice day of gossip, ladies. Stay warm." She turned the corner, away from their laughter. At the Russian supermarket, the mangoes were clumped in a refrigerated bin at the back, their skins green and uninviting. Their bodies were unyielding as stones. She would have to take the train to NetCost, she had barely enough time to do that.

On Kings Highway, the long row of Russian stores stretched before her, ones she usually avoided for their judgmental saleswomen who hinted she could lose a few pounds. The last time she walked this stretch of the street she was pushing Grisha's wheelchair, and she didn't expect the grief that overtook her as soon as she stepped onto the familiar sidewalk. There was the pharmacy where she picked up his insulin, the bookstore where he bought the latest Akunin mystery. She could picture the back of his head as they walked, the shape of it, the tufts of gray encircling a bald field at its center. The cane he held in one hand, swirling it in circles as if a baton. Then also, the pus that dripped out of his eyes, the red bruises that ran up his arms, the smell of urine that had seeped into the mattress.

"You're not looking too shabby this morning, Nadia Andreevna," he might say, no matter what condition she found him in. "Shall we proceed immediately to get our marriage license or shall we milk the anticipation by waiting until after lunch?"

Grisha, you are too much. Her response was so close to the surface, she was almost mouthing it. But she looked down for his response and his ghost was gone.

NetCost was not crowded on a weekday, a handful of people were milling around the produce. A voluptuous woman in a tiger-print blouse was manning the closest register, which meant she was idly flipping through the pages of a glossy magazine, a phone attached to her ear. The entire scene calmed her somehow, hid her from view.

"Dobroye utro," the woman said as she passed, without looking up from her magazine. It was an unusual note of kindness that Nadia took for a positive omen.

"Good morning," she replied.

Over the store's intercom, Vera Brezhneva was singing her latest pop hit, this one with a pop electronic beat. The lyrics seemed to be about long-distance romance, *When I'm away from you, and the world becomes too small for me.* Was she happy to be separated from her beloved? Did she prefer a relationship of phone calls? The singer's feelings on the subject were impossible to discern. *I return home, to love and spring and my entire life.* Larissa would have to explain her affection for Vera Brezhneva, argue its cultural importance point by point.

She pulled out a cart and directed it toward the produce. The voices of two women her age were saturating the store. Both were under the misconception that they were in their early twenties, one in jeans ripped at the knees, the other in a ribbed turtleneck dress that expanded past the intentions of its sizing. "So I'm trying this new diet," she was saying. "It's so easy. I'm not eating after six or before ten in the morning. But within those hours, I can eat what I want except sweets. Maybe a *zephyr* here and there, they are so low in fat. Don't we larger-boned ladies need to have some pleasures too? But what am I supposed to do about the white-dress fiasco?"

The friend looked horrified. "The bride is making you wear white? What kind of sadism is that? You should tell her where to shove those suggestions. Brides these days are so bossy. It's all about them, as if you should be dropping hundreds so they can have the perfect day they envision. It's just one day, am I right?"

"You tell her, will you?"

They parted ways at the citrus, the ladies inspecting peaches, and Nadia discovered the small mango section, the fruit not much more appetizing than they were at the local supermarket, their skins pocked with the same dots, a ring of black around the stem. But at this late point, they would do just fine.

"Well, look who it is." Aneta was standing right in front of her, leaning against the handle of a wheelchair. Inside it, an old lady's lap was tucked under a brown plaid blanket. Aneta was using the basket behind the wheelchair as a shopping cart, piling apples and bananas behind the woman's back. The months have imprinted no kindnesses on Aneta's face. It was still too crackled by sun, her mouth set as straight as a ruler, hair slightly more graying around the places pulled tightest by her bun.

"How are you, Aneta?"

"How lovely of you to ask. Funny that I haven't received any phone calls from you after I was pulled off the Grisha job."

Never has the word "lovely" emerged so poisonously from anyone's mouth. For a few beats, they stood there while Brezhneva mercifully sang over them.

Nadia tried again. "Family doing well? How's your niece liking America?"

"So your Jewish boyfriend is dead and here you are shopping like nothing happened."

It has been a while since she warred with Aneta and a protected place near her heart felt exposed, instantly wounded. "I am not shopping like nothing happened. He was not my boyfriend."

"Probably not rich enough for you. I suppose you found some muzhik to take care of you, eh? I always suspected you were wily, a little something on the side."

She did not expect to do it, to reach across the wheelchair, above the head of the frail dozing lady, and push Aneta. It was meant to be nothing more than a symbolic gesture, a hollow threat. She did not expect her former colleague to lose her balance so quickly, to go careening into the row of pineapples lining a cheerful yellow display promising FROM THAILAND. At first it was satisfying to see the wobble, the leg in the air, the flailing hands of shock. To see Aneta trying to steady herself on the cardboard and come flying to the ground, pineapples, placards, and all. The dieting friends were pointing, hands across their mouths, and she saw the woman at the register run toward them, a signal that it was too late to undo whatever she just sent into motion.

"I'm so sorry," she cried, offering her hand. "Please, Aneta, let me help you up."

"Don't touch me, you monster. Did everyone see that? Did anyone get photographic proof?"

Aneta was untangling her sweater from the prickly skins of pineapples. She looked entirely unharmed, not that this would stop her from trying to extract a letter from some quack of a local doctor who would testify to a sprained back. Nadia really did have the worst luck.

"What the hell's going on?" A man joined them from a set of double doors at the back wall. This manager was wearing dress pants and a tank top that hadn't been white in years, glancing at each of them for the exact amount of time, as if implicating them all as fellow conspirators. "What happened here?"

"It was this lady, I couldn't believe it. She seemed so normal coming in." The register employee in the tiger print was pointing at her, a phone in her hand. Nadia burst out with excuses—her daughter was coming from Ukraine—and dashed toward the door.

"Ukrainians," she heard the man say in his crisp Saint Petersburg Russian to the shoppers at large. "What do you expect?"

The unmarred perfection of the morning was turning humid with a gauzy slickness in the air. It was the perfect place to calm down, to regain perspective. Now that Larissa was on her way over, it felt like Aneta could pose no significant threat other than the financial. Which was not nothing, of course, but still. It was at least something she could control.

The beach was crisp and churning with refreshing wind. Brighton Beach was best in the fall and winter when all those bodies littering the beach in the high season returned to work. In the summers, she was too timid to join their ranks, all those people from the former Soviet Republics whose speech she understood too well, the black and brown people from places bewildering to her, the odd Americans planting themselves inside this beautiful orgy of foreignness. She preferred the Rockaways, where the Russians made room for you. But in the winter, she could stroll right off the boardwalk and directly onto the sand and make her way to the shoreline. From here she could imagine the approach of her daughter and the realization that the main thrust of her last seven years was dissolving. What do you fight for after your most important demands are met?

It felt good to sink inside the cold stretch of beach. To slip off her shoes and socks and bore her toes into the wet sheet of sand. A small plane created an arc across the sky, trailing an advertisement she could not understand. Now her own need to learn English would be less sharp and urgent. With the war back home deflated down to occasional sparks, the new administration revealed to be as corrupt as the old administration, empty talk about changes that will never happen, all of that would begin its slow fade. Yes, many things here would become less sharp and urgent.

She looked at her watch. Boris should be pulling up in front of her building by now, and here she was still a half hour away from her place. There was nowhere to wash off the sand and the coarse pebbly coating of it chafed her feet inside her shoes. "So live a little and take them off," Grisha proclaimed, materializing again before her. "What are you doing wearing those ugly shoes with your elegant feet anyway? You deserve someone to take care of you for a change."

She hurried away, running for the boardwalk. Her daughter was supposed to pass security and see her immediately on the other side of the checkpoint. She should be entirely in white, holding mangoes. Now Larissa would have to wait, wondering where her mother was, why she had failed so miserably in this historical greeting.

"We have to turn around," she said as they screeched around the corner. She felt a thousand needles boring into her heart. "I forgot. I think I forgot my charger and my phone is almost dead. What if she's trying to find me?"

Boris ignored her, pulling out onto the wide lanes of Ocean Avenue. "This is third time you forget something. I was here on time just like you wanted and now we are going to be seriously late."

The car smelled of oily Chinese food, a cuisine she knew Boris enjoyed eating alone in the backseat of his car between jobs. He had recently taken to driving passengers around the city on top of his importing/exporting and other mysterious methods of employment. How could passengers tolerate this sticky smell? On her lap was a plastic bag full of mangoes and a knife. She started to wonder why mangoes had been such a priority in the first place. Well, for Larissa fruit was always a special treat; hadn't she loved those illicit mandarins Nadia brought from the factory?

They joined the crawling cars on the highway. Before them snaked a long line of flashing red lights. The squat homes peppered into rows were witnesses to their misery. Boris impatiently jerked his foot on and off the brake. "We should have left sooner. Where did you disappear to?"

"I had a million things to do."

"Like what?"

"You should have helped me with all the errands, you know." She felt guilty about flinging her guilt back in his direction. This was between her and Larisska.

They slid through the mystery borough called Queens, a series of car repair shops and fast-food restaurants and cemeteries. Billboards and houses stacked next to each other. A mustard brick sameness to the architecture. If Yulia saw it, she would remind her of their night at the Kiev Opera House where even poor people could immerse themselves in opulent luxury.

The time for Larisska's arrival came and went, and Boris was banging his palm against the wheel, jutting his foot against the brake, the horn sounding like an angry whine.

The last time she'd stood in this very same airport was upon her own arrival. She knew she'd hardly had the look of the grateful immigrant. Her clothing was disheveled, hair sticking out of her pins, wet with perspiration beneath a too warm sweater. Dragging two suitcases in each hand, one of them entirely filled with albums and useless gifts for her sister from Ukraine. *Psyanka* cookies she would find out later littered Brighton Beach like musty, undesirable mementos. Her sister looked shocked at her wild appearance, but tried hiding it under a stream of empty chatter. Yasha tugged her luggage across the linoleum floor. As they traversed the terminal, Olga kept blathering about how wonderful it would be here, the opportunities, why didn't she move to Cleveland, how she bought entire gallons of blueberries at some great supermarket called Costco.

"Why is that so great? Why do you even need so many blueberries?" Nadia wondered. But Olga waved her away, chuckling at her naïveté. Of course they did not need the blueberries, but they ate them anyway. That was the entire point! Just the other day, she brought home an entire crate of mangoes she did not need. She bet Nadia had never even tried a single mango but in fact they were delicious.

What did she care about mangoes? Just fifteen hours before, she'd walked into her daughter's room for the last time. Larissa was completely shrouded by her duvet cover, back turned to the door, face almost entirely pressed against the wall. Hair coiled around her neck. Even breathing, whether real or manufactured, was making her shoulders rise and fall. Nadia wanted to drop her bags right there, climb into the bed with her daughter, and tell her she would never leave without her. She wanted to curl behind her, feel the soft downy hairs of her arms, pile her head on top so they lay ear to ear. Their separation was temporary, she reminded herself. Together, they had already been on the waiting list for so long, Larissa would probably be placed on some short, expedited line. They would come together again as soon as the paperwork came through. "Laris, wake up. I have to go, you know."

"*Poka,*" her daughter's voice replied. "See you later." It was clear, unblurred by sleep. It was a voice that was modulated toward indifference, toward causing pain.

"Larisska, get up. Say good-bye properly. What kind of farewell is this? Were you raised by wolves? Didn't I always teach you to say good-bye properly, at the door?"

"Obviously I was raised by wolves." Her daughter remained in position, her face more fully tucked into the crevice of her own arm.

Nadia shook that shoulder with more energy. "You are not a little girl anymore and yet you are being petulant and silly. How is this a way to behave? What about coming to the airport and seeing me off?"

"I'm working today, I told you."

"You couldn't switch, you couldn't call in sick."

"No, I couldn't. It's a new job, you know. Can't make a bad impression." Larissa finally sat up in bed and tossed off the covers. A ghostly light shimmered up the blanket toward her veiny legs, the translucent skin Nadia kept trying to expose to as much vitamin D as possible.

"All right then. Next time I see you, we will be reunited in New York." Nadia's pain was pressing against her side with so much force, it took all her effort to lend her words the perfect casual lilt. She bent over to hug the girl, and in response she received a tiny press of the arms, a vague feeling of obedient hands sweeping along her back.

"Fine, see you then." *I will not forgive you.*

She could feel all that anguish spilling over, self-pity mingled with hopeless love and guilt and horror at what she was doing. But her child was technically an adult, and everyone assured her that what she was doing in the short term would be the best thing in the long term. The Orange Revolution had turned out to be a disappointment. Nothing changed, just a steady rotation of corruption. Ukraine was a land parceled out to rich cronies, nothing left for hardworking citizens. And how many stories had she heard, the meteoric rise in fortune of immigrants in America? It was the only story she ever heard.

So why was every step out that door so impossible? Yulia and her mother basically carried her out to the car, transported her to the airport. Her mother's embrace could squeeze the life out of a person, full as it was of worry and a resigned grief. The plane window was misted over with morning dew, another frozen, dull day. Her sweater was barely keeping her warm here. Every few minutes during the flight, she would startle, sure she had forgotten something crucial, left a vital body part behind. All she wanted was to remain in one whole piece.

And in the airport, her sister going on and on about mangoes. How juicy they were when they were ripe, how exotic. And Nadia finally snapping, "Can't you shut up for a minute. I don't give a fig about mangoes."

It would take at least a year and a half until she tasted an actual mango. A few of them were lying in a bowl on Regina's table and it was her third week of work so she called to ask her permission to consume one. Regina sounded circumspect (was she a crook who could not be left alone?), but said, of course. At first she tried biting into it, but when that proved untenable, she scraped the skin and pared off a piece with her knife. As her sister promised, it was like nothing she'd ever tasted. It was mushy and sweet and stringy. By then she had learned to appreciate the splendor in foreign flavors, and eventually she bought a few of her own.

Now, she was the moron slapping around an airport with a bag of mangoes, inserting herself into groups of blond people that could have come from her homeland and asking each one, "Ukraine?" No, they said. Sweden or Finland or some such nonsense. How did anyone ever meet up before phones? Oh, this was not at all the greeting she envisioned. After the disorienting encounter with Aneta at NetCost, it turned out she was wearing the furthest thing from white, her black scalloped sweater and an old pair of itchy wool pants.

She squinted at the board for the flight from Kiev. It was complete chaos with drivers accosting passengers, calling out deals on drop-offs with their stenciled signs. Unclaimed bags were piled high, a security guard standing over them with a walkie-talkie. In a whirl, she passed a group of college kids, a pregnant woman dragging a suitcase across the floor, a loud family arguing about taxis. She heard "Mama," but it was coming from an unexpected direction, from an area she had recently scanned and abandoned.

"Mama," it said again.

The word was coming from the mouth of the very pregnant lady with the bag, and on closer inspection the pregnant lady was Larissa. "You ran right past me," she said. She was unrecognizable even from Moscow, even from Skype. Her face full and even more freckled than before, her hair natural and blond and thick down her back. The constellations around her eyes were slightly deeper.

"Oh my dearest girl." Larissa was pregnant? She groped for air, for some solid surface. Her first thought was diabetes, the high risks her daughter must be facing. They would have to go to the hospital at once! Her second thought was about the father, his identity. But then something else overtook her, a feeling so tender and caved in, so sweet and briny. Her daughter was going to be a mother; there was a baby cleaving to Larissa right now. She and Larissa were both mothers. She and Larissa were, like her own mother, single mothers.

"I've been here forever. I thought you got the dates wrong." Larissa said this peevishly, but then noticed her mother's scrutiny over her belly. "I know. I should have told you."

She had remembered language, that it was made up of words. "Of course you should have told me. Why were you saving this for a surprise?"

"I don't know. I was paranoid. That they wouldn't take me or not let me leave. That I'd lose it. That you'd be mad."

Larissa was not holding her gaze steady but flinging it around the terminal, toward the loud drivers barking names, the cabs pulling up outside the tinted automatic doors where Boris was circulating to avoid security. It looked to Nadia like a means to escape. She forced her brain to work, to put the baby into the proper category.

"Aren't you going to say something? I was too scared to tell you."

Her daughter was finally staring directly at her, a look all muddled by fear and knowledge of a parent's wrath and the steel gate of self-protection. It would be so easy to say the words that easily presented themselves to her tongue. But her daughter was scared and angry, and she was the cause. Nadia had to select them with care.

"Are you well? Have you received good care? How's the diabetes?"

"Glucose under control. I've got to take more insulin. There's a risk of preeclampsia, they say. It will probably be a C-section, but I was prepared for that."

Nadia remembered the mangoes. Suddenly they didn't seem like a good idea. She hid them back in her bag.

"What was that?"

"Nothing. Come here." She stretched out her arms. Then she said something she heard all the mothers saying again and again on the Brooklyn playgrounds, something not as casually woven into the Russian vocabulary. Just two years ago, she thought the sentiment vapid and too easily spoken, but now mastering it felt like the only way forward with Larisska. "I love you."

She prepared herself for the pushing away, the rejection, or for the mealy hug of her departure. But Nadia realized that Larissa was hugging her back. Actively, shyly but with intent. She understood then in a single breathless moment: her daughter was almost thirty. She was separate from her and that would be something to get used to.

Suddenly Nadia didn't care if the child was that terrible Slavik's. Or even that Sergei's, who, it was told to her secondhand, never loved her daughter but had plucked her daughter's *vinok* out of the water to make the girl who looked like Yulia Tymoshenko jealous. Or if that meant that they would now have to put his name or some other name on a list and wait seven more years until the number of the father of the child came up. She supposed the baby would delay Larissa's ability to work and Nadia would have to stay employed at Regina's and VIP for the foreseeable future. None of those details were important now.

All that mattered was the breathing body between her arms and now, amazingly, the breathing body inside that body. It was unharmed and it had the capacity to love.

Would Nadia forget the completeness of this moment and would life once again splinter into a thousand mundane pieces of work and its ticking clock of boredom, into petty grievances and a million new bureaucratic forms and the never-ending scraping for a little bit of savings? She had no idea. It would be everyone getting to know each other again, feeling gingerly around the new, redrawn borders of their love.

As she and her daughter stepped out into the icy flat air of New York City, she craned her neck for Boris but his car was not there. She felt a mild panic at the omission, an instant mistrust. Could he have just left? Where was Boris, for God's sake? And her phone almost depleted of its charge.

The phone buzzed in her hand before she could dial him first. In the background she could hear the loud noise of shuffling cars, the cacophony of automotive logistics. Angry men flinging obscenities at other angry men.

"Talk quickly," she said. "Just tell me where you are."

But Boris was screaming into his phone as if she couldn't hear him.

"They shooed me away from the front door but I'm coming back around. I'm coming to get you, do you understand? Do you hear me? Don't go anywhere. I'll be there soon."

She raised her voice to match his. "I hear you. Yes, yes. We're waiting right here in front of door number three."

Her daughter was crumpled into herself, her spine the curved shape of a hook. A plane was taking off and the trajectory of its ascent into the sky seemed to be occupying her full attention. One of her hands was draped across the top of her belly, the other leaning against the handle of her luggage. Wisps of sun-flecked hair framed a gleaming forehead. She was smiling, lost in thought, but also drained, it seemed, by the effort of leaving. Watching her, Nadia recognized the true cost of reunion, of bringing back together what was once—reluctantly, violently, unnaturally—wrenched apart.

Acknowledgments

I'm grateful for the support I've received from so many people during the writing of this book. In particular, I would like to thank my writing group, Allison Amend and Amy Brill, for their brilliant input draft after draft. Angie Cruz, Peter Trachtenberg, Paul W. Morris, and Claire McMillan also offered invaluable advice. Immense thanks go to Maryna Yarmoshevych and Tetyana Yarmoshevych. The University of Pittsburgh, Ledig House, and Brooklyn Writers Space provided me with the time and space to dream.

Thanks to Ladette Randolph from *Ploughshares* and Michael Dumanis from *Bennington Review* for believing in this story enough to excerpt chapters.

Kimberly Witherspoon and David Forrer at Inkwell continue to be the very best literary advocates any writer could hope for. Thanks to Laurie Chittenden for believing in the project, and Vicki Lame, Jennie Conway, Jessica Preeg, and everyone at St. Martin's and Picador for such an enthusiastic and welcoming home.

Thanks to my family for their deep wellspring of love and support, including Mark Reyn, Elizabeth Reyn, and Sonya Bekkerman. This book is dedicated to mothers and daughters, particularly to my mother, Gina Reyn, and daughter, Simone Lowenstein. I feel lucky to share the everyday with Adam Lowenstein. He infuses the journey with magic.